W9-BIT-337

"Last night we were both unmindful of propriety and plain good sense, and the idea that because of that we should wed— why, the very idea is ludicrous." Linnet looked at him in cold, frigid silence for an endless moment, their gazes locked as they assessed one another.

Lord Blakely's face was a cynical mask. "You're absolutely right. It is ludicrous. And yet all these years I've been harboring the delusion that all young ladies yearn to snare wealthy and titled husbands."

"I'm not like other young ladies," Linnet shot back while wanting nothing more than to fling herself into his arms. She knew all about the kinds of ladies he referred to and, had she been higher up the social scale, perhaps she would have been just like them. But she wasn't like them—she never would be—and she couldn't bear the humiliation of being forced into marriage because they had shared a simple kiss.

"I sensed that from the moment I met you," Christian remarked.

Author Note

The Governess's Scandalous Marriage is set in the Regency period. It begins with a masquerade ball to celebrate the Duke of Wellington's success in the Peninsular War.

When Christian, Lord Blakely, comes across Linnet in Lord Stourbridge's room of antiquities, his initial suspicion is that she is there to steal something. Of course, he could be mistaken, but whatever the truth of the situation, their lives become inextricably linked. This is a story of two people's passionate search for love and happiness. With unhappy memories of his parents' turbulent marriage, Christian is in no rush to step up to the altar, but Linnet is a challenge he has not bargained on.

There are many twists and turns as both Christian and Linnet are beset with emotional conflicts that must be resolved before they can emerge victorious in the battle for their love.

HELEN DICKSON

*The Governess's
Scandalous Marriage*

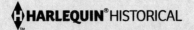

If you purchased this book without a cover you should be aware that this book is stolen property. It was reported as "unsold and destroyed" to the publisher, and neither the author nor the publisher has received any payment for this "stripped book."

Recycling programs
for this product may
not exist in your area.

ISBN-13: 978-1-335-63532-7

The Governess's Scandalous Marriage

Copyright © 2019 by Helen Dickson

All rights reserved. Except for use in any review, the reproduction or utilization of this work in whole or in part in any form by any electronic, mechanical or other means, now known or hereafter invented, including xerography, photocopying and recording, or in any information storage or retrieval system, is forbidden without the written permission of the publisher, Harlequin Enterprises Limited, 22 Adelaide St. West, 40th Floor, Toronto, Ontario M5H 4E3, Canada.

This is a work of fiction. Names, characters, places and incidents are either the product of the author's imagination or are used fictitiously, and any resemblance to actual persons, living or dead, business establishments, events or locales is entirely coincidental.

This edition published by arrangement with Harlequin Books S.A.

For questions and comments about the quality of this book, please contact us at CustomerService@Harlequin.com.

® and TM are trademarks of Harlequin Enterprises Limited or its corporate affiliates. Trademarks indicated with ® are registered in the United States Patent and Trademark Office, the Canadian Intellectual Property Office and in other countries.

Printed in U.S.A.

Helen Dickson was born in and still lives in South Yorkshire, with her retired farm manager husband. Having moved out of the busy farmhouse where she raised their two sons, she has more time to indulge in her favorite pastimes. She enjoys being outdoors, traveling, reading and music. An incurable romantic, she writes for pleasure. It was a love of history that drove her to writing historical fiction.

Books by Helen Dickson

Harlequin Historical

When Marrying a Duke...
The Devil Claims a Wife
The Master of Stonegrave Hall
Mishap Marriage
A Traitor's Touch
Caught in Scandal's Storm
Lucy Lane and the Lieutenant
Lord Lansbury's Christmas Wedding
Royalist on the Run
The Foundling Bride
Carrying the Gentleman's Secret
A Vow for an Heiress
The Governess's Scandalous Marriage

Castonbury Park

The Housemaid's Scandalous Secret

Visit the Author Profile page
at Harlequin.com for more titles.

Prologue

Cairo, Egypt—1814

The Englishman heard the wail of the muezzin and the cries of the street pedlars hawking their wares up and down the narrow alleyways. Neither the grilling heat, which beat down on his head with relentless force, nor the persistent flies had the effect of delaying him. Beggars tugged at his clothes, whining for alms, but he paid them no attention as he carried on his way. Tall, with broad, muscular shoulders, deep chest and narrow waist, his handsome features, bronzed by the Egyptian sun, were ruggedly hewn. He was Lord Blakely of Park House, situated in Sussex, England.

There was an urgency about him. If he delayed any longer the ship would leave without him. All passengers were bidden to be aboard by five o'clock. Two hours.

Hailing an empty *hantoor*, drawn by a skinny

horse, he gave the driver an address and told him to hurry.

The man nodded vigorously. 'I take you there.'

The Englishman didn't ask how much it would cost him, he simply climbed aboard. The conveyance made good speed, the horse clopping briskly through the narrow streets with their pungent smells of spices mingled with open drains. Obstacles got in their way—bullock carts and laden donkeys, crowds of men and women with baskets on their heads and hips, myriad children, their dark eyes ringed with kohl, who ran beside the cart holding out their hands for the Englishman's coin.

At last the cart halted in front of a house set back from the road behind high iron railings. Asking the man to wait and telling him that he would pay him handsomely if he took him to his ship, the man climbed down and rang a bell attached to a tall gate. A stout middle-aged Egyptian waddled down the path and opened the gate.

'I have business with the lady, Mrs Marsden,' he said. 'My name is Christian Blakely. My ship sails shortly and I am pressed for time.'

The Egyptian smiled. 'Mrs Marsden is expecting you,' he said in excellent English.

Christian followed him up the steps of the veranda and through a bead curtain.

An elderly Englishwoman dressed entirely in black appeared holding the hand of a young girl.

'Mrs Marsden?' Christian said, not having met her before.

'Yes—I am Mrs Marsden and this is Alice.'

Christian's manner was brusque. Seeming reluctant to look at the child with a shock of black curling hair, not unlike his own, and large brown eyes regarding him with an inquisitive melancholy stare, he felt his face harden into an expressionless mask. He had not set eyes on the child before either. He remembered the day five years ago when he had learned of her birth. He knew he would never again feel the anger, resentment and wretchedness that had seized him then.

The child's mother was Selina.

Selina, the ambitious daughter of a military man, had been his father's mistress, a woman whose sole interest in life was money and position. His father had both, but since he already had a wife the position as Lady Blakely was denied her. She was much younger than his father and he had been completely dazzled by her—there was something about her that would convince a man he would find warmth in her arms. She had wheedled money out of him at an alarming rate—especially when the child came along. Selina made her daughter a bargaining tool that she used to the full. It was unfortunate for her that his father had died, but, not one to rest on her laurels, Selina had soon found another lover to fund her needs.

Christian had encountered her on several occasions and had summed her up immediately. Selina was beautiful, but there was a coarseness about her that his father seemed oblivious to. Aware of Christian's disapproval—he made no attempt to conceal it—she would fix him with a bold and penetrating stare, leaving him in no doubt that she would happily and brazenly exchange the father for the son if he showed willing.

At the beginning of his father's affair with Selina, Christian had tried to reason with him. He had begged his father to leave her and return to his mother, but to no avail. A furious row had ensued with his father, a powerful and controlling man, telling Christian that he forgot himself, that his private life was not his concern and neither was his mistress. A keen Egyptologist, his father had left for Cairo shortly after this bitter confrontation. Selina, already carrying his child, had accompanied him.

Such a course was unbelievably cruel to his mother. Christian had watched her endure the pain of marriage to a man who had nothing but contempt for her. Why a woman whose nature was tender and loving continued to harbour any affection for him, since his father was a blackguard whose treatment of her was deplorable, was one of life's inexplicable mysteries. She had died shortly after his father had left for Egypt for the last time. Christian was certain the cause of her demise was a broken heart.

His father's actions destroyed what feelings Christian had left for him. Frequent absences from his life as a boy and later as a youth had prevented a closeness from developing between father and son. On the occasions when Christian had been at home, his father's controlling attitude and insistence that Christian learn everything there was to learn about running the estate so that he could pursue his own pleasures had instilled a deep resentment within him. As a result of his father's behaviour, Christian had no appetite for marriage, which to him didn't seem a source of happiness. When he married he would not be doing so expecting to be made happy by it. He would prefer not to marry at all, but if he was to secure an heir he could not postpone the inevitable indefinitely.

'We are ready to leave,' Mrs Marsden said.

'Where is she—Selina? She hasn't come back?'

Mrs Marsden shook her head. 'No. She isn't coming back.'

Christian picked up the baggage waiting by the door and carried it out to the *hantoor*. Mrs Marsden followed him, asking him to help Alice. This he did, placing her on the seat. He looked at the child and quickly looked away, trying to defend himself against the rising and violent tide of anger directed against this small being, whose entry into the world had destroyed so much that had been precious to him.

Angry, relentlessly so and unable to understand why he should feel like this for an innocent child who had not asked to be born, his face resolute and without expression, Christian ordered the driver to head for the ship which was to carry them to England.

Chapter One

London—1814
A ball held in honour of the Duke of Wellington's
return to England following his success in the
Peninsular War

Lord Blakely, the Earl of Ridgemont, idly looked into the hall below. He was the stuff ladies' dreams were made of, fatally handsome and with the devil's own charm. Here was manner, bearing and elegance that could not be bought or cut into shape by a tailor. He was one of those enviable individuals whose breeding would show through even if he were dressed in rags. Christian was a fiercely private man, guarded and solitary, accountable to no one. To those who knew him he was clever, with an almost mystical ability to see what motivated others. To his business partners it was a gift beyond value, because it provided insight into the guarded ambitions of his adversaries.

The Christian Blakely who had recently returned

from Egypt was very different from the one who had left a year ago. The changes were startling. In contrast to the man who had lounged about the gentlemen's clubs and ballrooms with bored languor, it was a more serious Christian Blakely who had returned. Deeply tanned by the Egyptian sun, he was muscular and extremely fit, sharp and authoritative, and although he charmed his way back into society, there was an aura about him of a man who had done and seen all there was to see and do, a man who had confronted danger. It was a reserved aura that women couldn't resist and which added to his attraction.

Christian was as quick as any other man to look at a beautiful woman. Raising a lazy brow, with mild interest he watched one now passing slowly among the throng. With a good deal of pleasure he allowed his gaze to dwell on her. She was petite, like a girl, with a hand-span waist. There was elegance and grace in every step she took and she had a perfect, unselfconscious way of walking. In the company of an older woman wearing a striking black and red mask and a young gentleman who bore a similarity to the object of his gaze, she was surrounded by other beautiful ladies. She held her head confidently high as she appeared to mingle with the other guests, a slight smile playing on her pretty lips.

A white wig, short and softly curled, covered her hair. Long white gloves encased her arms and the mask covering the upper part of her face matched the pale gold of her high-waisted dress and the series of ribbons and bows that decorated the bodice and puffed sleeves. Her only adornment was a scintillating teardrop pearl on a thread of gold nestling comfortably in the shadow of her pert young breasts. For a brief moment their eyes met and then he looked away when she passed from view.

A solid block of elegant equipages, stretching all along the street, deposited the cream of London society and foreign dignitaries before the portico of Corinthian columns of the very grand and awe-inspiring Stourbridge House on the Strand. Lord and Lady Stourbridge were giving a masquerade ball at their magnificent residence to celebrate the return of the Duke of Wellington to England following his success in the war against Napoleon Bonaparte in the Peninsula. All England was rejoicing and no one could talk of anything else.

Light streamed from large windows and the moon reflected its silver sheen on surrounding rooftops. The black and white marble hall was filled to capacity with guests greeting each other and being received by their perfect hosts. Lady Stourbridge, one of London's most popular socialites, was tall and statuesque and attired in blue satin, her light brown hair fussily plumed and bandeauxed. Lord Stourbridge, a man who believed his worth was measured by the cut of his cloth, was pink cheeked beneath his elaborately curled wig and corpulent—a result of too many excesses at the dinner table. He was a pompous, grandiose character, his appearance impressive, from his high collar and bright yellow waistcoat, to his buckled shoes. He was smiling broadly, looking genial and avuncular as he and his wife gave their complete attention to their guests, making each one feel like the most important person in the house.

Lord Blakely watched as the guests strolled along corridors and spilled out on to the wide terrace, descending the shallow flight of stone steps into the torch-lit gardens below. The buzz of chatter and laughter drifted in through the open doors. Pausing at the entrance to the ballroom, he glanced inside without much interest. Two huge chandeliers with crystal drops hung from the stuccoed ceiling, flowers were bursting out of urns and music filled the air. This whole affair was like attending a magnificent theatre and no expense had been spared.

The ladies were attired in their finest, their heads adorned with elaborate swaying plumes and ribbons, their throats and fingers dripping with exquisite jewels. Christian's gaze lingered on those expensive gems, calmly assessing their worth, before moving on to admire and evaluate the fine paintings adorning the walls. A lady brushed against him. He turned to look at her. She was an attractive woman, but it was not her pretty face that caught his eyes. It was what she was wearing about her throat. He stared into the verdant depths of an emerald necklace. Gleaming with regal fire, it motivated him into action, but he was not interested in rubies or diamonds but something else—something much more valuable to him.

The masked ball was filled with beauty and elegance. Footmen in scarlet and gold livery stood to attention. Finding it all magically impressive, Linnet Osborne absorbed every detail. Above her head chandeliers, dripping with hundreds of thousands of crystals, were ablaze with blinding light. She could not have imagined such a spectacle. It was the most lavish affair she had ever attended. There was such gaiety and so much colour, the people behind the masks inspired with a sense of boldness, of daring as the carnival atmosphere of the ball invaded each and every one of them. But she became increasingly apprehensive as she mingled with so much elegance and wealth and felt a strong impulse to run from it all and leave. She was conscious of the simplicity of her attire among so much flamboyance. Unfortunately she was wearing the one and only gown she owned that was suitable for such an occasion and she could not afford another. For her the evening could not be over soon enough.

Suddenly her feminine senses tingled. Sensing she was being watched, Linnet looked up at the gallery that circled the upper storey of the house. She looked straight into the eyes of a stranger. He was leaning against a marble pillar, an expression of utter boredom on his handsome face. He was extremely tall with powerful shoulders. Through the balustrade she saw that white-silk stockings encased his muscular calves. Unlike the other gentlemen, who were dressed like peacocks in a multitude of bright colours, he was clad in a blue-velvet coat and breeches, the curve of the cut of the coat allowing full display of the gold embroidered waistcoat. Her attention was focused entirely on him. Had she wanted to look away she could not have done so. She had never seen such a figure of masculine elegance. He looked so poised, so debonair. His habitual air of languid indolence hung about him like a cloak. His thick hair, drawn back and secured at the nape, was as black as the mask which covered the upper part of his face, his taut skin, a dark bronze.

The cold eyes behind the mask made her shiver. As he met her gaze, the expression in his eyes was half-startled, half-amused, and something else—something slightly carnal that stirred unfamiliar things inside her and brought heat to her cheeks. It was impossible not to respond to this man as his masculine magnetism dominated the scene. She was struck by the arrogance in his stance, an arrogance that told her he knew everything about her, which made her feel uneasy. Perhaps, she thought, he would have looked at her differently had he known how miserable she was, her heart heavy like a stone in her young breast. Love and passion were unknown to her—waiting to flourish in the warmth of a man's eyes.

Quickly she looked away.

Stiffening her spine, Linnet snapped open her fan. She picked up her skirts with her free hand, and followed in the wake of her Aunt Lydia with her brother Toby by her side along with her cousin Louisa and Harry Radcliffe, the young man Louisa was to marry. As she began to ascend the elaborate marble staircase, Linnet assumed an expression of fashionable ennui. The beautiful setting and the laughter spurred her on through a sea of nameless faces into the ball-room, where she was swept along by the music and the dancing. She didn't lack for partners.

It was during the break for refreshments that Linnet realised she hadn't seen Toby all evening.

Noting her unease, her aunt tapped her arm with her fan. 'What is it, Linnet? Is it Toby you are looking for?'

'Yes. I—I don't know where he can be.'

Although a smile stretched her lips, her aunt's eyes were cold. She looked at Linnet with disdain. 'Perhaps you should try the card room, Linnet. Isn't that where he spends most of his time?'

Linnet's heart sank. 'I—I hadn't thought... He said he wouldn't...not tonight.'

'Really, my dear,' her aunt said, with a meaningful lift to her brows, 'you know him better than that.'

'Yes, I do, Aunt. Excuse me. I—I will go and look for him.'

Linnet was relieved to escape her aunt's overbearing presence. Tall and statuesque, Aunt Lydia was a striking woman with dark brown hair and pale blue eyes. Her sole ambition in life was to entertain and ingratiate herself with the social elite and she was a stickler for propriety. Her husband had been killed in a riding accident, leaving her an extremely wealthy widow—a widow who saw that none of her wealth reached her impoverished niece and nephew at Birch House in Chelsea. Lydia's dislike for Linnet and Toby—the poor relations—radiated from her.

Linnet knew this, but there was nothing she could do about it.

Anger and disappointment at her brother's recklessness burned inside Linnet. At twenty years of age, Toby was two years younger than Linnet. Toby was a man of expensive tastes and, in his reckless desperation to improve their lot, he was in danger of gambling everything away, including their wonderful home in Chelsea, where they lived alone, now their parents were both dead.

Ever since their father had died when Toby was a youth, leaving them almost destitute—their situation worsened by Toby's propensity to gamble—Linnet's life had been a constant worry. No one knew what the wrenching loss of both their father and his income had done to her and Toby, or understood the humiliation, shame and heartbreak of it all and how it felt to be forced to live in shabby, penny-pinching gentility.

Trouble was looming, which would be too big for Linnet to handle. Her greatest fear was that they would be left with no choice but to sell the house, which would break her heart. Every day was a struggle to make ends meet, a struggle in which it seemed that defeat was waiting to mock her. Linnet felt as if she were constantly banging her head against a stone wall—and there had been too many stone walls of late. She had contemplated seeking work of some kind and would consider anything that would bring her some income. If only she had someone to talk to, someone to advise her. She was sick with worry and striving and she felt tired. What would become of them?

Linnet had begged Toby countless times to give up his reckless way of life, for if he did not heed their situation then he would find himself in gaol—or worse. But Toby was so wrapped up in his own self-indulgent world he always became angry and defensive and found Linnet's persistence to try to reform him extremely irritating. Now, her resolve to find him before it was too late sent her towards the room where the card tables had been set up, believing she would find her brother there.

Inside the room the noise was muted so as not to distract the players. There were a lot of people throwing away their money sitting around the green baize tables, and even more standing around watching the games of whist, Hazard and other games that took the guests' fancy in this paradise of chance. Standing in the doorway, Linnet scanned the groups of people clustered around them, where several games were in progress, but there was no sign of Toby.

Relief flooded through her, but she was left wondering where he could be. She did not linger, not wishing to draw undue attention to herself, but it was no easy matter for Linnet was exquisitely attractive, a figure of elegance, one who instinctively drew a second, lingering glance. There was not a thing she could do about it, for it was innate, like drawing breath. She was unaware that in her plain gown she was scintillating and far more alluring than if she had been adorned from head to toe in jewels.

She was also unaware of the attention of the gentleman who now observed her appearance in the card room—the same gentleman who had noted her arrival at Stourbridge House, his eyes following her with an interested gleam. Linnet was in no mood to return to the ballroom, so she turned away from the card room and wandered from room to room, looking for her brother.

She wandered into a quiet part of the house, where the passageways were dimly lit. When a door opened further along she paused and watched in amazement as her brother emerged, his hand in the pocket of his coat. There was something furtive in his movements and the way his eyes darted up and down the passage. Linnet was immediately suspicious that he was up to something.

'Toby! What are you doing here? I've been looking for you. Why are you not with the other guests?'

'Linnet—I—I was just—'

'Just what? What have you got in your pocket?'

Toby's face reddened. 'Nothing—nothing at all.'

'Yes, you have. Show me,' Linnet demanded, holding out her hand.

Knowing she wouldn't let him go until he'd showed her the contents of his pocket, Toby slowly pulled out what looked to be a piece of jewellery.

Linnet stared at it, not fully comprehending at first what it was. But then something she had heard her aunt talking about resurrected itself and she could not believe what she was seeing—what Toby had done. Lord Stourbridge was a keen archaeologist and loved all things Egyptian. He was excited and vociferous about the artefacts he had recently brought out of Egypt and he proudly boasted of his finds to all and sundry. His treasures were much talked about, especially a recently acquired necklace of solid gold.

Linnet looked at him accusingly. 'So, not only do you gamble away every penny we own, now you are a thief. How could you, Toby? How could you do this? I have no doubt you are not in this alone and that one of your associates has put you up to it. How did you know where to look?'

'It wasn't difficult. I gained inside knowledge of the house from one of the footmen employed by Lord Stourbridge.'

'I imagine the footman was well paid for the information and the man who would be guarding the room has gone for his supper.' Hearing laughter coming from close by and being quick, efficient and decisive, she snatched the necklace out of his hand. 'Go back to the ballroom and show your face to Aunt Lydia. I'll put this back.'

A look of panic appeared in Toby's eyes. 'You can't. There are others depending on this.'

'If they want the necklace, then they can come and get it. I will not see you go to prison, Toby. Where did you get it from? Tell me.'

'There's a small black box in the chest facing the door,' he told her petulantly. 'You can't miss it.'

Linnet watched Toby hurry down the passage before opening the door to the room he had come out of. Attaching her fan to her reticule, with her heart in her mouth she slipped inside, closing the door softly behind her.

There were lighted candles in sconces on the walls, casting light and shadows in the room. Looking around, she saw it was a treasure trove of antiquities. Lord Stourbridge was very proud of his collection of ancient relics. The walls were hung with all kinds of artefacts, from African spears and shields to brightly coloured frescoes depicting Egyptians' daily lives and mosaics from ancient Egypt and ancient Greece. Stuffed animal heads leered down at her. Shoving herself away from the door, she slowly moved into the centre of the room, pulling off her gloves and shoving them into her reticule. Amulets of ancient gods, bronze figurines, wooden statuettes and objects taken from Egyptian tombs that the dead had used and enjoyed in life, were displayed on plinths and shelves.

Moving across the room, Linnet was unaware of the door opening and a tall figure slipping inside. She stood quite still, the music from the ballroom fading as she gazed in awe at what she saw. She had never seen anything like it. Brought from her reverie by laughter somewhere outside the room, Linnet told herself she would have to hurry if she was to accomplish her task successfully. Almost at once she recognised the wooden chest Toby had described to her, one Lord Stourbridge had recently brought from Egypt that held his latest collection of treasures.

With her heart beating loudly in her ears, Linnet quickly moved towards it and lifted the lid. Looking inside, she did a quick search of the contents. Seeing a wooden box, tentatively she lifted it out and looked inside, certain this was the box where the necklace belonged.

Removing the box, she looked at the necklace in her hand, letting it trail through her fingers in solitary splendour. It was a lavish piece of jewellery, made up of five rows of solid gold links inlaid with lapis lazuli and joined by a central gold clasp in the shape of a scarab. Each lapis lazuli stone was like no other in a combination of blue, black and gold. It was truly magnificent. Even to her inexperienced eye Linnet knew it would require a significant level of skill to produce. Out of interest, there were other items in the chest she would have liked to look at more closely, but she told herself she had to hurry. Time was of the essence. The longer she remained in the room, the greater the risk of her being caught. She was about to place it inside the box when a voice rang behind her.

'I wouldn't do that if you value your life,' it said.

She felt a frisson of alarm as all her senses became heightened. She spun around to see who had spoken. A man emerged from the shadows and moved menacingly towards her. Edging into view with a cynical twist to his lips, he allowed the shifting light of the candles to illuminate his features. As she watched him her throat tightened and fear jabbed her in the chest. It was the same man who had drawn her attention earlier. The closer he came brought a waft of gentle cologne that touched her senses and she became aware of his catlike litheness. She could feel the energy flowing from him and could sense the danger.

He hardly made a sound as he walked towards her, his eyes never leaving her face, his step surprisingly light for his size.

Linnet had to look up into his face, he was so tall. He was close, so close she could see the fine lines at the corners of his mouth and the glitter of his black eyes behind the mask. They seemed to bore through her, the gaze so bold and forward that her eyes slowly widened and for a brief moment she held her breath, frozen by his steely gaze.

The man saw the wary look of a trapped but defiant young animal enter her transparent eyes, eyes the colour of a tawny owl behind her mask. Her face was uptilted—deep inside he felt something tighten, harden, clarifying and coalescing into one crystal-clear emotion. He found himself wishing he could see her face. Her eyes blazed with defiance. There was an elfin delicacy from the little he could see of her face and a pert little point to her chin. Her lips were full and the straight cut of her gown revealed the curves of her slender body beneath. He knit his brows as he searched her eyes.

'Do you normally inspect the ladies you meet with such thoroughness?' Linnet demanded suddenly, with a voice like frosted glass.

An impudent smile curved his lips. 'You don't like it?'

'Not one bit.'

His smile broadened. 'Whoever you are, you look extremely lovely—as rare a jewel as the one you are holding. Too bad you are a thief. I like what I see.'

Her lips tightened at the chauvinistic remark. 'Things aren't always what they seem.'

'No? My eyes do not deceive me. But please do not be alarmed. You will come to no harm if you behave yourself.'

The sound of his voice, deep and resonant, sent a thrill of fear down Linnet's spine, and she trembled for some unknown reason. He continued to look at her searchingly—the warm liquid of his dark gaze missed nothing. 'Behave myself?' she uttered bravely. 'If you lay one finger on my person, I swear I will scream.'

'I have no intention of touching you,' he replied calmly. 'Be assured that nothing was further from my mind and to scream would be your greatest folly. What do you think would happen to you if Lord Stourbridge should find you—an intruder, if my judgement serves me correct—in this room, about to steal his greatest prize? A most foolhardy act.'

Linnet's fear increased, pricking her consciousness that she had been caught in what must seem to be a criminal act. The certainty of what would happen to her was beginning to loom monstrously large in her mind. Her mind tumbled over in a frenzy. What could she do? With the man blocking her way to the door, it was impossible for her to escape. Straightening her spine, she faced him with outward calm, looking at him for a long, thoughtful moment, estimating her chances of getting out of that room with her dignity intact.

'This isn't what it looks like,' Linnet said, hoping to convince him. 'I wasn't stealing it.'

'No? Try telling that to a magistrate. My eyes did not deceive me. I caught you red handed.' Taking the necklace from her, he held it up to the light, the gold links trailing through his fingers like droplets of shining water. He sighed his appreciation, his casual manner and his outward calm out of keeping with the seriousness of the situation.

'It's a beautiful piece—hard to believe it's been buried for nigh on three thousand years. Do you know anything about it?'

'No—only that it is worth a considerable fortune.'

He smiled thinly. 'Of course you do, otherwise you would not be here to steal it. Allow me enlighten you. Jewellery made of lapis lazuli was a status symbol in ancient Egypt. It was a symbol of power and status. The Egyptians believed it offered protection and symbolised truth. They valued it more highly than gold. The scarab you see is believed to ensure resurrection and eternal life and generally to bring good luck. Amulets in the shape of scarabs were used in connection with burials and were intended to protect the dead from all dangers which faced them in the future life.'

'Really?' Linnet remarked with a hint of sarcasm. 'Thank you for the lesson, but do you mind telling me what you are going to do?'

'What do you expect me to do? You are a common thief—and not a very good one otherwise you wouldn't have been caught out.' Holding her gaze, he moved closer. 'Mention this to anyone, Miss Whoever-You-Are, and you can kiss your freedom goodbye.'

Linnet blanched at the threat and stepped away from him. 'Will you tell Lord Stourbridge?' Fear filled her heart, but she would not make a spectacle of herself with weakness and tears.

He looked at her, so small and slender. There was a sweet elfin delicacy to what he could see of her face below the mask. He wondered at the colour of her hair beneath the white wig and he knit his brows as he studied her. She was studying him with equal measure. Drawn to her eyes, peering at him through the holes in her mask, he'd never seen such incredible eyes—they were indeed the unusual shade of tawny, he thought, and they had depth and glowed, almost as if they had hot coals burning behind them. When he had made his presence known, she had looked agitated and her expression had been one of intense fear.

'I haven't made up my mind.'

Suddenly a thought occurred to Linnet and her eyes opened wide. 'Why are you here, sir, in this room? Are *you* by any chance a thief also?'

'All I will say is that I am here to claim what is rightly mine.'

'Which is?'

'This,' he replied, indicating the necklace.

'How do I know you are telling me the truth? People are not always what they seem—and not to be trusted.'

'You will simply have to take my word for it.'

'I can't do that.'

'I give you my word as a gentleman.'

'A gentleman does not steal other people's property.'

'I told you. I am not a thief.'

'Then I can see we find ourselves in something of a dilemma.'

'Why? Because you are here for the necklace and you do not like to be cheated out of it? You may not be so eager to take possession of it if you knew more about it,' he remarked, with a quiet casualness as he admired his possession.

'What is there to know?'

'That a curse is believed to be cast upon any person who seeks to own it. The curse does not differentiate between archaeologists or common thieves. Allegedly it can cause bad luck, illness and even death.'

Linnet blanched. Even though the knowledge of the curse terrified her, she refused to let that terror overtake her. 'You are only telling me this to scare me.'

Shrugging his shoulders, the man shook his head. 'Not at all. I am merely stating a fact. Ancient Egyptians believed that they should protect their tombs by magical means or curses. Curses are placed on sacred objects and possessions to stop people from disturbing them. Inscriptions on tombs often speak of the deceased coming back to life to seek revenge should anyone dare to desecrate their resting place. The curse is what will happen to anyone who does not heed the warning.'

'Do you believe the curse exists?'

'I know of at least two men who took possession of the necklace who met untimely deaths—one violently and the other died of a mysterious disease.'

A cold tremor trickled down Linnet's spine. The stranger turned his dark eyes on her. She looked away, biting her lip—there was something unpleasant about what he said that put a different slant on the necklace. Telling herself it was all mumbo-jumbo, she shook herself and looked at him. The line of his jaw was hard and behind the cold glitter of his dark eyes lay a fathomless stillness.

'It is an interesting tale, but I think it is just superstitious nonsense. I do not believe that beings can exact revenge from beyond the grave.'

'Beings that possess unknown and seemingly evil qualities,' he stated flatly, keeping his voice soft, knowing he was deliberately trying to make her question her desire for the necklace.

'Nevertheless, it was all a long time ago and Egypt is a long way away. I am not afraid of such things. I refuse to let them scare me.'

'Then does that mean you are unwilling to relinquish your claim?'

'Yes.'

His voice was condescendingly amused as he tried not to look too deeply into her eyes, eloquent in the fear she was trying so hard to hide. He smiled. 'Then I suggest we play for it. Would that be agreeable to you?'

Christian knew he should not give her the impression that he was a thief, that he should explain his reason for taking the necklace, which was completely innocent and that he was its rightful owner, but he found he was enjoying teasing her and could think of nothing that would please him more just then than to prolong their encounter. There was something about her that touched a hidden spot within him that he had not felt for a long time. It would give him no pleasure to have her arrested. No pleasure at all.

'If you refuse to relinquish it to me, then I will have to. What do you suggest?'

'A wager,' he suggested.

Linnet's eyes narrowed. If playing for the necklace was the only way she could secure it and put it back in its box, then that was what she must do. 'What kind of wager?'

A leisurely smile moved across the stranger's face. 'By your actions you seem to be hell bent on self-destruction.'

Linnet's eyes flashed with a feral gleam. 'That is my affair.'

'I agree, but you cannot deny that you have got yourself into an impossible situation. You are too reckless by far.'

'What is life without a little danger?' she replied wryly.

Christian laughed lightly. 'My feeling exactly. So—let us play a game of chance. The best of three.' Putting the necklace back into its box and placing it on top of the chest, he produced two dice from his pocket.

Raising her eyebrows, Linnet gave him an ironic look. The man was infuriatingly sublime in his amusement. She was self-willed, energetic and passionate, with a fierce and undisciplined temper, but her youth, her charm and her wit had more than made up for the deficiencies in her character. She was proud and spirited and so determined to have her own way that she had always been prepared to plough straight through any hurdle that stood in her path—just as she was about to do now. It dawned on her that she was making an idiot of herself, but her wits had been put somewhat out of sorts by their exchange so far. If she weren't so desperate to replace the necklace that Toby had stolen, she'd cheerfully tell the man to go and jump in the Thames.

'You even came prepared, I see.' Linnet glanced at the dice suspiciously. Should she ask to inspect them? she wondered. On second thoughts, perhaps not. They looked quite ordinary, yet she was hardly an expert in these matters—Toby would have been able to tell if they were loaded at a glance. It would appear that she would have to trust this infuriating stranger.

The handsome stranger stepped towards a table. She followed, feeling his eyes intently upon her. His hands were the hands of a gentleman, his fingers long and tapering. But if he was a gentleman—a nobleman for all she knew—then what had turned him into a thief? She looked up at him, meeting eyes as black as his mask. He was tall, lean, muscular, giving the appearance of someone who rode, fenced and hunted. She recognised authority when she met it and his personality was so strong that she was certain that with a lift of one of his arrogant eyebrows, or a flare of a nostril, he could make one tremble with fear. She guessed him to be in his late twenties.

There was an aggressive confidence and strength of purpose to him. She detected an air of breeding about him, a quality that displayed itself in his crisp manner and neat apparel. His eyes, holding hers captive, seemed capable of piercing her soul, laying bare her innermost secrets, causing a chill to sear through her. She felt overwhelmed by his close presence and he seemed to invade every part of her. She thought it miraculous that she managed to keep her head.

'Would you like first throw?' he asked.

'No, you can go first.'

'I must point out that I never wager on uncertainties.'

'That's an arrogant assumption. Are you saying that I will lose?'

He bowed his head in deferential respect. 'I would not be so bold. I would not dare. I suspect it would be more than my life is worth. All I am saying is that I intend to win.'

Clearly in no hurry, he caressed the dice in the palms of his hands and then rolled them over the table's polished surface. They rolled over and over before finally stopping close to the edge, showing two and five. Next it was Linnet's turn. Collecting the dice herself, she rolled them carefully, breathing a sigh of relief with the dice showing six and three.

'The first roll to you,' he said, scooping up the dice masterfully in his hands.

His second throw showed five and five. Linnet followed with a disappointing three and one. There was a certain sense of triumph in the look he gave her. He was confident. He believed he would win.

'We are even,' he said. 'Well—this is it—the decider.'

Holding her breath Linnet bit her lip as she watched his throw. Six and five. Picking up the dice, she sent up a silent prayer, knowing in her heart that she wouldn't match his high score. The dice seemed to roll for ever. At last they stopped rolling and showed double five.

'Oh, dear,' she said as disappointment swamped her.

'Oh, yes,' he mocked, scooping up the dice. Losing no time in claiming the necklace, he slipped it into his pocket along with the dice.

Linnet watched him, feeling anger towards the stranger for catching her, but most of her anger was directed against Toby for putting her in this position and also at herself for getting caught and being bested at the dice. She tightened her lips. Resentment burned in her breast and heated her cheeks. 'I don't suppose you would change your mind and take something else?' she suggested, knowing it was a futile question, but hoping he would.

Behind the mask his eyes went darker than dark and his voice was soft but cutting. 'No, I'm afraid not.'

'What would you have done had I won?'

His lips curved in a slight smile. 'As to that, little lady, you will never know.'

Christian saw the intensity in her eyes, the defiance to accept that she had lost and the ill-concealed anger. Her hands were clenched. He had watched her soft white hand as she had rolled the dice and he got the impression that this young woman was like two people—outwardly she was like the consummate actress, but underneath there was something else—something he now picked up on and it wasn't the underlying steely quality he'd expected.

She was small and slender, her hands small like a child's that could easily slip into a pocket—a necessary asset to a thief. This was not a woman who lost easily. 'Of course you could choose something else to steal—although I wouldn't advise it. Should you be caught and a constable called, then the consequences for you would be dire indeed.'

'As they will for you, should you be caught with the necklace in your possession. I do not believe you have a claim to it, otherwise you would have taken it without rolling the dice. You are a thief, sir, and as likely to hang as any other thief.'

He laughed in the face of her ire. He knew he should enlighten her and tell her he was no thief. He should explain that his father had unearthed it in Egypt. Aware of the value of this precious object and knowing it was a target for thieves, he had approached Lord Stourbridge, also in Egypt, who was to return to England before him. He had given it to him for safekeeping and this ball to which Christian had been invited, with Lord Stourbridge's lawyer's permission, had been the perfect opportunity to retrieve it. Yes, he should tell her the truth, but he was enjoying her company and wished to prolong it a while.

'Dear me. You have a strange preoccupation with seeing me hang. As a gentleman and a peer of the realm, I assure you that will not be my fate. You must know that London is a dangerous and corrupt city. Crime abounds and though the legal system has its limitations, allowing criminals to flourish, that does not mean that they cannot be caught. So have a care lest I inform Lord Stourbridge of your intention to steal from him.'

Linnet's face blanched beneath the mask. The utter humiliation of being arrested and publicly conveyed out of the house by a constable, and subsequently brought before the magistrate and thrown into prison for thieving, would be mortifying. 'I will not take anything else,' she said quietly, the words almost sticking in her throat. 'There is nothing else that I want.'

Having got what he wanted, Lord Blakely was surprised to find he was reluctant to leave his female thief. A vision of what she might look like without the concealing mask caught hold of his imagination. He knew nothing about her, yet the strength of his desire was unexpected. He was certain this young woman possessed a healthy concern for her skin and he felt that fear was the determining factor in her decision not to take anything else from Stourbridge's collection.

'The evening need not end here.' He moved closer, his eyes appraising.

* * *

His voice was deep and seductive and brought a warmth to Linnet's cheeks. She stood in shock beneath his leisurely perusal—and was she mistaken, or did his gaze actually linger on her breasts? His close study of her feminine assets left her feeling as if she'd just been stripped stark naked. The gall of the man, she thought with rising ire. He conveyed an air of arrogance and uncompromising authority which no doubt stemmed from a haughty attitude which was not to her liking. Recognising his obvious admiration, she suddenly became aware of the boldness in his eyes, his masculinity and the impropriety of being alone in this room with this stranger.

'Please don't come any closer,' she murmured, her tone less commanding than she'd intended.

The huskiness of her voice entered Christian's ears like a caress. It was as tempting and appealing as her body and the lustrous eyes looking back at him from behind the mask. Both aroused him in an unexpected way and this bewitching young woman aroused a hungering ache he hadn't known in a long time. Lust and desire were collecting heavy and thick deep in his body and he sensed she could fulfil his needs and bring some brightness to his life after many months of darkness. The conviction was profound. He narrowed his eyes, mentally stripping her of her delectable gown, draping her instead in a diaphanous fabric that was so light her body would be open to his gaze. The thought warmed his body and encouraged his erotic thoughts. Alluring and provocative, she was a natural temptress. Christian had to fight the insane impulse to take hold of her lithe, warm, breathing form, crush it beneath him and kiss her soft, inviting lips. He wanted her and he had methods of persuasion and powers of seduction to call on if necessary. Thoughtfully he contemplated the young woman before him and, drawn by an urge that was stronger than reason and eager to see the fullness of her features, he raised his hand to remove her mask. Aware of his intent, she immediately shoved his hand away and backed away.

'Please don't touch me.'

His smile was slow, sensual and brilliant. 'I would dearly like to see your face. I am more than willing to take you under my protection for the time you are here.'

'I am perfectly capable of protecting myself,' she retorted, shocked by his temerity, 'and I do not intend remaining longer than I have to.'

'Pity. I was already imagining an evening of pleasure.'

'With a thief, sir?'

'If that is indeed what you are,' he said softly, 'then yes.'

His eyes captured hers, a lazy, seductive smile curving his lips. His stare travelled over her before coming back to her face. He lifted one eyebrow slightly in a silent challenge. Something in his stare quickened her pulse. There was a sweet warmth in her chest. They stared at each other for a moment, with just two yards between them. Linnet barely realised she was holding her breath. Bowled over by the delicious magnetism of the man, she felt herself being drawn towards him, knowing she should step back and walk away, but she was too inexperienced and affected by him to do that. 'You don't even know me.'

'No, I don't, but I am willing to remedy that situation. What is your name?'

'That is for me to know, sir. I do not intend sharing the personal details of my life with a perfect stranger.'

Lord Blakely tilted his head to one side and regarded her with a critical, masculine eye. He was becoming more intrigued by her by the minute. He wondered who and what she was. Earlier he had seen her with an older woman and assumed she was this young lady's chaperon. It would appear he had been mistaken. An unprotected female roaming the passageways of Stourbridge House led him to think that perhaps she was an actress or even a courtesan, forced to earn her living as best she could. She had charm and feminine graces in abundance—eminently agreeable qualities in a mistress.

Linnet drew a deep breath. Those dark eyes seemed to see more than she wished him to see. She was aware that her body trembled slightly as she tried to figure out a way of extricating herself from this situation that seemed to be running away with her. This man seemed determined to detain her and she suspected he did not give up easily. 'If you are suggesting what I think you are, then your proposal is most indecent. If you are here in pursuit of pleasure, then you must look elsewhere.'

Even as she said the words Linnet knew that because of the inferior role she had assumed he could not be faulted and the difference in their social status— if indeed he was a peer of the realm, as he professed to be—was an open invitation to seduction. Ladies did not infiltrate events such as this alone and with criminal intent.

'I'm sure we could come to an arrangement that would suit us both. I assure you that you will find me most generous.'

'I do not think I would care for your kind of generosity.'

'Are you not tempted to know me better? I think you would find it interesting to discover more.'

'I doubt it. You think too highly of yourself, sir.'

'*That* is a failing indeed.'

He shocked her when he touched her gently under her chin. Linnet caught her breath sharply as he tilted her face upward and looked into her eyes.

'Perhaps you are afraid, is that it?'

Her heart pounded at the light but sure pressure of his warm fingertips against her skin, but she managed to meet his gaze squarely. 'I'm not afraid of you, sir. I'm not afraid of anyone.'

'I'm relieved to hear it.'

He continued to peer down at her, into her very soul. A lazy, seductive smile passed across his mouth, curling his lips, and Linnet felt herself being drawn towards him, knowing she should step back and walk away, but she was too affected by him to do that. Feelings she had never experienced before began to appear within her and she could not deny that she was attracted by him. Belated warning bells screamed through her head and her eyes became fixed on his finely sculptured mouth. As he came closer still, to her helpless horror she knew he was going to kiss her.

When he reached out and took her hand, drawing her into his embrace, she knew she was trapped as securely as a rabbit in a snare.

Chapter Two

Linnet was mesmerised by him. He was standing very close. She could smell the sharpness of his cologne and feel his presence. Like a magnet, it was drawing her to him and she hadn't the will to resist, nor did she want to. A smile played on his lips, curving gently, a lovely smile, and an errant wave had fallen across his brow. The heat of his closeness was making her warm and the feelings coursing through her body spoke of desire, not love, not even infatuation. It ached for him to touch her, her lips ached for him to kiss her. Her heart suddenly started pounding in a quite unpredictable manner. He was looking into her eyes, holding her spellbound, weaving some magic web around her from which there was no escape.

'I—I should go,' she whispered. 'Please let me go at once.'

'Not a chance,' he murmured. With his arms around her he held her tightly against his chest.

The strength of his embrace and the hard pressure

of his loins made her all too aware of the danger she was in, that he was a strong, determined man, and that he was treating her as he would any woman he had a desire for. Resolutely she squirmed against him. A strange feeling, until this moment unknown to her, fluttered within her breast and she was halted for a brief passing of time by the flood of excitement that surged through her.

'It's useless to resist me,' he said huskily. 'Relax. I'm not going to hurt you.'

The darkening of his eyes, the naked passion she saw in their depths drew her even more to him, but it was his tone and not his words that conquered her. She relaxed against him, her entire body beginning to tremble with desire. Her head swam and she was unable to still the violent tremor of delight that seized her, touching every nerve until they were aflame. There was nothing she could do to still the quiver of anticipation as he lowered his head and covered her mouth with his own. The shock of his lips on hers was one of wild, indescribably sweetness and sensuality as he claimed a kiss of violent tenderness. In silent permission she opened her mouth to his and what followed evoked feelings she had never felt before. That was when she realised the idea of resisting him was ludicrous and a gross miscalculation of her power to deny him, for the kiss went through her with the impact of a broadside.

His lips caressed and clung to hers, finding them moist and honey sweet, and for a slow beat in time hers responded, parting under his mounting fervour.

She leaned against him, melting more closely to him, as though the strength had gone from her. All her will began to crumble and disintegrate. The moment was one of madness. The sweetness of the kiss, the yielding to it, of willingly parting her soft lips for his searching tongue, made her confused with longing. Unconsciously, and too naïve to know how to hide her feelings, her arm rose and slid over his wide, masculine shoulders and she slipped her hand behind his neck, a movement which, in her inexperience, was an act of pure instinct to Linnet, unaware that it might convince this stranger that she was no different to any other woman he had made love to. Seemingly aware of her weakening, he raised his head and stared down at the softness in her eyes.

'Please,' Linnet whispered, trying to sound firm but without conviction. 'We should stop. This game has gone on long enough.'

'Games are for children. This is something between a man and a woman.'

'But…'

He silenced her with his lips, kissing her long and deep and hard. He closed his eyes, intense desire for this woman torturing him. As he caressed and kissed this sweet young woman, his flesh betrayed his need, rising up against his will. He was hungry for her and could hardly restrain himself from flinging her down on to the floor and making love to her.

Imprisoned by his embrace and seduced by his mouth and strong, caressing hands, which slid down the curve of her spine to the swell of her buttocks and back to her arms, her neck, burning wherever they touched, Linnet clung to him, her body responding eagerly, melting with the primitive sensations that went soaring through her, her lips beginning to move against his with increasing abandon as she fed his hunger, unwittingly increasing it. When he slid one hand down to her buttocks and pressed her to him, she became acutely conscious of her innocence. She was lost in a dreamy limbo where nothing mattered but the closeness of his body and the circling protection of his arms.

Not for a moment did he break the kiss that was inciting her. His mouth was hungering, turning to a heated, crushing demand. What she had felt in the beginning became raw hunger, cindered beneath the white heat of their mutual desires. It was sudden, the awakened fires, the hungering lust, the bitter-sweet ache of passion such as Linnet could never have imagined.

When he finally drew his mouth from hers an eternity later, Linnet reluctantly surfaced from the glorious Eden where he had sent her, her face suffused with languor and passion, her eyes luminous.

'Well, well,' he murmured, lightly touching her lips with his own. 'I seem to have awakened a temptress. You're the most direct, self-willed woman I have ever met, traits I admire in any woman, but you are also so damn lovely and desirable.'

His words affected Linnet like a douche of cold water. Stepping back, she glared at him, trying to re-

gain control of her rioting emotions. 'You should not
have done that... We—we shouldn't...'

Struggling for control, finding it with effort, Christian swept a lock of dark hair from his brow. 'Come
now,' he managed to say, smiling, though he himself
was shaken by the moment. 'It was only a kiss—an
innocent kiss, nothing more sordid than that.' But he
was not convinced by his words. With her ripe young
body, moist lips and large liquid bright eyes, he was
led to think that he had never caressed any woman that
had evoked his imagination as much as she did. The
lingering impression of her lips on his, of their thighs
pressed together, had done much to awaken a manly
craving that had gone unappeased for some months.

'You call what you just did innocent?' Linnet whispered, still trying to come to terms with what had just
happened between them.

Raising his hand, he traced a finger gently down
the curve of her warm, flushed cheek. 'It was a kiss—
a kiss that could lead to other things—if you would
let it.'

Linnet looked at him with a renewed light in her
eyes, under no illusion as to what he was asking of
her. He was smiling now, a lazy, masculine, supremely
confident smile, a gentle promise in his expression
and the flickering depths of his eyes that drew her
in. It held her spellbound for the longest moment as a
plan began forming in her mind, a plan so shocking
she hardly dared enlarge on it. It caused her heart to

pound so hard she could scarcely breathe, for it was a plan no gently bred young lady would dare think of, let alone consider.

She had been raised to believe that young ladies of quality must not abandon the restrictive codes of behaviour that governed their conduct without fear of censure, but with one stroke, this stranger had presented her with an answer to her problem. Despite having caught her in the act of what he mistakenly thought was stealing, he was obviously attracted by her. On a stroke of desperation all her fears and wretchedness, all the worries for the future, came hurtling back to her and she thought that maybe she could turn the situation to her advantage. By giving herself to him on her terms, perhaps she could retrieve the necklace, return it to its rightful place and exonerate Toby of any wrongdoing.

The plan sent a chill down Linnet's spine, but it did not shock her. The misery that Toby's gambling had caused her over the past months had come to a culmination when this man had made his presence known to her and drained her of all feeling so there was hardly any emotion left in her. If her capacity to feel had been intact, everything inside her would have protested and rebelled against the plan forming in her mind. But with her feelings and emotions subdued by the anxiety of the situation her brother had created, Linnet's thoughts were entirely practical. She was driven by desperation. She and Toby had been impoverished for a long time and she was determined they would not become beggars. If there was a way of saving herself and Toby from homelessness and starvation, then she would do everything in her power to do so. Afterwards, the shame would be something she alone would have to live with.

'I am not afraid and I have a mind to test your generosity and exact my revenge—to recoup what I have just lost to you. If I were to lay down terms of my own, would you accept them for an evening of pleasure?'

'Terms?'

'An evening of pleasure in return for the necklace you have just taken from me?'

He frowned. 'And your terms are not open for negotiation?'

'No. Take it or leave it,' she said, her voice low and direct, her lovely eyes challenging.

He had to give her credit, Christian thought to himself, fighting down a rush of disgust. At least she was honest about what she wanted. And he had to respect her honesty and courage, if not her standards. Her decision to consider his offer was anything but respectable. He wondered how, in a matter of moments, he had gone from thinking of her as a thief, then as an opponent in a game of chance, to seriously considering inviting her to share an evening of pleasure.

He had not had a serious relationship with a woman in a long time, nor had he wished to. All his romantic entanglements had not been permanent and were soon forgotten. As a youth when he had witnessed his father's affairs and his mother's heartbreak, he had spent years of evasion, trying to avoid affairs of the heart, ignoring the whispers and sighs of women eager to shackle him with matrimony. And he had succeeded, believing himself immune. Deep inside, what his father had done, his betrayal of his mother and the tragedy of her death still haunted him. He had deliberately put the memory away, not wanting to look too carefully, but now, when he looked at this young woman whose name he did not know, he found it rising to the fore. He had always diligently avoided becoming deeply involved with any woman in the romantic sense and it would be no different with this young woman, should she consent to his request.

Christian still didn't want that kind of relationship. But he had only recently returned from Egypt after an absence of almost a year and if he was to dispel his dark thoughts, how much easier he would find it with a lively young woman such as this with sweet young flesh as a diversion. Despite her illicit occupation, there was a forthright quality about her, a freshness with an intriguing hint of mischief in her lovely eyes that drew him like a moth to a flame.

'I am tempted,' he replied.

Feeling somewhat light-headed, and unaccustomedly bemused, held by his intense gaze, Linnet knew that if she was not careful she would fall under his spell. Sensual pleasure still spiralled through her and her body ached with a need she had never experienced before. If she were honest with herself, she would admit to feeling a measure of curiosity about what an evening of pleasure with this man held. Feeling slightly faint, shocked at the extremely unladylike drift of her imaginings, Linnet looked away. It was madness, she knew, but she didn't want to leave him, to widen the distance between them. She looked at him once more, the sheer wickedness of the slow, lazy smile he gave her making her catch her breath. She was trapped by the dark eyes behind the mask that were searching her face intently, a question in their depths, a question she could not have answered even if he'd asked her. She was surprised when, seeming to come to a decision, a change came over him and he stepped away from her.

'As much as I would like nothing more than to share an evening of pleasure with you, I regret I must decline. The necklace is important to me.' Turning from her, he strode towards the door. 'I advise you not to linger in this room and from this moment on take on a more suitable occupation for a young woman. 'Tis a dangerous profession you have chosen. You appear to be intelligent, so I am sure you care about yourself, about what you do—but not enough, it would seem, if you decide to carry on stealing other people's property. Perhaps you don't have enough faith in yourself—or pride.'

'I do believe in myself,' she confided softly. 'You were mistaken in what you saw. I didn't steal the necklace. I was putting it back.'

He turned and looked back at her, reminding himself that here was no innocent. But he could not help but wonder at the gist of what she had said. He was troubled by the intensity of her statement. It had been a flash of unguarded candour—and honesty, maybe?—which surprised him. It was born of deep conviction—and perhaps more than a little pain. There was an intensity in her eyes behind the mask, showing in their depths a strong will that as yet knew neither strength nor direction. He was surprised at the feelings of tenderness she aroused in him.

'Perhaps what you say is the truth. How would I know? I only know what I saw. But a word of warning. Those who make thieving their profession are destined for an early death on the gallows. Think on. If you are indeed a thief, then the next time you get caught, the person you rob will show you no leniency.' Christian inclined his head slightly. 'It has been a pleasure meeting you. I doubt our paths will cross again.'

On that note, giving her a farewell salute and a cheeky, knowing wink—a playful, frivolous gesture that infuriated her—he went out, closing the door softly behind him.

Unbeknown to Linnet, had she told him the truth about her reason for being there, he would have readily alleviated her fears and given her an explanation of his own purpose for being in Lord Stourbridge's Egyptian room. This being the case, she could have left knowing Toby would not be arrested for theft. As it was they had both misinterpreted the other's reasons and parted taking their mutual distrust with them, and she was left with the nagging fear that Toby was not out of the woods.

Making his way to the ballroom, Christian saw Lord Stourbridge strutting and posing among his guests like a colourful bird of paradise. Despite his flamboyant, larger-than-life appearance, he was a shrewd businessman who had made a large fortune in clever investments. He was also, like Christian's own father had been, interested in ancient relics and was a keen collector, often travelling to the Holy Land and Egypt with the hope of discovering some precious relics to add to his private collection. The two men had been drawn together by their shared interest.

On seeing Christian, Stourbridge moved towards him.

'Why, Blakely. It is a profound pleasure to see you again. So glad you came.'

'Thank you for inviting me.'

'Lord Stourbridge fixed Christian with an investigative stare. 'Your father's death must have come as a shock to you. What was it? His heart?'

Christian nodded.

'Unfortunately it's one of the hazards of being in Egypt—the heat, you know. Although there are other hazards that play havoc with travellers and explorers alike. They are likely to encounter serious difficulties and indeed great dangers.' He smiled blandly. 'Might I say that like so many persons of our mutual acquaintance I am totally sympathetic to what happened to your father. We met out there. As I believe my lawyer has informed you, I have some of his artefacts among my own collection. The necklace in particular is a beautiful piece, of great value. Thieves are a problem out there. He wanted to make sure it was brought back safely. I was glad to be able to help.'

'I thank you for that and I trust you won't mind if I tell you the necklace is now in my possession.' He patted his pocket. 'Father bequeathed it to the British Museum, along with some other pieces he uncovered. It will be on display shortly.'

'I'm happy to hear it.' Lord Stourbridge was about to turn and walk away when he paused and asked almost hesitantly, 'What about the child—Alice? I seem to recall…'

'She is with me—here in London,' Christian quickly replied. 'I—trust I can rely on your discretion on that matter, Stourbridge.'

He nodded, thoughtful. 'You can depend on it. Wouldn't want to besmirch your father's memory, Blakely.'

'Thank you. I appreciate that.'

As Christian walked away, he put all thoughts of the child from his mind. Instead his thoughts were of the young woman he had invited to spend the night with him. A smile touched his lips. He had enjoyed deceiving her into believing he, too, might be a thief. He need not have challenged her to a roll of dice for possession, but he had enjoyed playing the game. It had been worth it.

Alone now the stranger had left her, fully aware of the enormity of what had just happened, Linnet realised how fortunate she had been to be let off so lightly. The man could have raised the alarm and had her arrested and she would have been unable to prove her innocence. Instead he had bested her and taken that which she had gone to great pains to replace.

The more she thought about it, the more she became convinced that whoever the man was, he was still a thief and if the roll of the dice had gone in her favour—which she doubted—he would not have given her the necklace. It had been important to him. Realising how stupid she had been and that he had duped her, Linnet stared at the closed door with a firestorm of humiliated fury.

Returning to the ballroom, she was impatient to leave. She found Toby and told him to summon the carriage. Thankfully they had come in their own carriage so they didn't have to wait for Aunt Lydia. Behind the mask Linnet's eyes searched the lively, chattering throng, looking for the tall, black-haired man. At first, to her immense relief, she failed to locate him, then, just when she was beginning to think he had left, she saw him.

He stood with a boisterous group of young gentlemen on the other side of the room, a head taller than any of them. With a crush of people milling around them, it couldn't be better for her. Linnet was calm now, icy calm. She had been thrown by his surprise appearance, it had unnerved her, but now she was back in control. She made her way out of the ballroom, eager to put as much distance as she could between her and the irascible gentleman. She was on the point of leaving the ballroom when the dance ended. She paused and glanced back, seeing the stranger's head above the crowd. At that moment he turned his imperious head and his bold, rebel's eyes locked on to hers and he smiled, raising his fingers to his head in a salute, a lazy cocksure smile, with humour and a warning of the danger to them both if anyone should discover what had transpired between them in Lord Stourbridge's Egyptian room.

Audacious as ever, she thought, as she watched the lazy, confident smile on his face. How she would like to wipe that smile from his handsome face. She returned his smile and turned away, becoming swallowed up in the crowd of people vacating the dance floor. No one tried to apprehend her as she left the house.

Linnet hoisted herself into the carriage. The agonising tension she had been under since she had entered Lord Stourbridge's Egyptian room still showed on her face. She saw the anxiety on Toby's face. He clearly regretted stealing the necklace and, despite everything, she knew he cared about her safety and would be vastly relieved to see her back safe.

'Did you manage to put it back?' he asked.

She nodded. 'It went to plan,' she said, looking away. Toby didn't have to know what had happened in Lord Stourbridge's artefacts room. Besides, she didn't want to talk about it.

'I'm sorry, Linnet. I don't know why I agreed to do it.'

Linnet believed him. Toby indulged in any form of gambling, but stealing other people's property was not his forte. Ever since he had fallen in with a wrong crowd—young men who drank, gambled and seduced their way through life—he had changed. Being masters of manipulation the crowd played on Toby's desperation and knew how to use the right combination of charm and menace to ensure his absolute loyalty to the group. Toby also owed them a fortune in gambling debts, which made it impossible for him to refuse whatever they asked him to do. If it were not for the china and other quality objects in the house which Linnet sold off from time to time without Toby's knowledge, they would be unable to make ends meet.

'You know I hate what you do, Toby. I shudder to think what Father would say.'

Clearly feeling guilty, Toby looked away, unable to look into her eyes. 'I know you do and I will try to make things better.'

'It's about time you did,' Linnet said sharply. 'Do you take so little interest in my happiness? I hated what I had to do tonight. I hated it—the anxiety and the misery of it all. I thought I would die a thousand deaths. I will not do anything like it again. You can't steal, Toby. It's a terrible thing to do.'

'Damn it all, don't exaggerate! The theft of the necklace was to have been my friends' biggest haul yet and would have brought a sizeable fortune.'

'For them, Toby. Remember that. What worries me is that if you carry on gambling as you do, your luck will run out and you will be thrown into a debtors' prison.'

Toby turned to her, his eyes holding a hard glitter. She was accustomed to the mask-like expression he used when he didn't wish to discuss what he did, things of which he was ashamed.

'Stop it, Linnet! Don't make a fuss. That won't happen, I'm going to make sure of that. Besides, what other way is there if one wants to gain greater position and a place and power in society?'

'Work, Toby. Honest work. You cannot go on as you do indefinitely. There are lots of people who prefer good honest work without resorting to gambling and stealing other people's property.'

'What kind of work could I possibly do?' he protested crossly. 'I'm not one of the labouring classes, I'm a gentleman—'

'A penniless gentleman,' Linnet was quick to remind him. 'Grow up, Toby, and take responsibility for yourself. There must be something you can do.'

'I am a connoisseur of wine,' Toby retorted, raising his arm with a flourish. 'I suppose I could look for something in that line if the fancy takes me.'

Linnet threw him an exasperated look. He could be such a child. It was always the same when she tried to make him discuss things seriously. However, he was speaking the truth. He had been trained for nothing but how to be a gentleman of leisure. As much as she loved her brother, she had no illusions about him and could not ignore the fact that he was inclined to laziness.

Linnet hated the influence of the men he had become involved with. Some of them had been dragged up on London's meanest streets and were scoundrels, thieves and gamblers of the highest order. Toby had met them in the gambling haunts he frequented with his rakish friends and had been quickly seduced by their gains at the tables. They talked of riches and offered to help pay off Toby's debts, debts he could repay when his circumstances improved, and Toby fell for every word that dripped from their mouths. He steadfastly believed that his association with his new friends was a new and profitable beginning for him and further confirmed the belief that he was in full control of his own destiny and could have whatever he desired. How wrong he was.

Linnet absently pushed back a strand of honey-gold hair that had escaped her wig. The problem of how they were ever going to pay off Toby's debts weighed heavily on her mind. 'I fear greatly what will become of us, Toby. Perhaps you should consider contracting a favourable marriage to help pay off the debts.'

Toby shrugged. 'I've thought of it, but, apart from Caroline, who as you know I would gladly settle down with at the drop of a hat if her father would allow it, there is no one else I wish to marry.'

Linnet knew this to be true. Caroline Mortimer was the youngest of Sir George and Lady Mortimer's five daughters. Toby had become smitten with her when he had met her at a social event twelve months earlier. She was the one good thing that had happened to him in recent months. She was quiet and gentle and he professed to love her dearly. Sir George and his wife were in favour of a match between them, but

Toby knew that if Sir George became aware of his gambling debts he would pull back.

'You should marry, Linnet—someone with money.'

'Without a dowry who would marry me?'

'Someone who would wed you for your own sweet self. If you were to marry a man of means and consequence the creditors would back away.'

'But I have no desire to marry. Must I remind you that the mess we are in is of your own making. They are your debts, not mine,' Linnet remarked, raising her chin and looking away from him, hoping it would indicate the depth of her disappointment in him and that when he realised it, he would begin thinking differently, which he did. He immediately looked contrite and, taking her hand, he gave it a gentle squeeze.

Aware of the intensity of her feelings and her fear, Toby softened. 'I'm sorry, Linnet. None of this is fair on you, I know. If anyone's to blame for tonight it's me. I will try harder. I promise.'

From the way he looked at her Linnet knew that he recognised the truth contained in her words. 'I know you will,' she replied while not holding out much hope. Exasperating as she found it, she loved her brother more than anyone else and couldn't imagine living without him. But she was afraid, more afraid than she had ever been in her life. Afraid not just for Toby and herself, but for the whole future.

'Look, I know how difficult this is for you,' Toby said. 'I've been thinking. I know we said we wouldn't accept Aunt Lydia's invitation to go to Richmond for the celebration of Louisa's betrothal to Harry, but maybe we should. It was good to see them tonight. Cousin Louisa is your age and it benefits you to have some female company.'

Linnet could not deny that the idea of visiting her cousin appealed to her. She was piercingly lonely. She lacked female companionship and the love and affection of their mother, who had passed away several years earlier, followed so quickly by their father. She and Toby both knew the invitation to Louisa's betrothal celebrations had been issued half-heartedly. Aunt Lydia, their mother's sister and a widow of eight years, was a hard, unfeeling woman who looked on them as poor relations she would rather distance herself from than have in the house. She had offered to chaperon Linnet to the ball tonight under sufferance and both Linnet and Toby were aware of that. But they were her nephew and niece and she was duty bound not to ignore them. She toadied to the elite—money and position carried more weight than goodwill and good intentions.

Besides, Caroline Mortimer was Louisa's friend so it was highly likely that she would be present, which would cheer Toby.

Three days after the Stourbridge ball found Linnet accompanied by Toby going into the city to make one or two small purchases. Linnet loved to come and browse the shops, with everything the merchants possessed displayed behind windows along the Strand and the courts and passages leading off it, even though she couldn't afford to venture inside most of them. Today the Strand was crowded and bustling, with carriages and drays and sedans passing to and fro in a never-ending stream. Merchants and traders and hawkers of wares mingled with people of all occupations and positions and gentlemen in military uniforms. She breathed in the different smells from freshly baked bread and hot pies.

Suddenly confusion erupted when a dog appeared out of nowhere, yapping ferociously and baring its teeth. It ran into the street in front of two stationary bay horses hitched to a carriage. One of the startled horses gave a snort of alarm. It reared in the shafts, its hooves awkwardly flailing the air, before coming down to earth and lunging forward, unsettling the other horse. It tossed its head back and forth, the whites of its eyes rolling. The open carriage swayed precariously, the driver losing hold of the reins as he was flung out on to the ground, while the elderly lady and small child inside the carriage gripped it for dear life.

Linnet had completed her shopping and was heading towards the carriage further along the street where Toby had told her he would wait, when she paused to watch what was happening. Seeing the horse's nostrils flared and its ears pulled back, Linnet suspected the horse was about to bolt with its partner in the shafts meaning the lady and child were in danger of being flung out on to the street. She had to try to prevent it from happening. Linnet was accustomed to handling horses, so, acting swiftly and unafraid, she dropped the bag that held her few practical purchases on the ground and stepped into the path of the agitated horse, holding her arms wide and uttering soothing words in an attempt to calm it down. Thankfully it seemed to work for the horse became still. Taking hold of a loose rein, Linnet continued talking to it while she ran her free hand gently along its quivering silky neck.

The driver had picked himself up and come to her aid, calming the other horse.

'It's all right, miss. I'm grateful to you for calming him down—that wretched dog, running out like that. I'll take him now.'

Linnet passed over the rein and, retrieving her purchases, went to make sure the lady in the carriage was unhurt. She had a comforting arm around the child—a girl perhaps four or five years old with curly dark brown hair peeking out from beneath her bonnet. Her face showed confusion and she was clearly anxious and frightened. A tear rolled down her cheek. Linnet climbed up into the carriage and sat facing her. Leaning across, she smiled at the weeping child, producing a handkerchief. 'Here, let me wipe your face.' Gently she dabbed at the tears of the child, who was looking up at her with solemn brown eyes that reminded her of a wounded puppy. 'What is your name?' she asked.

'Alice,' she whispered.

'Is that so. Well, I think that's a lovely name.'

Linnet directed her gaze at the lady, who was of slight build and in middle age, dressed in black and unadorned—the same clothes a nursemaid or a housekeeper would wear. Her eyes were grey and melan-

choly surmounted by firm arched brows. The general
impression was of physical frailty, but the face revealed pride and obstinacy, although she did look
slightly shaken as she tried to comfort the child.

'Everything is all right now,' Linnet told her,
speaking quietly in an attempt to calm the lady. 'Your
driver is with the horse.'

'I can't thank you enough for your brave interven-
tion. But for your prompt action we would have been
tossed out of the carriage. I am so grateful.'

'You have no companion with you?'

'Oh, yes. My employer is conducting some business further along the street. He will be back shortly.'

'Then if you like, I will wait with you until he re-
turns.'

'I would appreciate that. You are very kind.'

Linnet smiled into the lady's kindly face. Despite
the shock of being rocked about in the carriage, she
now sat ramrod straight. Apart from her hat being
slightly askew she appeared recovered.

'It's the least I can do.'

'This is Alice,' the lady said. 'She is my charge
until my employer can find a governess for her. I am
Mrs Marsden.'

'You are Alice's nursemaid.'

She nodded and smiled. 'I suppose I am—although
I'm getting a bit long in the tooth now to be looking
after little ones. I'll be able to take a back seat when
she has a governess to take care of her.'

Linnet glanced at her sharply. 'Your employer is
looking for a governess, you say?'

'That is correct.' Seeing she had pricked Linnet's interest, she tilted her head to one side and studied her with interest. 'Do you know of anyone who would be interested by any chance?'

'Why—I—I was thinking of myself. I have been considering seeking employment for a while now.'

'Do you like children, Miss…?'

'Osborne. Linnet Osborne and, yes, I do like children.'

'And your education?'

'I was educated at Miss Reid's Academy in Kensington.'

'Splendid. Well—if you are interested I will mention it to my employer—although he is a very busy man and tends to leave household matters to his housekeeper and where Alice is concerned to me, of course. Would you consider the position?'

'I will—although I shall have to speak to my brother. Since our parents passed on there are just the two of us.'

Mrs Marsden looked down at the child, who had been listening intently. A little smile tugged at the corners of her mouth. She seemed to be assessing her and when her eyes ceased to regard her so seriously and her smile gradually broadened, which was a delight to see, Linnet returned the smile.

Linnet enjoyed talking to Mrs Marsden. It made her realise how isolated she was at Birch House with just Toby and the housekeeper for company. Glancing down the street and seeing Toby striding towards their carriage, she excused herself on the understanding that Mrs Marsden would contact her at Birch House when she had spoken to her employer.

Having witnessed the entire incident, but being too far away to be of immediate assistance, Christian hurried towards the carriage which contained Alice and her nurse, their safety paramount to all else. He had seen a young woman step out into the path of the frightened horse and calm it down. He was too far away to see her clearly, but her prompt action had brought what could have been a serious situation under control, although it was an extremely foolish thing to have done. Stepping in front of an out-of-control horse was dangerous, but he was glad that she had.

Seeing that all was well and the normal order of things had been restored, he paused momentarily to acknowledge an acquaintance.

Walking in the direction of her carriage and seeing the tall gentleman ahead of her, Linnet's eyes opened wide in overwhelmed disbelief. Thankfully he was in deep conversation with another gentleman and was unaware of her presence. He had appeared too suddenly for her to prepare herself. Momentarily immobilised in the cataclysmic silence that seemed to descend on her, her right hand pressed to her throat, Linnet was incapable of speech or action as she stared at the man as though she had seen a ghost. There was hardly a moment when she didn't relive the humiliation of being caught by the stranger. Now, three days later, the scene was as raw and mortifying as it had been when it had taken place. The memory brought with it a black mask and dark eyes and the memory of frustration and desire mingled with her embarrassment.

As her mind raced in wild circles, her thoughts tumbling over themselves, Linnet thought she must be seeing things—that she must be suffering from some kind of delusion. But even without his mask, all her senses remembered the tall and arrogant-looking man with the dark penetrating eyes. It was the stranger she had met at the Stourbridge ball, the man who had kissed her so ardently and suggested she spend the night with him. She knew him by the rich, hypnotically deep voice as he spoke to the other gentleman and the sudden heat that sprang to her cheeks that was her own response to him.

Linnet had adamantly tried not to think of him, but despite herself a tremor of remembered passion and bittersweet memories coursed through her. The continuation of the desire he had awoken in Linnet confounded her. She was still reeling from the impact of him, shattered by the power of the physical attraction she felt for him. She had never realised she had been capable of such intense passion. Nothing in her experience had prepared her for what he had done to her, or the emotions he had aroused, triggering off an explosion of sensuality the like of which she could never have imagined, prompting her to respond in a way that astounded her. As shock waves tingled up and down her spine, she hurried on by, averting her face.

* * *

But Christian, his acquaintance having said farewell and gone on his way, had seen her and gave her his full attention. He saw a young woman attired in a dark blue informal dress, fitted jacket and matching bonnet covering her hair. Looking into her tawny-coloured eyes when she looked his way, he felt a frisson of recognition. It was the young woman who had so intrigued him at the Stourbridge ball. Even without her white wig and the concealing mask he knew it was her. He was as surprised as she clearly was and didn't realise she was the young woman who had just averted a major disaster when one of his carriage horses had nearly bolted.

Taking her arm when she was about to hurry on, he smiled. 'So, it is you. I thought I recognised you—even without your mask.'

The two stared at each other for a long moment and Linnet was conscious of an odd feeling wrenching her stomach as she helplessly berated herself and the instinct that had driven her to leap unthinkingly to the rescue of the elderly lady and child about to be flung out of their carriage. Pulling herself together, Linnet wanted to turn on her heels and run, but in a moment, common sense prevailed over the embarrassment which had taken hold of her.

Stepping back, she said, 'I beg you will excuse me, sir. I am in a hurry.'

'Not in such a hurry that you cannot pass the time of day with—how shall I put it—an old friend.'

'You are not an old friend and we have nothing to say to one another…'

His smile deepened and a look came into his eyes that Linnet did not care for. 'I seem to remember that we had a great deal to say to one another at the Stourbridge ball.'

Momentarily distracted, Christian glanced at the driver of his carriage who had climbed inside. Taking advantage of the distraction, the woman dragged her arm from his grip and turned and slipped into the crowd. By the time he looked again, she had disappeared. His eyes searched for her among the crowd of people milling about on the street, but there was no sign of her. His disappointment was profound. He could not believe that he had allowed her to slip through his fingers.

The simple truth was that he was strongly attracted to the young woman and she was far too beautiful for any man to turn his back on. Having seen her today without her disguise, he was astounded by the force of his feelings. He was quite bewildered by the emotion he felt in his heart. He couldn't really describe what he felt for her because he didn't have any words. All he knew was that he felt strange—different from anything he had ever expected to feel.

Only now when he had returned from Egypt after sorting out his father's affairs was he beginning to get his life under control. Eventually he would marry, but until that time he did not want a woman in his house, at his table or in his bed. He could satisfy his physical needs well enough with women seeking diversion for a few night hours, women who wanted from him what he wanted from them.

And yet he wanted this young woman whose kiss had roused emotions in him like no other woman ever had before her. He had to find out who she was. She had run from him but he was determined to find her. Someone must know who she was.

Reaching the carriage, Christian was relieved to see the occupants were no worse for the incident which could have resulted in injury but for the stranger's prompt action to calm the frightened horse.

Preoccupied as he was with thoughts of the young woman who had just escaped him and determined to find her—starting with Lord Stourbridge who might know the lady she was with at the ball—Christian only half-listened as Mrs Marsden gave him an account of the conversation she'd had with the young woman who had rescued them, telling him that she was well educated and was considering seeking a position as a governess. Christian knew by the hopeful expression when she looked at him that she wanted him to say he would consider giving her employment. He was to leave for his estate in Sussex the day after tomorrow and had no time to seek a governess for Alice. Trusting Mrs Marsden's judgement completely, he told her to go ahead and employ the young lady if she considered her suitable.

Chapter Three

Woodside Hall was the ancestral home of four generations of Miltons. It was a large, sprawling half-timbered structure and so beautiful that Linnet temporarily forgot her anxieties and looked forward to the next day's celebrations. They were admitted by the butler, who guided them into the drawing room. For the celebratory event the house was done simply but elegantly, each room decked with urns of fragrant summer flowers. The chandeliers, which maids had spent the week dusting, hung from the ceilings and wood polished to a warm sheen glowed in the quiet statement of elegance and quiet good taste.

Aunt Lydia stopped fussing with some flowers and came to greet them, although her attitude was cold and unwelcoming. With a twenty-four-year-old son as well as her twenty-two-year-old daughter, she had high hopes that they would both soon be wed. Her son William had inherited Woodside Hall, Lady Milton continued to act as mistress. When William took a wife, she would retire to the Dower House.

'Thank you for inviting us, Aunt Lydia,' Toby said. 'We are both happy for Louisa and Harry is such a grand chap.'

'Yes,' Linnet agreed. 'Louisa is so fortunate.'

'So is Harry,' Lady Milton remarked, 'to be marrying Louisa.'

'Yes, Of course,' Toby mumbled.

'I expect you would like to freshen up after your journey. The rooms I have allotted to you are on the upper floor—there will be a large complement of guests to accommodate. I know you will understand.'

Pride enabled Linnet to smile and pretend to ignore the insult. Where her aunt was concerned, wealth and position carried more weight than good intentions. She felt no surprise on being given rooms on the servants' floor. She had expected nothing better. If Aunt Lydia knew the true state of their affairs, she would have an apoplexy. Although if they didn't find a solution to their problems soon, then it was inevitable that she would find out and be sure to distance herself from them even further.

After freshening up in her room, Linnet went in search of Louisa. Louisa was the same age as Linnet, but unlike her cousin had a generous dowry. She was pretty, too, with a sweet expression and bright blue eyes. Linnet's mother had died when she was fifteen and her father had followed three years later. Afterwards, Linnet found living at Birch House alone with Toby difficult and was oppressed by a terrible feeling of isolation. During that time, Louisa had been her salvation. She was vibrant and charming and could not be found wanting in those accomplishments that characterise a young lady. Linnet envied her cousin her home and her closeness to her brother William, who adored her and showered her with many gifts.

'You'll have a beau soon, Linnet. You'll see.'

With the sun beating down on them, the two girls were stretched out on the grass in a quiet part of the garden.

Linnet gave a deep sigh. She didn't have a beau and nor was she likely to, yet thoughts of her encounter with the handsome stranger at the Stourbridge ball were never far from her mind. She remembered everything about him—how could she not after he had kissed her so ardently? His voice was deep and seductive and made her think of highly improper things. It had seemed to caress each word he had spoken and she knew there weren't many women who could resist a voice like that—especially if he were also over six feet tall and built like a Greek athlete of old. Linnet had not been immune to that potent allure he exuded.

Her cousin would be shocked if she knew the true nature of her situation. The truth of it was that she was envious of Louisa. Linnet was lonelier than she had ever been and it was beginning to take its toll. It frightened her to think about the future. She kept her fears to herself and no one saw the vulnerable side of her. She was in need of love and so afraid she would never find it, and she wanted to, so very much. Linnet sighed, a sigh of regret. There was no use wishing for things she could not have. She wanted to stay in the moment, with the sun on her face and the smell of roses and honeysuckle heavy on the air and listening to Louisa's happy chatter.

'It's different for me, Louisa. I have no dowry and, apart from you and William and Aunt Lydia, my only kin is Toby. I know he can be difficult sometimes, but it is fortunate that deep down he has a fondness for me and he can be considerate when he tries.'

'I'm so glad you like Harry, Linnet. He's so caring and charming. I can't wait to marry him and go to live in Kent. The betrothal party promises to be exciting. Mama has gone to a lot of trouble and expense to make it right.'

'Then that is what it will be.'

Louisa turned her head and looked at her. 'You never know, Linnet. There might be someone here who will draw your attention—a rich gentleman who is looking for a wife.'

Linnet laughed, closing her eyes and stretching her young body on the grass beneath her that felt like rich velvet. She was her own person and as isolated as she had always been. 'I really don't think so, Louisa. I'm not on the market for a husband—rich or poor.'

On the day of the celebrations the reception rooms were filled with people. Whenever Lady Milton entertained she liked to relax the rules. There was always plenty of amusement without any of the coarser element that vulgarised so many of the stately homes of England. She had sufficient force of character to steer clear of any such difficulties at her parties.

Lord Christian Blakely was impressed by the house and its prospect. He had been greeted by Lady Milton. After enquiring of Lord and Lady Stourbridge as to the identity of the lady, giving them a rather hazy description—although he did remember the red and black mask she had been wearing—Lady Stourbridge recalled Lady Milton had been wearing one just like it. She also told him that she had escorted her niece and nephew, Toby Osborne and his sister Linnet, to the ball. Convinced this was the young lady he was searching for they were happy to provide him with further information regarding Lady Milton. Her daughter Louisa was about to become betrothed to Harry Radcliffe and she was to host the celebratory event at Woodside Hall in Richmond.

Christian was impatient to see Miss Osborne again—he wanted to see her. He hadn't been honest with her when he had come across her in Lord Stourbridge's room of antiquities and it bothered him. As well as that, what she had said just before he had left her, that she hadn't stolen the necklace but was there to put it back—what if that was the truth? If so, he had done her an injustice. It was important to him that he set things right. He also wanted to gaze at her lovely face and lose himself in those tawny eyes of hers. As an acquaintance of Lord Radcliffe and after contacting him at his club, he had managed to have his name placed on the guest list for the betrothal celebrations.

He took casual note of the guests. Having recognised Miss Osborne without the mask she had worn to the Stourbridge ball, he now knew what she looked like.

Doors opened from the large, circular hall, the French doors from the long dining room opening on to the terrace. The trees in the gardens were hung with lanterns, which would be lit at dusk, when a hundred pinpoints of light would shine sharply as guests wandered along the pathways. Stepping out into the gardens, he exchanged smiles and polite greetings with other guests. Some of them he knew—those he didn't looked at him with open curiosity.

The lawns had been mown to resemble smooth velvet and the borders and terraces were ablaze with flowers and trailing roses and dotted with graceful sculptures. Most of the privileged, rich and well-connected guests had already arrived and spilled out into the gardens. Lady Milton flitted like a butterfly among the titled and influential people, their brightly coloured gowns, jackets and painted parasols echoing the bright colours of the flowerbeds.

With his hands behind his back, ignoring the scrutiny of the other guests, Christian's pace was slow as he looked for Miss Osborne. The sun was hot, the air heavy with humidity, which, he thought, might run to rain later. Conversations, laughter and the rustle of gowns eddied about him, competing with the hum of bees. Lords and ladies sat around sipping punch or lemonade from crystal glasses. Some of the fashionable, overdressed gentlemen were sprawled on benches and some stretched out on the lawn, drink-

ing wine and talking and laughing much too loudly
as the liquor loosened their inhibitions.

Hearing shrieks and giggles from behind a tall
privet hedge, he felt an invisible thread draw him in
that direction and entered an enclosed lawned garden. Bright sunlight illuminated a happy group of
young people playing a game, their faces alight with
laughter and flushed with exertion. In an array of
brightly coloured gowns and decorated bonnets, they
were circled around a girl in a bright yellow dress
who held centre stage. A scarf was tied around her
eyes, her hands held out in front of her, her mouth
stretched wide with merriment. Spinning on her heel,
she laughed and her skirts billowed out, exposing
shapely ankles encased in white stockings. Having
disposed of her bonnet better to accommodate the
scarf, her head was full of luxuriant honey-gold curling locks that bounced as she tossed her head.

Transfixed, Christian's gaze homed in on her, staring openly at her and savouring the supple grace in
the way she moved. The young ladies, as skittish as
ponies with the wind up their tails, paid him no attention, seemingly immersed in their game. He began to
move slowly across the grass, drawn compulsively to
the young woman in the yellow dress. His footsteps
made no sound and she was laughing, unaware of his
approach. He smiled for her laughter was infectious.
He stopped close to her, bewitched by this picture she
presented. He was aware of a surge of heat inside him
that had nothing to do with the warmth of the sun.
She reached out to clasp a player, only to find thin air

as her prey nimbly danced aside and others reached out to touch and tease her.

Coming closer to Christian, who stood perfectly still, she reached out her arms and one of her hands came to rest on his arm.

A bubble of laughter escaped her. 'At last,' she cried, her smile unfurling like a pennant on her lips. 'I have someone. Harry—it has to be you.'

Her hand moved from his arm to his broad chest and upwards, tentatively feeling his chest, his height. 'Oh—you are not Harry.' Her breath was a quiet whisper, her lips soft and moist and parted to reveal perfect teeth that shone like pearls. 'It is a gentleman, I think.' Her hands sought to identify this mysterious being, small fingers gently touching his face so far above her own—his cheek, the wide brow, the nose, the lips, lingering there a moment before moving to the other cheek, encountering a narrow scar.' She withdrew her hand fractionally. 'Oh! You've been hurt! I am at a loss, sir. I feel I do not know you.'

Quickly removing the blindfold, Linnet blinked her eyes a moment to adjust them to the bright light, becoming focused on the stranger—but he wasn't a stranger, not to her.

At first she was unmoving and lost in a confused welter of troubling thoughts, then all the feelings she had experienced since the night of the Stourbridge ball came rolling back. All she could do was stand and stare at him with her lips slightly parted, her heart beating a rapid tattoo in her chest.

Tall and straight, and with a whipcord strength, he emanated an aura of carefully restrained power. The area around them was so charged with tension it was as if all the air had been removed.

Linnet stepped back, unable to look away. 'Please forgive me…' she breathed softly. 'I—I did not mean…'

Inclining his head slightly, he smiled, giving no indication of recognition. For a moment she was allowed to hope this was just a chance encounter and he would continue on his way. She bobbed a small curtsy. 'E-excuse me…' she stammered.

Her haste seemed to amuse him. A smile lit his eye. 'Just one moment, if you please.'

Linnet looked at the girls standing around, but she couldn't get her eyes to settle on them for more than a few seconds. Sick with uncertainty, she waited for him to speak, clutching the scarf in her hands in front of her.

The man bent his head and spoke softly in her ear, his warm breath fanning her neck. 'Did you think you could escape me so easily? I'm hardly surprised to see you at such a fashionable gathering when there are rich pickings to be had.'

Indignation flushed Linnet's cheeks. 'I would not… I am hardly likely to… Oh, how dare you—'

'Oh, but I do dare, Miss Osborne.'

She stared at him in disbelief. 'You know who I am? How did you find out?'

He smiled down at her, enjoying her confusion. 'It wasn't difficult.'

'But—what are you doing here?' It was a coincidence. It had to be. 'Do you know Aunt Lydia?'

'We have not met until today. Lord Radcliffe is a close acquaintance of mine.' He glanced around, conscious of the young ladies observing their exchange in open-mouthed curiosity. 'We have an audience. We will speak later.'

Smiling, he met Linnet's stare, his eyebrows rising, and then without more ado he took his leave of her. For a long moment she watched him stride away. The next thing she was aware of was Louisa by her side, an excited flush on her cheeks.

'That was Lord Blakely and as handsome as a man can be, don't you think?' she uttered on a sigh, as struck as all the other females in their group gazing after him.

'Lord Blakely?'

'Christian, Lord Blakely. I think he's also an earl of somewhere or other.'

'Oh—I… I didn't know.' Blinking like someone waking from a dream, Linnet looked at Louisa for further information about the man in whose arms she had surrendered and even contemplated spending the night with without even knowing his name.

'Harry was surprised to see him here,' Louisa went on. 'He didn't know Lord Blakely was back in London and had no idea he had been invited, although I do believe he is a close acquaintance of his father. He's been out of the country for several months—in Egypt, apparently. He spoke to you so you must know him, Linnet?'

Linnet flushed, knowing how scandalised her cousin would be if she were to learn of the sordid circumstances that had brought them together.

'No—I—how could I? What was he doing in Egypt?'

'Rumour has it that his father died over there. He was an archaeologist, I think—loved digging for ancient relics and the like. Lord Blakely went out there to sort his father's affairs out, I imagine.'

Linnet shook her head, still feeling the after-effects of her encounter with Lord Blakely. 'What else?'

'Only that he is a man of considerable wealth. William is acquainted with him and from what I have heard him say a great deal of his fortune comes from land, taking no account of his industrial interests—which are considerable apparently—and the properties he owns, mainly in London.'

No longer in any mood to join in the games with the other young ladies, Linnet escaped to the house to prepare for the evening's festivities.

Entering the small room allotted to her in the upper reaches of the house, she discovered the maid had laid out her pitiful belongings. Her nightdress was folded on the bed and the pale gold gown she was to wear, the dress she had worn to the Stourbridge ball, hung pathetically on a hanger on the wardrobe.

She was just putting the finishing touches to her hair when Louisa burst in, brimming with happiness.

'Oh, there you are!' she exclaimed. 'I was wondering where you had disappeared to. You're not feeling ill, are you, Linnet? You did look rather pale earlier.'

'No, I feel fine,' Linnet said with a practised smile, giving Louisa no indication of the turmoil inside her.

'I'm relieved to hear it.' She cast a disdainful eye over Linnet's gown, a gown she had seen many times.

Fully aware of what her cousin was thinking, before she could make any comment, Linnet said, 'I know what you're thinking, Louisa, that this gown has seen the light of day many times, but I have nothing else suitable.'

'I would be more than happy to let you have some of mine. I'm sure Mama wouldn't mind if you—'

'No—thank you, Louisa. Thank you for your kind offer,' Linnet said in a low voice, 'but I will make do with what I have—such as it may be.' She had seen inside Louisa's wardrobe. Never had she seen so many fine gowns. 'I know you mean well, but I wouldn't hear of it. Our income doesn't reach to refurbishing my wardrobe at this present time—but I am sure things will improve.'

Louisa knew better than to make further comment and, clearly having no wish to offend Linnet, she changed the subject. 'I asked Harry about Lord Blakely. It appears he wasn't on Mama's list of guests.'

'Then how does he come to be here if he was not invited?'

'Apparently he approached Harry's father for an invitation—which is highly irregular. Although why he would want to attend a betrothal party when he is not acquainted with Mama is a mystery.'

'I suppose it is rather unconventional.'

'Mama doesn't mind in the slightest since Harry's father has a high opinion of Lord Blakely. Now I would like you to come down to the party with me at once. I wouldn't want you to miss me having the first dance with Harry. Mama insists that everything must be done right.' With happy laughter bubbling from her lips, Louisa took Linnet's hand, who allowed her to shepherd her merrily down to the salon.

Louisa went to find Harry, leaving Linnet to mingle with the large complement of guests making their way to the large drawing room in which the furniture and carpets had been removed to allow for the dancing. Louisa was clad in a peach-satin gown embroidered with pink roses that beautifully flattered her creamy complexion. Her cheeks were flushed and her eyes were shining with excitement as she sought her betrothed, finding him surrounded by a crowd of young men, all in high spirits before the evening had even begun.

Linnet blinked against the bright lights of the chandeliers that hung down from the ornately plastered ceiling, bearing innumerable candles whose illumination was reflected in the gilt-framed mirrors on the surrounding walls. Lords and ladies gathered round, the ladies complimenting each other lavishly on their gowns and eager for the small orchestra to begin playing, so they would be whisked away to dance a quadrille or a country dance.

Linnet immediately looked for Toby, finding him standing alone on the side of the room. He was observing the proceedings and in particular Caroline Mortimer. On her arrival with her parents and one of her older sisters, Linnet had watched as a joyful Toby had stepped forward to greet her. She had given him a shy look from beneath her lashes, flushing prettily at the attention he was showering on her.

Linnet's heart ached for her brother, wishing with her whole heart that things would work out for him and that he would eventually be granted his heart's desire and be allowed to make Caroline his wife. With her fair hair and deep blue eyes, she was a very pretty, happy and lively young woman. She had perfect manners, excellent conversation and highly developed powers of social observation—her talents made her therefore uniquely positioned to become a gentleman's wife—hopefully Toby's—and mistress of Birch House. But unless Toby's circumstances improved, then her father would never allow it.

In a brooding silence Linnet watched as a cool and serene Lady Milton, mother of the bride-to-be, presided over the occasion with her usual high level of competence. The music began and the newly betrothed couple stepped on to the dance floor. The room quietened for them for it was surely a match made in heaven. Harry held Louisa's hand as though she was his most treasured possession which at that moment she was. And there was no denying the look of melting love in Louisa's eyes when they settled upon Harry Radcliffe.

* * *

With a false smile pinned to her face, surrounded by the laughter and the warmth as the evening progressed, sipping her lemonade, Linnet didn't move far from Toby's side lest he wandered into the room that had been set aside for gaming. He had promised her he wouldn't and, much as she would like to trust him, she knew he was easily swayed and might succumb to temptation. The event was turning out to be a huge success, with weaving lines of dancers twirling around the polished floor, yet a wave of loneliness washed through her.

Wistfully she glanced around, wondering where Lord Blakely could be and hoping he had left. Then she saw him—tall and perfectly built and as virile as a Greek god. Her stomach lurched and the ballroom spun around her in a blur of colour. From the starched perfection of his neckcloth to his white-silk stockings and black dress shoes, he was perfection. She observed his popularity as he mingled with the guests. His arrival among them had caused quite a stir—it wasn't often that a man with so mysterious a background appeared among them.

He moved with the confident ease of a man well assured of his masculinity and his own worth. He conversed politely, seeming to give them his full attention. He threw back his head and laughed loud at something one of the gentlemen said to him, his even white teeth gleaming between his lips, causing everyone within close proximity to turn their heads in his direction, such was the effect this handsome, most popular bachelor had on others.

All the while the major part of Christian's attention and his mesmerising eyes were flitting about the room, looking for someone. When they came to rest on Miss Osborne his whole sum and substance had become concentrated on her. She drifted into his vision like a butterfly, completely at odds with the young woman he had come upon playing a game with the other young ladies earlier. She moved with a fluency and elegance that drew the eye. Her back was straight, her head tilted proudly and her small breasts, thrust forward, showed beneath the modest bodice of her gown.

A slow, sardonic smile curved his lips when he caught her eye and he inclined his head ever so slightly.

To Linnet the movement was like an intimate caress. She felt a flush start somewhere behind her knees and creep up her body. To her relief he made no move to approach her, but he seemed to be making sure she was always within his sights. She watched him perambulate among the guests, carrying his pride, arrogance in his attitude, aware of his superiority. His eyes followed her every move like a predatory hawk, his smile that of a hunter.

As the evening wore on and she could no longer see him, Linnet assumed he must have left. Toby moved away to dance attention on Caroline. Linnet danced two dances, a quadrille with Harry and a lively country dance with her cousin William that left her quite breathless.

About to go in search of Toby, she turned as a tall figure materialised from the shadows and came to stand in front of her. The musicians were beginning to play a waltz.

'Dance with me, Miss Osborne.'

His voice was deep and made Linnet think of thick honey. It seemed to caress each word he uttered. 'That would not be appropriate,' she said, having no wish to dance with him at all, especially not the waltz, a dance considered to be fast and daring and banned at Almack's.

Lord Blakely laughed. 'Why, what is this, Miss Osborne? Are you afraid to dance with me?'

'Not at all.'

His eyes shot to hers as an absolutely ridiculous thought suddenly occurred to him. 'You are familiar with the waltz? You do dance?'

With a sparkle in her eyes and a tilt to her head, the smile she gave him was sublime.

'Like a fairy,' she quipped.

He laughed. 'Thank the Lord for that,' he said, taking her gloved hand and leading her on to the dance floor before she could object.

Favouring the dance to become close to their partners, other couples crowded on to the floor. A huge sea of people seemed to press towards them and voices erupted as heads turned and fans fluttered and people craned their necks to observe the couple about to take to the floor.

Lord Blakely gathered her into his arms. Linnet wasn't at all sure she could do it, but the challenge in his dark eyes made demurring unthinkable. Giddiness threatened to take hold of her.

'Relax.' Lord Blakely looked down at her. She almost missed her step, but his arm tightened, holding her steady. 'Focus your eyes on me and follow my lead,' he said, steering her into the first gliding steps as the graceful music washed over her.

Linnet's feet followed where his led of their own volition, and her mind opened to the sensations of the dance. She was aware of the hardness of her companion's thighs against hers and the subtle play of her skirts about her legs. The scent of his cologne was fleeting, a clean, masculine smell. The seductive notes of the music were mirrored in their movements and the sway was a sensual delight. Lord Blakely's hand on her waist was firm, his touch confident as he whisked her smoothly about the floor.

After looking at them attentively, the couples on the dance floor renewed their interest in the music. Conversations were resumed and everyone got on with enjoying themselves.

When the dance ended, Lord Blakely put his hand under Linnet's elbow and guided her off the dance floor. When he suggested they dance the next, an allemande, laughter bubbled to Linnet's lips.

'Oh, no—the allemande is a dance with too much twirling and exchanging of hands. Please—can we abandon that idea?'

Lord Blakely willingly agreed. They were close to the doors opening on to the terrace and, feeling the heat of the room exacerbated by the dance, it seemed perfectly natural to step outside. With her Aunt Lydia's eyes fixed upon her from across the room, it was obvious Linnet was about to refuse until she caught the impassioned plea on his face and stepped outside.

A lazy somnolence had descended on the gardens and the perfume of roses was heavy and sweet.

Linnet inhaled deeply, gazing into the night. Conscious of Lord Blakely's silence, she turned her head. He was half-perched on the balustrade, watching her. Gone was the open hostility he'd shown towards her so far. In its place was something different, warmer, almost appreciative.

'Why do you stare at me?' she asked, finding it virtually impossible to ignore the tug of his eyes.

'Because, Miss Osborne, I have never met anyone quite like you.'

'Are you always so forthright? You are smiling—as if you are on the verge of laughing at me.'

'Not at you. For some unfathomable reason you surprise me at every turn—and if I am smiling it is because I happen to like you.'

'Why on earth would you?'

* * *

Because, he thought, she was exquisite and put all the pale, simpering, overeager English roses who came out each Season in the shade. He smiled, his pleasant thoughts of her bringing a warmth and humour to his face. Her mouth was full and a luscious shade of deep pink. He noticed, too, she had an unbelievably small waist and a long, lovely neck. Her tawny-coloured eyes were quite extraordinarily wide with a slight upward slant that emphasised her high cheekbones. Her skin was creamy smooth and rich with a translucency that had him wondering whether it continued beneath the gown she wore. He speculated and the thought put a covetous gleam in his eyes.

'Why shouldn't I like you?' he said, in answer to her question.

'Because there have been times when I have behaved as no proper young lady should.'

'I agree, but since you consented to dance with me then you are forgiven.'

'That's gracious of you to say so, but I really was quite horrid to you when we first met. I—also behaved in a most improper manner.' Linnet glanced at him and smiled, shaking her shining head as the memory of how she had looked and behaved that night assailed her, and when she met his eyes she saw that he remembered it, too.

'It will be imprinted on my mind for ever.'

'I sincerely hope you will forget it. I was quite shameless—we both were,' she murmured, licking her bottom lip, unwittingly unaware of how this simple gesture warmed Lord Blakely's blood.

'It wasn't like that at all. We kissed—by mutual consent as I recall. Although I recall my mother had other ideas on one's behaviour before marriage—both male and female. She was very strict and of the opinion that a young lady should live under the scrutiny of family members. Her acquaintances with the opposite sex should be selected and chaperoned, and if she is caught in any compromising situation her reputation would be ruined and she would in all probability see out the rest of her days in a convent.'

'Goodness! I find that a bit extreme, but then—my mother died when I was quite young so I missed out on the advice.'

'I'm sorry about that.' He was silent for a moment and then he said, 'I have a confession to make. I'm afraid I wasn't honest with you. I should have told you the truth about the necklace.'

'Oh?'

'My father discovered it in Egypt. As you know it is extremely valuable. Thieves abounded in the camps. Lord Stourbridge was a friend of his. He was to return to England before him and my father asked him to bring it to England for safe keeping—which he did. I was merely taking it back.'

'And you let me believe you were stealing it.'

'No. You assumed.'

'Like you assumed I was a thief.'

'Are you telling me you weren't there to steal it?'

Linnet was indignant. 'No—although I cannot

blame you for believing that was what I was doing. But I was there under duress. I told you I was there to put it back.'

'Yes, you did. I didn't know whether to believe you or not.'

'I was telling the truth.'

'Then if you were putting it back, someone must have stolen it in the first place.'

She nodded and turned away, struggling against the insidious feeling of shame which was steadily crushing her. Her immediate feeling was one of drowning—how could Toby have brought them to this?

Christian moved closer. Having made discreet enquiries into her family background, he knew the Osbornes were an old and distinguished family, but the extravagance of Toby Osborne and his weakness for the gaming tables had frittered away most of his inheritance, leaving his sister to live on a virtual pittance at Birch House.

'Would you care to tell me who that person was? Would I be correct in thinking it was your brother? I passed him in the passage returning to the festivities. I'm beginning to realise he had been visiting Lord Sturbridge's artefacts room. Lord Stourbridge is proud of his finds and it is unfortunate that he told all and sundry of the priceless beauty of the necklace, unwittingly making it a target for every thief in London.'

Linnet stared straight ahead of her, aware that Lord Blakely was standing directly behind her, almost touching her, so close that she could smell the tang of his cologne. How she would like to unburden herself, to tell him how she had begged Toby countless times to give up his reckless, expensive way of life, for if he did not heed the situation, then ruination would very soon be knocking on their door.

'It was Toby,' she confirmed quietly, turning to face him. 'He—he realises that what he did was wrong and he has never done anything like that before—or will do again.'

Christian watched the tension and emotion play across her lovely, expressive face and tried to put her at her ease. 'For your sake I hope he is sincere.'

'What I don't understand is if the necklace really did belong to you, what was all that nonsense with the dice?'

He laughed. 'I apologise. I couldn't resist teasing you.'

'Teasing? Is that what you call it? I was beside myself with worry. How could you take so much pleasure in my discomfort?'

'Believe me, I didn't. At least now the necklace is back where it belongs and will soon be on display in the British Museum.'

'When you suggested a wager, you knew you would win, didn't you?'

'I did.'

'Were the dice loaded?'

His look was one of mock mortification. 'Of course not. It is not in my nature to cheat.'

Linnet gave him a dubious glance. 'I suppose I shall have to believe you. You have recently returned from Egypt. You are much travelled, Lord Blakely— although you don't strike me as being a gentleman of leisure.'

'You're right. I'm not. I like to be busy.'

'And—I take it you don't have a wife,' she ventured to say, wanting to know all there was to know about this strange man who had seduced her on their first encounter.

'No.' One black-arched brow lifted in mild enquire. 'Why? Would you like to marry me?'

His question spoken in jest and with a twinkle in his eyes caused Linnet to laugh out loud and brought a sparkle to her eyes, yet somewhere deep inside her she could feel the first stirrings of discomfort. 'Of course not. What I mean is,' she said when he shot her a thoroughly amused look, 'is there a lady in your life—someone special?'

He met her eyes and the line of his mouth quirked in a half-smile. 'You are very inquisitive, Miss Osborne.'

Linnet let her eyes drift over him, noting the nobility and pride stamped on his handsome face. 'I'm sorry. It's in my nature.'

'Then the answer to your question is that there are many women in my life—but no one special.'

She glanced at him obliquely, a warmth beginning to suffuse her face that had nothing to do with the heat of the night. His voice was low pitched and, though she wasn't used to men like Lord Blakely, she knew it was sensual and was unsure how to respond to it. 'You are a curious gentleman, Lord Blakely, and as much a mystery to me now as you were on our first encounter.'

'Which adds to my appeal, I hope.'

'Appeal. What a strange word to use. I don't find you in the least appealing.'

'You don't?' he asked with mock disappointment, placing a hand over his heart. 'You certainly know how to wound a gentleman, Miss Osborne.'

'Now you're teasing. I hardly know you so of course I don't find you appealing.'

His eyes narrowed and darkened, becoming warm and seductive. 'And you are sure about that, are you?'

'Yes, of course I am,' she replied, laughing lightly in an attempt to reduce the effect his blatant masculinity was beginning to have on her, bringing her drifting spirit back to reality. Her dawning response to him was solid enough reason to return to the dancing. 'I think I should go back inside before Aunt Lydia notices my absence and comes looking for me.'

Excusing herself, she left him on the terrace not a moment too soon. As soon as she entered the house she was immediately claimed by her aunt, who had watched Lord Blakely lead her unceremoniously on to the dance floor before disappearing with her on to the terrace.

Taking Linnet aside, Lady Milton turned and gave her a baleful look.

'What is it, Aunt Lydia? Is something wrong?'

'I was wondering why Lord Blakely singled you out for a dance. He hasn't danced with anyone else. I have noticed that he has been watching you a good deal and the two of you certainly drew attention when you danced—and it was most inappropriate of you to go on to the terrace with him. He is only recently returned to London from Egypt. He is a powerful man and of course he is most welcome here today. His presence enhances any event and he is causing quite a stir among the ladies in particular. Although I am curious as to his interest in celebrating the betrothal of two people who are virtually unknown to him.'

'I understand he is a close acquaintance of Harry's father. Do you know him well, Aunt Lydia?'

'I'm afraid not,' she answered, flicking open her fan and working it vigorously to cool her heated face. 'He comes from a wealthy, respectable family and I understand his father spent a good deal of his time in Egypt, leaving his son to manage his affairs here. He is certainly a very attractive man, polite and extremely charming. His wealth and prestige cannot be overlooked and now he is back in England he will have every ambitious family with marriageable daughters clamouring to be introduced.' With her nose elevated to a lofty angle, she looked at Linnet. 'I advise you not to get ideas above your station, Linnet. It can only end in tears.'

Deeply offended, Linnet had to bite her tongue not to deliver an angry riposte. Pulling her emotions into a hard, tight knot of pride, after a moment, forcing herself to look her aunt straight in the eye, she smiled slightly. 'I understand exactly what you are saying, Aunt Lydia, but please don't worry. I am not in danger of becoming involved with Lord Blakely—not in the romantic sense or any other,' she answered, while trying to banish the vision of the man who had seduced her at the Stourbridge ball.

Chapter Four

The candles in the two huge chandeliers and wall sconces were producing an unbearable heat. The frenzy of noise from the musicians and the laughing, chattering guests jostling for attention threatened to suffocate Linnet. Passing her fingers over her brow, she felt it was moist. Feeling a strong desire to be away from the throng, she escaped into the lantern-lit garden. Glancing in Toby's direction as she went out on to the terrace, she was relieved to see him leading a happy Caroline in the intricate figures of a quadrille, her wide, generous mouth as she gazed at Toby curved upwards into a smile so radiant Linnet felt the heat of her personality from across the room.

There were few people strolling. Most of them were indoors and those who passed her were drifting back inside. She inhaled deeply, appreciative of the cool fresh air, although gathering clouds heralded a storm. The spell of the gardens, the darkness and the gentle spill of water in the fountain ahead settled over her. Reaching it, she paused and closed her eyes.

Time seemed to stand still. It was as if the garden was sealed off from the rest of the world in a time zone of its own, where normal rules and etiquette and doing and saying the right thing didn't apply.

An owl spilled its cry over the land and the trees rustled in a soft current of air. Somewhere in the distance a cow lowed, followed by the bark of a dog. A small flock of jackdaws rose protesting from the elms. She was unaware of the still, lone man standing with his shoulder propped against a stone plinth bearing a statue, a brooding expression on his face.

Christian had no wish for company. He was feeling irritable. The celebrations did not suit his mood, but since Lord Radcliffe had gone to the trouble of providing him with an invitation, it would be impolite of him to leave so early. Thankfully no one broke into his thoughts.

Hearing the sound of footsteps, and the soft rustle of a woman's dress, he turned his head and saw Miss Osborne. He held his breath, transfixed on seeing her again so soon. Every one of his senses clamoured for her. There was that same fierce tug to his senses on being near her as there had been on that first time he had seen her at the Stourbridge ball. Throughout the evening he had watched her with a patient, neutral gaze. He had enjoyed dancing with her and their light-hearted repartee on the terrace afterwards. She had the look of a girl, but he felt she was a woman in every sense of that meaningful word. Without the concealing mask and wig she had worn on their first encounter she was so astonishingly beautiful. Added to her perfect features was a sweetness and vulnerability whose impact was immediate. She possessed a poise and dignity and she was sexually elegant and extremely desirable.

Unaware of his presence, she continued to stand beside the fountain. Slight of figure, she stood straight and still, her hands pressing back the full skirts of her dress. He saw the rise and fall of her chest and the way the light from the lanterns illuminated her face turned up to the sky. The picture she presented reminded him of a heroine in some ancient romance, waiting for the return of her lover from battle.

Christian was aware of a sudden sense of guilt, as though he were spying on her privacy. He shrugged himself away from the plinth, intending to walk away, but she must have sensed his presence for she turned and looked directly at him. He heard her sharp intake of breath.

'Oh! Lord Blakely! I didn't see you there.'

'You looked lost in thought.'

'Yes—yes, I was. I have much to think about.'

'And the festivities?'

'I am in no mood to dance again tonight. But please don't feel that you have to talk to me. We said all there is to say earlier. I am sure there are people more deserving of your company than me.'

Christian looked at her intently, finding himself looking into two warm tawny-coloured eyes, opened wide in her strikingly lovely heart-shaped face. Her skin creamy was flawless, her honey-gold hair like a halo of light beneath the lanterns in the trees.

'Since we appear to be the only two people in the garden and I have no wish to partake of Lady Milton's entertainment, and you have said you are in no mood to dance, then the sensible thing would be for us to talk to each other. Come, walk with me.'

'I think it might rain,' Linnet remarked, glancing up at the sky.

'It's been threatening all day. I'm willing to risk it if you are.'

They walked on slowly in silence.

'I am surprised to find you are still here,' Linnet remarked at length. 'I—I thought you might have left.'

'I would have, only I went to a great deal of trouble to obtain an invitation from Lord Radcliffe, whom I have known for many years. It would be ill mannered of me to leave early. Lady Milton has kindly offered me accommodation. I shall leave first thing in the morning. And you? When do you return to Chelsea?'

'Tomorrow, also. What is your reason for being here? Unlike everyone else, you are here unaccompanied—and I do not think you are the kind of man to partake in the frivolities of a young woman's betrothal party.'

'I should have explained when we talked earlier. I'm to leave London shortly for my estate in Sussex. When I saw you in the Strand and you ran from me I couldn't leave it at that. I had to find you.'

Linnet stared at him in disbelief. 'Why would you want to do that?'

'Because you disappeared before I had a chance to find out more about you. Given what you told me before you left Lord Stourbridge's artefacts room—that you were there to return the necklace, not to steal it—I thought that perhaps you were telling the truth and that I had misjudged you.'

'I was not lying. It was perfectly true.'

'I'm beginning to realise that.'

'How did you find me? How did you know I would be here?'

'I obtained information as to your identity from Lord and Lady Stourbridge. They are acquainted with your aunt and they informed me she was to hold a betrothal party for her daughter and Harry Radcliffe and that, being family, you would be present. Lord Radcliffe and I are old friends. I approached him for an invitation.'

'I see. You seem to have gone to an awful lot of trouble to find me.'

'It wasn't difficult. You live in Chelsea with your brother, I believe.'

'Yes.'

'And your parents?'

'They died several years ago. There is just Toby and me now.'

'And is there a young man in your life, Miss Osborne?'

'No—and nor is there likely to be in the foreseeable future.'

'Oh? And why is that, pray?'

'I have no dowry, Lord Blakely. In fact, our situation is so dire that I am considering applying for work, even though I do so with great reluctance.'

'You are? What kind of work?'

'A governess—or something along those lines. I would certainly consider anything. My brother is a gambler—and not a very good one. He can think of nothing else. If we are to pay off the creditors and Toby's debts, then it is necessary for me to find some kind of employment.'

'Does your brother know this.'

'I have mentioned it to him, but he doesn't believe I will. I often dream of better things and keep hoping something will turn up, but I very much doubt it.' She sighed, looking beyond the gardens to the fields beyond. How could she tell this man how heavy her heart felt in her breast? She was weary and sick, both mentally and physically, at the prospect ahead of her and fearful of the future. 'Our situation is so bad that there may come a time when we have no choice but to sell the house,' she said quietly, 'even though it will break my heart to do so. I will fight tooth and nail not to let that happen. It's filled with so many memories—of a happy childhood and my mother and father always there.'

The intensity of Christian's stare didn't waver. 'I am heartily sorry things are as they are for you, but there is nothing wrong with having dreams and longings, Miss Osborne. We'd be nowhere without them.'

'I know, but unfortunately dreams don't pay the bills. In the end I have to be realistic. No one's going

to wave a magic wand. I can't see my situation changing in the foreseeable future unless I do it myself.'

'Your brother doesn't deserve you. He should be
the one seeking an occupation. I wish you luck.'

'I have been well educated—my parents saw to
that. I live in hope that something will turn up.'

Recalling his intention to find someone to relieve
Mrs Marsden to take care of Alice, it did cross his
mind that he was in a position to offer her employment. But then he mentally listed all the reasons why
he was reluctant to even consider her as a governess
for Alice. When he recalled the manner of their meeting and that she had considered climbing into his bed
to regain what he believed she had stolen, her weak
moral standards left her wanting in his eyes. And
yet as she stood there, looking into the distance she
looked so very vulnerable. Her air of impregnable
self-sufficiency vanished and Christian saw a troubled and extremely desperate young woman.

'Even though that would be a blow to your pride?'

'Oh, no. I'm truly not proud. I am many things,
Lord Blakely—stubborn, headstrong, frequently ar-
gumentative and endowed with a boldness unbefitting
a young lady—at least that's what Toby says—but
not, I think, proud.'

'Will you allow me to help you?'

The question was so unexpected, the tone of his
voice so soft and inviting, that Linnet thought how
wonderful it would be to accept his offer, but since
she did not know him well she could not turn to him

for safety or security. The whole thing was hopeless, a hopeless never-ending worry to which she could see no end. Her life was one endless spiral of debt and more debt.

Giving Lord Blakely no notion of her thoughts, she pinned a smile to her lips. 'Things always have a way of working out in the most unexpected of ways. Toby is always telling me that I worry too much.'

She was looking at him straight in the face, and there was a look deep in her eyes that was almost appealing, asking for help. And, strangely, he did want to help her, but he didn't know how to. At least not yet. He noticed how the moonlight illuminated her face. It was achingly lovely. The soft tawny eyes, the arch of her brow, the gentle curve of her cheek and lips, the stubborn chin. Ever since his father's death and the misery his affair with Selina had caused him and his mother, he had been emotionally frozen, but now something warm was beginning to creep into his heart.

A breeze rustled the leaves on the trees and from the stables could be heard the whinny of a horse and the thumping of hooves against the stall. Linnet turned her head in the direction and smiled. 'That will be Cousin William's horse—Sampson. He's a frisky beast at the best of times. He always gets restless about this time and starts rattling the boards of his stall.'

'Do you like horses, Miss Osborne?'

'Yes, very much. I was brought up with them.'

'Do you ride?'

'Yes. My father taught me when I was a child. He bought me my first pony when I was three. With no land of our own he would often let Toby and me accompany him to Woodside Hall. I would ride with Louisa while he and Toby took part in the hunt. When he died, Toby... He—he found it necessary to sell the horses—apart from the carriage horse which I ride sometimes when he is not pulling the carriage.'

They walked on in silence until they came to the rotunda on a rise, where they stopped and looked back at the house. Light blazed from the windows and music drifted to them on the air. Rain began to fall sharply which they would be foolish to ignore.

'We have walked further than I intended,' Lord Blakely said. 'To avoid a drenching, I suggest we shelter in the rotunda.' He drew her between the stone columns into the dim interior.

Linnet looked about her. It was not a large structure, but it was dry and surprisingly clean. Side by side they watched the rain slanting down, bouncing off the ground. Hopefully it would soon be over.

'Did you really think I was a thief when you saw me in Lord Stourbridge's artefacts room? Did I look like a thief?'

'No, you did not. But a woman's face may be deceptive.'

There was an underlying meaning to his reply, but Linnet failed to detect it. She gave a hard, contemptuous little laugh. 'Especially when she is attired in ribbons and lace.'

'Exactly.' He looked at her intently. 'Would you really have given yourself to me that night?'

An appealing flush crept over her cheeks and she lowered her eyes. 'In all truth I don't know what I would have done. You found me in very straitened circumstances. I really was quite desperate not to get caught.'

'Then I curse your brother for placing you in an impossible situation. The least he could have done was to put it back himself. That you would rather contemplate giving yourself to a complete stranger to right the wrong he did is unforgivable. I can only apologise for putting you in such a dreadful position.'

The softness of his tone, his dark eyes, shook Linnet out of her melancholy. He was searching her face intently, a faint scowl between his brows, as if he might by sheer force of will drive away her unhappiness. 'It wasn't your fault. You didn't know me—who I was or anything about me. But had I known that you were the rightful owner of the wretched thing I would not have entertained your proposition. I was afraid that if you took it, when Lord Stourbridge found it was missing, because Toby had gained information about the house from one of the footmen, he would not keep his mouth shut and the finger would be pointed at him.'

Something in the despairing words touched Christian. He saw how his words had deepened the sadness in her eyes, but at the same time stiffened her spine. Her decision to return what her brother had stolen was as bizarre as it was unexpected. But then, with the threat of arrest hanging over both her and her brother should it come out, it wasn't surprising. She was a strange young woman. He had never encountered her like before.

'The incident is over. Don't let it worry you further. You have nothing to fear.'

She jerked her head up. 'Fear? Fear is always close when the threat is to someone you love. I fear for my brother, about what will happen to him—that he will be thrown into a debtors' prison should he continue gambling until we have nothing left. I doubt you know the meaning of fear, sir.'

Christian ignored the sarcasm because he knew it came from a place of hurt. She had given him an insight of what lay behind her fear. Had it been anyone else he had caught in Lord Stourbridge's Egyptian room he would not have let them off lightly. But he felt this young woman had far too much to contend with and there were times in life when there was more to be gained by giving a little. Her brother was a different matter and he blamed him entirely for placing his sister in such a dangerous situation. Had anyone else happened to come across her that night, they would have shouted thief and she would be locked up now.

The idea of scoring off Toby Osborne appealed greatly to his sardonic sense of humour, knowing how immensely satisfying it would be to avenge himself in some way for his disgraceful treatment of his sister. But, on reflection, all such dealings were abhorrent to him. He had many faults, but it was not in his nature to inflict injury or insult on any man or woman who was guilty of wrongdoings against him.

'You are wrong, Miss Osborne. I have known fear. And I know what you fear. I give you my word that I have no intention of exposing your brother,' he said quietly.

'And at what price?'

'There is no price.'

'I thought every man had a price.'

'And every woman,' he replied softly.

The melancholy note that had crept into his voice stoked her curiosity. She realised how little she knew about him.

'Did your father spend a lot of his time in Egypt?' she asked.

His expression changed abruptly and became guarded, his eyes brittle and cold as glass. Moving away from her, he propped his shoulder against a pillar and folded his arms over his chest. 'He was rarely at home—not even when I was a boy. Oh, I loved him well enough then, but I did not love his inconstancy. At eighteen years of age I felt the weight of responsibility foisted on me during his long absences.'

'You were resentful, I can tell.'

His eyes narrowed with pain as he stared out at the night. 'Resentful because he put his love of all things Egyptian before me and my mother and the estate.

It was something I could never understand or become reconciled with. He could not have cared less about what was happening at home.'

'And you carry your hurt and bitterness around your neck like a millstone.'

His smile was one of cynicism. 'Does it show all that much.'

'No, not at all, but I can hear it in your voice.'

'There are some things, Miss Osborne, that cannot easily be put aside.'

'Did he ever take you to Egypt as a boy?'

He nodded. 'One time—before my mother died, we travelled to other places—Venice and Padua in Italy, the Holy Land to name but a few.'

'It must have been a difficult time for you when your mother died.'

He smiled at her. 'As you would know, having experienced the same kind of loss yourself.'

'Yes, that's true, but we all deal with death in different ways.'

Christian searched her face with something like wonder in his dark eyes. There were depths to Linnet Osborne that every woman he knew lacked and she never ceased to amaze him. 'You confound me, Miss Osborne, do you know that? I came here because I wanted to see you, to see if my memory of you had changed.'

'And has it?'

He shook his head. 'You risked your good name and arrest when you took it upon yourself to right a wrong for your brother. What an amazingly sensitive, perceptive, wise young thing you are, Linnet Osborne.'

'If I were wise I would have done what my father asked of me before he died—to look after Toby and not allowed him to notch up so much debt. That is a millstone around my neck I have to bear.'

Standing beside him, Linnet became silent, content for the moment to remain in his still presence and let the silence of the night surround her.

'Tell me, Miss Osborne,' he said, gazing at her, 'does not the London scene and all its frivolities beckon?'

'Not really.'

'That's a pity,' he told her, 'for you would be an enormous success in St James's. In no time at all you would endear yourself to every male who crosses your path. You would slay the lot of them with your beauty.'

'Lord Blakely, please don't exaggerate.' She stepped away from him to hide her confusion, aware of the magnetic charm he was exuding and beginning to think it was time she returned to the house.

'I don't. You would bowl them over and down they would fall like skittles. No doubt they would all turn poets overnight and express their love for this bright new star in their midst.'

'Really?' She smiled, her eyes slanted, and a quietly teasing feeling of treacherous warmth seeped through her. 'And would you pen one yourself, Lord Blakely?'

He grinned. 'You would break enough hearts without wanting mine. I did not realise when I saw you at the Stourbridge ball that your mask concealed so much beauty.'

Linnet felt her face flush red. 'I thank you for your kind remark, but I assure you that my looks—good or bad—play no part in my everyday life. I am quite content to remain at home. I visit Louisa from time to time and she often comes to me.'

'You will miss her when she marries Harry and goes to live in Kent.'

'I will, very much.' She glanced sideways at him, mindful of his proximity in several ways, not least of which was his close attention to her problems and the spicy scent of his cologne.

'Was your father a gambler, Miss Osborne?'

'No, a businessman. In the years following my mother's death he lost interest in his work and made some bad investments. They were close. He loved her so much he couldn't bear being without her. Before he died he paid little attention to what was happening in the financial world until it was too late to do anything about it.'

'So it is your brother who is the gambler.'

'I'm afraid so and it does nothing to improve things.'

'It appears to me that you are the sensible, practical one.'

'As much as I can be, although it is difficult at times.'

'Your brother is a grown man. He knows perfectly well what he is doing when he stakes his money.'

'Gambling is a temptation which Toby cannot resist—to gamble and to go on gambling.'

'You do know, Miss Osborne, that there will come a day of reckoning for your brother.'

'I know,' she said, quietly. 'I know what you must think of Toby. You can say whatever you like about him. He is a gambler, and he is weak and easily manipulated by any unsavoury character that comes along. But whatever he is, whatever he has done, I will forgive him because I happen to love him. All I want is for him to stop gambling.

Her eyes brimmed with tears. It was unexpected and it saddened Christian. Her open emotion and obvious declaration of love for her brother were distressing. This lovely young woman was suddenly more vulnerable than any woman he had ever met. In the few moments of silence which fell between them, he bore witness to her tortured thoughts.

Pulling herself together, Linnet glanced at her companion and was unable to look away. He was still leaning against one of the pillars with one booted foot crossed over the other. A tree lantern threw a slant of shadow across the hard line of his cheek. He confounded her with emotions which were alien to her, emotions that overruled all common sense. She cast the thought away, furious with herself at her inability to be physically indifferent to him. The expression in his eyes was disconcerting.

They must have been sheltering for at least half an hour when the rain finally stopped. Taking advantage of the respite they stepped out of the rotunda. Linnet looked down at her dancing slippers which were inadequate on the wet ground, but there was nothing for it but to walk on. They began to make their way back to the house, unconsciously taking a darker, longer route back along a path that was unlit by tree lanterns and the ground uneven. Suddenly, slipping on the wet ground and tripping on a tree root that snaked beneath the surface, with a cry Linnet tumbled to one side, falling and becoming entangled in a large rose bush, its cruel barbs hooking into her gown.

Immediately Lord Blakely was beside her, seeing the danger posed by the vicious barbs. 'Hold still. Let me help you. I'll have you out in a trice.'

Bending over, methodically and deftly his long fingers pulled away the offending branches. Linnet remained as still as she was able, feeling foolish over losing her footing and more than a little of her dignity. She watched his hands working quickly to release her, seeing they had the strength in them of a man who was not afraid to dirty them, yet giving the impression of refinement. Eventually she was free and, taking her hand and hoisting her to her feet, he held her steady. His senses were invaded by the smell of her. It was the soft fragrance of her hair—the sweet scent of roses mingled with a musky female scent—that made his body burn. Curling his long masculine fingers round her chin, he tilted her face up to his.

'Thankfully there doesn't appear to be any lacerations, but the same cannot be said of your gown.'

Stepping from him Linnet surveyed the damage.

The bodice was torn, a flap of material exposing her undergarment. The skirt had also suffered, with tears on either side and mud clinging to the hem. Some of her hair had become snagged and long tresses trailed to her shoulders.

'Goodness! What a sight I look. Thank you for getting me free. Are you hurt? Those barbs are pretty sharp—but look at the sorry state of my gown.'

Looking at his companion, Christian frowned. Her gown had suffered badly and her wet skirts clung to her in a most provocative way. He took a moment to appreciate the shapely figure beneath. 'Your gown is wet and torn, but it will mend.' Without thinking he reached out and tucked a lock of hair behind her ear, feeling the velvety softness of her skin against his fingers.

'That may be so,' she said, achingly aware of his touch. A tautness began in her breast, a delicious ache that was like a languorous, honeyed warmth. 'I only hope I can make it to my room without being seen.'

Linnet raised her head and looked at him, conscious of his close proximity. His eyes were deep and piercing and she was unprepared for the thrill of quivering excitement that gripped her now, beginning in her chest where her heart lay, and radiating to every part of her body. His tall figure was dark against the shadows, with just enough light from the moon to see him by. She did not move away when he reached out and drew her to him. He looked steadily at her, then moved his head closer to hers.

Hypnotised by the warm dark depths of his eyes coming ever closer, Linnet found she couldn't move—

she had neither the desire nor the strength to do so. His penetrating eyes were searching her face. She was not imagining his interest in herself. She might have no experience of men, but she was perfectly able to recognise admiration in a man's eyes. Suddenly it was like being on an obstacle course of emotions that left her confused.

'You must think me very stupid, falling into that bush,' she said softly, taking a step back. She looked away and stiffened her spine.

'No, I don't. You couldn't help it. These things happen.' For a moment he studied her with heavy-lidded, speculative eyes. Stepping close to her again, he cupped her chin in his hand. 'Look at me,' he said, in a low, velvety, unfamiliar voice that sent apprehensive and exciting tingles darting up her spine. 'Ever since our conversation on the terrace earlier I've been wanting to kiss you. Now I think I will.'

Linnet raised her eyes to his. Although no one but this man had ever kissed her before, she took one look at the slumberous expression in his eyes and was instantly wary. 'You will?'

A slow, lazy smile that made her heart leap worked its way across his face and Linnet was unable to drag her eyes from his hypnotic gaze. 'Yes. Do you mind?'

She swallowed audibly. 'I—I don't know.'

Her reply, spoken in complete innocence, caught Christian completely off guard. Every feminine ploy in existence had been tried on him in the past, but without success—and yet this artless young woman, her candour combined with her upturned beautiful face and alluring body, acted like a powerful aphrodisiac. Standing there, wide-eyed and vulnerable and lovely—dear Lord, she was lovely and he wanted her with a fierceness that took his breath away.

'I don't think you will be disappointed,' he murmured, his arms folding around her, his face moving closer. 'You certainly didn't object when I kissed you before.'

Still cupping her chin, he took a moment to peruse her face. The insistent pressure of his body, those feral eyes glittering with power and primeval hunger, washed away any measure of comfort Linnet might have felt. A familiar feeling fluttered within her breast and she was halted for a brief passage of time when she found her lips entrapped with his and, though they were soft and tender, they burned with a fire that scorched her. Closing her eyes, she yielded to it, melting against him. His kiss was both gentle and compelling. His lips moved on hers, the fierceness changing to softness, the velvet touch of intoxication. His hand was splayed across her lower spine, forcing her closer to him, and she unwittingly moulded her melting body to the hardening contours of his. The trees and the darkness around them seemed to vanish, leaving only the two of them locked together in a charmed circle against reality which fell away. He deepened the kiss. It was long and tender and devouring, his mouth insisting, stirring, demanding, working their pagan magic on Linnet.

She was aware that this was a moment of great importance, that she stood on the threshold of a great revelation, but could not understand the substance of it. Her heart swelled with an emotion of such proportions she was overwhelmed as she allowed herself, just this once, the forbidden, fleeting joy of his mouth and his body close to her—never had she been so conscious of the nearness of another human body. She was astounded at her own body's reaction to this man. A touch, a look, a kiss, and he could rouse her. She was suddenly swamped with a swirling turbulence of longing, a longing for something she had never known before, but which only this man could provide. She was conscious of the hard lines of his body pressed close to hers and how tall he was. Her mind cried out with agonised yearning. She strained against him. Beyond her will her slender arms snaked up and around his neck, her fingers feeling the thickness of his hair at his nape. Her body was like a yielding, living substance as she gave all her desire and passion, responding to his inner heat.

He was a complex man who would be as elusive as smoke, a man who would break the heart of the woman who loved him. She felt she should be nervous, in the semi-darkness and all alone with him, but he offered no threat to her. They looked at each other with startled eyes, a look that lasted no more than a moment and yet seemed to last an eternity before he released her chin and pulled away.

Fighting back the wild desire to thrust her down on to the grass and take her there and then, Christian drew a long, steadying breath. He studied the flushed contours of her face, the thick crescent of her lashes and the fine line of her eyebrows. Her lips were soft and tender from his assault, her eyes warm and glowing with desire. He longed to run his fingertip down the slender column of her throat and to continue downwards until his hand cupped her breast. He imagined how it would be to have her in his bed, to take her in his arms and draw her to him and devour her with a passion he had not felt in a long time. What a glory that would be. She would make a magnificent bed partner—he had sensed it the instant her mouth had responded to his kiss. It would happen. He would make it happen if he expired with the effort.

Kissed and caressed into almost unconscious sensibility, a moment passed before Linnet opened her eyes in a daze of suspended yearning, newly awakened passion glowing in the velvety depths of her eyes.

'Dear Lord,' he murmured, looking down at her upturned face, his gaze smouldering, his breathing ragged, the throbbing ache in his loins reminding him how much he wanted to make love to her. With her hair tumbling around her face, she stood like a beautiful, pagan goddess. The return of the moon contending with the glow from the occasional lantern enhanced the warm glow in her eyes. He was tempted to caress the delicate, unblemished cheeks. Her features were perfect, her soft pink lips slightly parted, tantalising, moist and gracefully curving. Her eyes stared back at him, open, yet as unfathomable as any sea he had gazed into. 'I think you will have to fall into a rose bush more often—providing I am on hand to pull you out.'

Surfacing slowly from the depths of desire, Linnet dazedly gazed up at him with hypnotic eyes—still dark from the mysterious forces of passion, as if she could not comprehend what had just happened between them. She was astounded at her body's reaction to this man. A touch, a kiss, a look, and he could rouse her and something rose and shouted for the joy of it.

'I should not have let you kiss me.'

'No, you shouldn't—any more than I should have attempted to. Do you mind?'

She shook her head. 'No—at least I don't think so.'

'Then there's no harm done.'

'No, none at all,' she said, unaware as she said the words of the quietly giggling young couple who had witnessed their kiss and were already returning to the house to recount what they had witnessed. Lord Blakely thought he heard a sound, but looking into the darkness of the tall shrubs and seeing nothing untoward, thought nothing of it.

'Thank you for pulling me out of the rose bush,' Linnet went on, 'but if you don't mind, I think I should be getting back.'

They walked side by side in silence, each trying to analyse their thoughts after what had just occurred between them. Walking through a dark tunnel of high laurels, Lord Blakely reached out to take her hand. Linnet knew she should refuse to take it. Instead she gave a tiny laugh, trying to make light of it.

'What is this, Lord Blakely? Are you afraid I might fall into another rose bush?'

There was a long, strained pause and he never took his eyes off her. 'I am not afraid of what you might do, Miss Osborne. It is what I would do, or might not be able to stop myself doing if you were to do that.'

There was another strained pause as they continued walking towards the house. They didn't speak. Linnet didn't know if it was the warm, damp air or the churning of her stomach, but she was finding it hard to breath because she wanted him to touch her.

Turning her head, she glanced at him, noting the silver scar on the side of his face, and wondered how he had come to be wounded. The disfigurement did not detract from his good looks—in fact, in some strange way, it enhanced them. She found herself wanting to reach up and trace it with her fingers, remembering its smoothness when her eyes had been covered by the scarf when she had been playing the game with the other girls.

'You're wondering how I came by my scar, aren't you?'

Linnet almost gasped at being caught out, but found herself smiling instead. 'One can't help but notice something like that? I—hope you are not offended.'

'Not at all. The answer is very simple. As a seven-year-old boy I fell on the ice when I was attempting to skate. So, you see, no tales of fencing or any other act of bravado, I'm afraid.'

That might be so, Linnet thought, but she was certain Lord Blakely would be well skilled in the art of swordplay.

Reaching the terrace, hearing the music, the clinking of glasses and laughter, Linnet became still, reluctant to become a part of it.

Christian stood quite still, studying the exposed flesh of her neck and watching the dappled lantern light bring out a multitude of glorious lights in her hair. Fashioned in intricate curls, what had not become loosened in the rose bush was held in place by small, decorative tortoiseshell combs. He wanted to remove them so that all her hair could fall free, so that he could run his fingers through the heavy mass.

'Will you not go inside?' he asked softly, sensing her reluctance.

She laughed lightly. 'Looking like this?' she said, indicating the sorry state of her gown. 'No. I think not. I will go to my room by a staircase used by the servants and hope no one sees me.'

'Will your aunt not query your absence?'

'No. Believe me, Lord Blakely,' she said, looking at his deep, dark eyes fringed by long silken lashes and well-defined brows, 'I am the last person my aunt will miss.'

He looked down at her upturned face and then, quite unexpectedly, he took her fingers in his and kissed her hand gently. She smiled suddenly. Clearly the pleasure of his touch, of his lips on her flesh, took her by surprise. The intimacy of the moment reached out to some unknown part of them both, which they had not been aware they possessed. It touched and lightened some dark place they had not before now been aware of, but it was elusive and was soon gone when he released her fingers.

'Goodnight,' she said softly. 'Perhaps I will see you at breakfast.'

'Perhaps—although I intend leaving early.'

On that note Linnet left him standing in the shadows on the terrace, completely unaware as she did so of her Aunt Lydia regarding them from the terrace with an attentive expression in her eyes, having watched as Lord Blakely raised Linnet's hand to his lips and lingered on it overlong, and Linnet was content to let him.

Linnet would have been mortified to know that her aunt was not the only witness to the touching goodnight scene between her and Lord Blakely. Several guests had come out on to the terrace and, from the expressions on their faces as they glanced from Linnet's torn gown to the impeccably dressed gentleman kissing her hand, it was obvious that they had drawn their own conclusions, ranging from amused curiosity to censorious.

Christian watched her go, feeling bemused and intrigued in a way he hadn't felt in a long time. He smiled, pleasantly uplifted by the time he had spent in her company and hungry for more. She was truly a delight and alluring. The scent of her gentle floral perfume still clung to him. The kiss had affected him more than he realised. He felt burned—scorched— by her beauty. He was quite bewildered by the emotion he felt in the part of his body where he supposed his heart lay.

He couldn't describe what he felt because he didn't have any words. He was drawn by the sincerity in her gaze. The primal rush of attraction he felt for her surprised him. He wanted her with a kind of hunger he hadn't known in a long time. A good deal of it was sexual, but not all of it. He was aware of a swelling ache in his groin, but his desire went deeper than lust. For a moment he felt his resistance waver. It pulled him up short. It was a warning, but a warning all the same.

He intended leaving the next day. And yet he wasn't ready to give up this bright-eyed young woman just yet.

Chapter Five

Not until she was in her room with the door closed did Linnet's mind come together from the far reaches of her senses, where it had fled the instant Lord Blakely had taken her in his arms, and realise the full impact of what she had done. As she sat in front of the mirror staring at the devastation of her hair, she took a moment to consider her situation. She was disquieted. She remembered how it had felt to be held by him, how secure she had felt in his arms. Despite her sorry state after falling into the rose bush, she had been almost smothered by his nearness, by the heady smell of him, a clean masculine scent that had shot like tiny darts through her senses and evoked a rush of pleasure that flooded through her. He had been so close he seemed a part of her.

As Linnet went from day to day with no other thought in her head than how she was going to make ends meet, she had not thought for one moment that she would meet a man of Lord Blakely's ilk. Because she had no experience of men like him, being gullible and blind to everything but the devastatingly handsome man she had met at Stourbridge House, she had been drawn to him in the most inexplicable way.

When she finally climbed into bed, she closed her eyes. Again she saw the dark eyes and sighed deeply, a ragged sigh that tugged at her chest. It had been wrong of her to divulge so much about herself and Toby's affairs to Lord Blakely, but he had a way of drawing a person out of one's self.

Unable to sleep, she got up and went to the window, pulling aside the heavy curtains and looking out at the moonlit garden and seeing and hearing a few late revellers continuing to enjoy the festivities. A curious warmth crept through her body and again she sighed and went back to bed. Nothing helped her. She could not sleep. She could do nothing but think about Lord Blakely and that warm rush of feeling when he had kissed her. His kiss had been lethal, stripping away her resolve, and she realised she had cause to fear for she had become susceptible. He had aroused a yearning inside her for a repeat of his attentions. She realised she was in danger of falling in love with him and it scared her.

She mentally shook herself as she realised where her mind was wandering. How could she think of him in that way? What did any of it matter? If she didn't see him at breakfast, then she would probably never see him again.

The following morning before breakfast Lady Milton summoned her nephew and niece to her presence in a small sitting room set aside for her personal use. She was seated in her favourite chair by the window overlooking the gardens and did not trouble herself to rise when they entered. The coldness of her expression conveyed very clearly that what she had to say to them would not be pleasant.

'Sit down.' Doing as she ordered, they sat together on a sofa, facing her, unable to conceal their unease. 'I have been approached by Sir George Mortimer, Toby, with regards to his daughter. It would appear she is quite enamoured of you. It did not escape my notice that you were together a great deal during the dancing. I have to ask you if you reciprocate her feelings?'

'Yes, Aunt Lydia. Yes—I mean—I do have feelings for her,' he confessed. 'I admire her enormously.'

'Well, it is high time you settled down and the Mortimers are a respected and high-born family. As a British diplomat Sir George is highly thought of in government and aristocratic circles. Indeed, we have been friends for many years. Your parents are dead, so as your aunt I feel an obligation to take an interest in what you do and I have to say that your lifestyle concerns me deeply. It has been brought to my notice that you spend a good deal of your time gambling and that you are in debt. Just how bad are things?'

Linnet looked at Toby, at his flushed face and the way he shifted with embarrassment beside her. With a sinking heart, realising the situation called for the truth, raising her head she looked straight at her aunt. It was a difficult moment for Linnet. She wanted to maintain an air of cool disdain, to face her aunt in calm defiance, but her mauled pride and an aching distrust of the future assailed her senses.

'I'm afraid they could not be worse, Aunt Lydia.'

Lady Milton's expression didn't alter, but her eyes hardened. 'Worse? Kindly explain yourself, Toby. Am I to understand that you persist in continuing to throw money away at cards?'

'We no longer have any money to throw away, Aunt Lydia,' Linnet explained quietly, never having felt so degraded in her life.

The blood drained from Lady Milton's face. She was furious. It was a predicable reaction.

Toby stared at her, silent and helpless, waiting for her to speak.

She looked from Linnet to Toby for a long moment. 'I see. By that I take it to mean that you are penniless? You foolish man. What a disappointment you have turned out to be. You had every opportunity to make something of yourself when your father died. Instead, you have thrown it all away for the amusements to be found in London. And the house? Is it mortgaged?'

'No, Aunt Lydia,' Toby mumbled.

'Well, I suppose that's something to be thankful for. However, Sir George would be horrified at the prospect that his daughter would marry anyone who would be unable to support her in the manner to which she is accustomed. You have no money and no prospects. Do you want Caroline Mortimer or don't you?'

'Yes—of course I do.'

'Then you had better pull yourself together. He will not consider a match between you and his daughter as things stand. Indeed he would be horrified if he knew your present situation. You have to change from a profligate young man who cannot stop gambling into a sober adult. It is important to me that you further your advancement. We must salvage what we can. My bailiff will be leaving shortly. I will arrange for you to work with him, show you how to go on, and when he leaves you may have learned enough to take over. Your cousin William will help you all he can and help you with the business side of things so that eventually you can be what your father once was—a man of independent means. You will work hard and show me you have the ability to progress.'

'But, Aunt Lydia, I know nothing of—'

'Then you will learn,' she uttered forcefully. 'Now listen to me and listen carefully. You will not go near a gaming room. There will be no more gambling. You will behave. If you cannot conduct yourself like a gentleman, then I will have to rethink the situation. Is that clear? I know nothing of your debts. You will bring me the statements of tradespeople who are owed and I will see that they are paid. When this is done I will settle a sum of money on you. How many gambling debts do you have?'

'They—they are considerable.'

'I expect they are. Find out. If you work hard, you will, in time, earn a comfortable living.'

'But, Aunt Lydia,' Toby said, sitting on the edge of the seat, 'with no money to bring to the marriage,

Sir George will not allow a marriage between Caroline and me.'

'I will see that you have enough to satisfy Sir George. It is a risk I shall have to take to stop our honourable name being dragged down into the mire. Besides, Caroline is the youngest of his five daughters and I know he is eager to get her off his hands. You will be thankful that I am offering you a way out of the mire you have got yourself into.'

Linnet was overwhelmed with gratitude. She was unable to believe that the one person she had believed would not help them had astounded her by offering them a way out of their predicament. It forced her to see Toby and herself and their situation clearly and she was ashamed of what she saw.

'Aunt Lydia, I—I don't know what to say... It is indeed generous of you. We never expected... Toby?'

Lady Milton looked at them coldly. 'I am not doing this for you. It is for the family. The Mortimers are to go to the Continent for several weeks. You will spend the time putting your house in order. Do you understand me, Toby? If you fail, then I shall wash my hands of you.' Her eyes shifted to Linnet. 'And you, Linnet. Last night I saw you return to the house with Lord Blakely. It was not appropriate for you to be alone with him in the gardens for so long—and apparently there were witnesses who saw you embracing.'

She went on to deliver a blistering tirade, denouncing Linnet's disgraceful behaviour. Pale faced, Linnet endured her aunt's chastisement without offering a word in her defence, knowing that to do so would only incite her to further anger.

'The absence of the two of you was commented on—your return in a state of undress and your general lack of modesty and decorum when you allowed him the liberty of kissing your hand was scandalous.'

Linnet stared at her in disbelief. 'I—I didn't know I was being observed—I didn't think…'

'No, you did not, that is clear. Do you know what you have done? You've disgraced yourself. People are talking about you as if you were a—a woman of ill repute.'

'But I am not. It began to rain. We sheltered in the rotunda…' She fell silent when she saw the look of horror on her aunt's face.

'Are you telling me that the two of you were alone all that time?'

'It was raining.'

'That is beside the point. He was seen kissing you—touching you.' Lady Milton saw the shadow of guilt in her niece's eyes and her face hardened. 'So—he did take advantage of you.'

'No—no, please believe me when I say it was quite innocent. We did nothing wrong.'

'You may not understand that what you did was wrong, but a man as experienced as Lord Blakely will have known that you do not disappear for a prolonged period of time in a darkened garden with a respectable young lady. He took advantage of your innocence and naivety. The guests could speak of little else for the rest of the evening. He has ruined your reputation and any chance you had of making a decent marriage.'

'But nothing happened.' Linnet was adamant. 'The simple truth is that I fell into a rather large rose bush. That's how my dress became torn.' Remembering the kiss, she was horrified to think they had been seen. 'I sincerely hope you haven't spoken to Lord Blakely about this. I have no wish to cause him embarrassment.'

'That is the least of my worries. I will speak to him. Last night he retired to his room when he came in from the garden so I was unable to approach him. Before this unfortunate incident I had already decided that you must be found a husband. You cannot continue living at Birch House when Toby is married. It is high time you were wed. If Lord Blakely won't have you and you cannot acquire a husband yourself, then I will do it for you. And soon.'

Linnet sat perfectly still, her hands clenched in her lap, her lovely face pale but composed as she squared up to her aunt. Reflecting on the time she had spent with Lord Blakely in the garden, she marvelled at her gullibility and naivety. Secretly, all her life she had dreamt of experiencing the feelings Lord Blakely had woken in her with that first kiss. The desire and its result were a wonder to her and had completely overwhelmed her. For the first time in her life a man had made her feel like a real woman.

But marriage? No, she would not be united with any man under such circumstances as these. She was a nobody. She had nothing. He was a peer of the realm—an earl, Louisa had told her. She would never be able to live up to his position.

'I feel I must remind you of our conversation earlier, Aunt Lydia. What was it you advised? That I should not get ideas above my station.'

Her aunt stiffened. 'I have not forgotten, but that was before you went wandering off into the garden with him. You compromised yourself. You are absolutely ruined unless he marries you.'

'He wouldn't even consider it.'

'We'll see about that. If Lord Blakely thinks he can ruin my good name by seducing my niece and then go flitting off to wherever he is from, he is grievously mistaken.'

'I will not be forced into this.'

Aunt Lydia looked at her coldly. 'Not forced, Linnet. Persuaded. You will see the sense of it in time. You must face the fact that your father left you in a fix with no dowry and without a penny to your name. There isn't a man of note that will marry you without one. The lord knows what a task it will be for me to find you a decent husband if Blakely won't have you.' She sighed heavily, as if tired of her burden. 'Besides, if I am to help your brother out of the mess he has made of things then you must play your part. Marriage will be the best thing for you—I suppose I shall have to provide your dowry to bring that about.'

It wasn't her aunt's coldness Linnet resented, or her sudden decision to take control of their lives. She did see the necessity of discipline where Toby was concerned. But being ordered to acquire herself a husband to take her off her aunt's hands was too much to bear. The sooner she could find herself employment the better.

'What you suggest is quite preposterous. I have told you I wish to marry no one,' Linnet said, only to realise that her aunt wasn't listening to her and, with a sense of utter despair, she realised her own impotence. What could she do? What could she say against Aunt Lydia who was planning her future with an utter disregard for her own feelings on the matter?

Linnet glanced at Toby. He looked vulnerable and desperately unhappy. She would not argue with Aunt Lydia just now but she would not be coerced into a loveless marriage of convenience to Lord Blakely or one of the stuffy gentlemen of her aunt's acquaintance to suit her. When the time came she would have a say in who her husband would be and if, as Aunt Lydia said, her reputation was ruined beyond recall, then so be it.

Less than half an hour later Linnet and Toby entered the crowded breakfast room. That was the moment she was made painfully aware of the extent of her disgrace. The story of the episode in the garden had been circulated, but more damning by far was the titillating gossip that, after spending some considerable time alone with Lord Blakely, she had returned to the house with her dress in tatters and her hair in complete abandon. She could feel the stares and whispers. The younger members of the guests, who would have loved to ask what the handsome Lord Blakely was really like, were not as judgemental as the older set, who didn't hesitate to cast scathing glances her way.

'You look terrified,' Toby remarked. 'If you feel like running away, I wouldn't blame you.'

Linnet took a deep breath and squared her shoulders, knowing that if she left the room now, she would cover herself in further ridicule. 'I've never run away from anything in my life, Toby, and I do not intend to start now.'

Refusing to be shocked by what everyone was saying about her cousin, Louisa rushed up to her and gripped her arm, and in a whisper enquired if there was any truth in the gossip. 'I don't know what got into you last night, but Mama is in quite a lather about it.'

'Please be assured, Louisa, that my walk in the garden with Lord Blakely has been blown out of all proportion.'

'Still,' Louisa remarked, 'you were in the garden quite some time with him—and he *is* wondrously handsome. There's something dangerous about him, too—which I am sure you must have detected for yourself,' she said with a shiver of delight. 'Mama is quite bemused as to why he is here at all. It would appear Lord Radcliffe invited him, but why he would want to be here when he is unattached and a stranger to almost everyone—unless he had an ulterior motive—is a mystery.'

'Are you implying that his reason for being here is to see me, Louisa? Because if so, then you are quite mistaken. Lord Blakely is a stranger to me, so why on earth would he seek me out?'

'I was hoping you could tell me—after all, there was that little altercation between the two of you when we were playing the game yesterday. What did you talk about when you were alone in the garden last night?'

'It might have escaped your notice, Louisa, as a newly engaged lady, but there was a downpour and we had to shelter until it was over. As a matter of fact Lord Blakely is quite a gentleman and was extremely considerate and attentive.'

Louisa gave her a dubious look. 'To be sure, he is handsome to look at, not to mention extremely wealthy and probably a brilliant catch. Can you tell me you don't find him attractive?'

Linnet glanced abashedly at her cousin. 'No, Louisa, I'm afraid I can't.'

'Linnet!'

'Well—I can't help it!' she exclaimed, flushing like a green girl.

'Oh—so you do like him? How exciting!'

Linnet winced and clamped her lips together, refusing to admit it aloud.

Louisa giggled and waved to Harry, who had just entered the room. 'There's Harry. He's looking for me. I think Mama will want to have a word with you, Linnet, so prepare yourself. I'll catch up with you later.'

A buffet breakfast had been laid out in the dining room. Toby helped himself to ham and devilled kidneys, eggs and mushrooms, while Linnet, who had no appetite and was impatient to leave, settled for bread and butter and coffee. Determined to put on a brave face and keeping her head high, in a state of consuming misery she sat with Toby and ignored what was going on around her. She raised her head when Lord Blakely strolled in, nodding his head in acknowledgement of those he knew. She noted that he did not receive the same censorious treatment as she had—in fact, quite the opposite—which raised her ire.

Christian helped himself to a light breakfast and took a seat beside Toby.

'Is it my imagination or has something occurred that I should know about?'

'You will soon find out,' Toby informed him, chewing on his bacon. 'It's to do with you and Linnet. Apparently you were seen when you brought my sister back to the house after your walk in the garden. It's stirred a great deal of gossip among the guests, who didn't fail to notice the state of Linnet's gown.'

Lord Blakely's expression hardened. 'I beg your pardon?'

'According to Aunt Lydia, and the look on everyone's faces in this room, it's definitely the main topic of conversation this morning.'

When Lord Blakely's eyes finally moved to Linnet, his granite features softened, as if he understood the reason for her silence and how humiliated she must be feeling. He understood why she would naturally dread being the focal point of so many fascinated gossips, but not until she actually lowered her head and bit her trembling lip did he realise that her embarrassment was going to be compounded a thousand times now she was thrust into the limelight.

'I'm sorry. It must be quite upsetting for you.'

Touched by his concern, Linnet sighed. 'It's all right. We'll be leaving after breakfast. They'll forget all about me when I've gone.'

'Don't be too sure about that, Linnet.' Toby looked at Lord Blakely. 'I think Aunt Lydia wants to see you. She's none too pleased about what happened and wants you to explain yourself.'

'Does she, indeed?' Lord Blakely said tightly, tossing his napkin on the table and pushing his chair back. 'Then the sooner we sort this out the better. Excuse me.'

Some of the guests were leaving once breakfast was over and went to their respective rooms to prepare for their departure. Aunt Lydia appeared in the hall.

'Linnet, would you come in here.'

Linnet followed her aunt into her private sitting room for the second time that morning. Her heart sank when she saw Lord Blakely. He was standing by the window, his hands behind his back, his body taut. He turned when she entered. He bore little resemblance to the man who had teased her on the terrace after their dance and had laughingly pulled her out of the rose bush before kissing her. At that moment he was an aloof, icy stranger.

Lady Milton looked from one to the other. She was most put out that this unfortunate matter between Lord Blakely and her niece was taking precedence over her daughter's celebrations and was impatient to have order restored so it could continue.

Linnet steeled herself for the unpleasant scene that was about to occur. Her aunt stood stiffly in the middle of the room with the unshakeable confidence and poise that came from living a thoroughly privileged life, sure that the interview that was about to occur would go her way.

'Lord Blakely, I am most displeased. I welcomed you into my home and in return you have ruined my niece's reputation.'

'I did *what*?'

'You took a naïve young woman into the garden after dark and when she returned her appearance left much to be desired. Indeed, she was in quite a state.'

'He did not take me into the garden, Aunt Lydia,' Linnet protested indignantly. 'I was already there. I walked with him of my own volition and as for my dress—I told you I tripped and fell into a rose bush. Lord Blakely very kindly extricated me from it.'

'Maybe that is what happened, but no one will believe it. There were witnesses who saw you kissing. As a result of what happened, Linnet has been left open to censure and ridicule.'

'I have no doubt she will survive,' Lord Blakely

ground out, meeting Lady Milton's manner with cool disdain.

Linnet looked at him, her entire being engulfed in mortification, her misery increasing a thousandfold as she met his gaze. His features were drawn into a tight mask.

'Do you mind telling me what it is you wanted to speak to me about, Lady Milton?' he asked.

'I recognise that I must lend all my support to my niece at this time. I don't know how the two of you met, but it was evident to me when I saw the two of you dancing that there was already a familiarity between you. When you met her in the garden you should have seen to it that she returned to the house immediately. There was nothing discreet in your return under the watchful eyes of my guests and the servants. Servants talk.'

'Servants can be trusted to keep quiet.'

'It's not just the servants. There are others involved. I have a moral code, Lord Blakely, and you publicly breached that code by exposing my niece to scandal.'

'I realise how it must seem, Lady Milton. Our meeting in the garden was not prearranged, I assure you, and had it not started to rain then she would have returned to the house immediately.'

Lady Milton looked at him, her piercing eyes alive with anticipation. 'But she didn't and when she did return her dress was in tatters—which will provide society with enough bait to feed off until someone else causes a scandal.'

'I have listened to you while you have taken me to task, Lady Milton,' Lord Blakely said with strained patience. 'What is it that you want from me?'

'I pride myself on being realistic, Lord Blakely, and what is important now is how to extricate my niece from this sordid affair without complete ruin to her reputation. I am suggesting that you marry her.' Lady Milton clearly wanted this and seemed to sense victory already, perhaps convincing herself that Lord Blakely could not refuse to marry Linnet after last night.

Christian stood like a statue, his jaw clenched so tightly the corded muscles stood out. Anger flared in his eyes. 'What? You cannot be serious.'

'I assure you that I am perfectly serious,' Lady Milton said firmly. 'You have compromised the reputation of a young lady and you are honour-bound to marry her—to protect her good name as well as your own. What you have done will ruin her absolutely. There are many kinds of persecution that are not readily apparent, such as the whispered conjectures, the gossip and subtle innuendoes that can destroy a reputation and inflict a lifetime of damage. Society will assume her character must indeed be of the blackest nature and she will summarily be dropped. If you refuse to do the honourable and marry her, then you will destroy any chance of her making a decent marriage.'

Christian struggled to calm his temper. When he next spoke, his jaw was set in a hard line, his face a taut mask of controlled fury. 'Forgive me, Lady Milton. Since your suggestion is not what I expected, I must take a moment and consider the possible repercussions that may occur because of it.'

Pushed beyond the bounds of reason by her aunt's demands and shamed to the depths of her being, Linnet faced her aunt squarely. Her firm conviction that she would marry Lord Blakely, that she had no choice but to marry him, was more than she could bear just then. 'Aunt Lydia, I think you have got this out of all proportion.'

'No, Linnet, I don't think so. If Lord Blakely has any sense of responsibility, he must marry you.'

'But—I have no desire to marry him any more than he wants to marry me. You must let me choose, let me decide.' Her voice held no intonation. Total control was all she could bear. To allow any emotion through would weaken her. Dignity was a kind of refuge. 'Last night we were both unmindful of propriety and plain good sense, and the idea that because of that we should wed—why, the very idea is ludicrous.' Linnet looked at him and in cold, frigid silence, for an endless moment, their gazes locked as they assessed one another.

Lord Blakely's face was a cynical mask. 'You're absolutely right. It is ludicrous. And yet all these years I've been harbouring the delusion that all young ladies yearn to snare wealthy and titled husbands.'

'I'm not like other young ladies,' Linnet shot back while wanting nothing more than to fling herself into his arms. She knew all about the kind of ladies he referred to and, had she been higher up the social scale, then perhaps she would have been just like them. But she wasn't like them, she never would be and she couldn't bear the humiliation of being forced into marriage because they had shared a simple kiss.

'I sensed that from the moment I met you,' Christian remarked blandly.

Linnet heard the reminder of their unfortunate first encounter in his smoothly worded agreement and almost choked on her chagrin. 'Then that's plain enough. We won't wed.'

'Good. I'm glad that's sorted.'

'Thank you,' Linnet retorted with angry sarcasm, ignoring her aunt's sharp eyes that were telling her to be quiet.

'I am glad we are in accord. When I eventually take a wife it will be in my own way, with the woman of my choosing, and not when someone is holding an axe over my head, which is precisely where all my male instincts rebel.'

'So you intend to go on your way without righting the wrong you did,' Lady Milton retorted coldly, unable to conceal her mounting wrath at what she evidently thought to be Lord Blakely's lack of concern. 'You should have known what the consequences would be of dallying with an innocent, respectable young woman, that it could alter your life in a permanent way.'

'As far as I am concerned, Lady Milton, I have done no wrong. Had I done so, I might have even considered marrying your niece if she had acted as if she desired marriage to me. It is an unfortunate occurrence, I grant you, but I do not feel committed to marry her.'

'And the scandal?'

'I am certain that when your guests and whoever listens to their gossip has chewed over the incident, in time, when another scandal hits the scene, it will blow over and be forgotten as they get on with slating someone else.'

His arrogant calm was too much for Lady Milton. 'How dare you refuse to give the respectability of your name to Linnet—to take advantage of her and then to simply cast her off...' She halted, breathing heavily as she struggled to bring her anger and her emotions under control. She had failed in her effort to get Lord Blakely to wed Linnet. Her arguments had slid off him like a smooth, frozen block of ice. She seemed to realise she could not compel the man to marry her niece.

Suddenly Linnet, concerned by her aunt's outburst and fearing the situation was about to get out of hand, said, 'Please do not upset yourself, Aunt. I am sure all this can be sorted out in a calm and reasonable manner.'

Drawing herself up straight and squaring her shoulders, she fixed Lord Blakely with a direct stare. The whole situation was ridiculous. With no dowry, no connections and a mountain of responsibilities, how could she expect Lord Blakely to take her as his wife? Yet she did find him desirable—highly so. She had kissed him and was intrigued by him, but that did not mean she wanted to marry him. Although, if he showed any sign that he would not be averse to her, then she might be persuaded.

'I can understand your reticence to marry me, Lord Blakely, and you know I have no more desire to marry you than you have to marry me. You can take your leave of us now and no more will be said about it.' She looked at her aunt. 'I will go and find Toby. I think we should leave. I will go and say goodbye to Louisa.'

Linnet looked squarely at Lord Blakely as he held the door open for her to pass through. He turned and bowed his head to her aunt, thanking her for her hospitality and that he regretted the way things had turned out.

Christian was impatient to be away from Woodside Hall and the overbearing Lady Milton. Self-disgust and burning fury coursed through him, reality crushing down on him as he suddenly found his life infuriating and complicated. Everything was out of control and in utter confusion—and all because he had been unable to keep his hands off Linnet Osborne.

He had spent years of evasion, trying to avoid a situation such as this, ignoring the whispers and sighs of women who did not interest him eager to shackle him into matrimony. But it had taken only the curve of Linnet Osborne's lovely lips, for him to fall into a trap of his own making. If the incident had involved any other woman he would have cursed himself for a fool, but too often of late he had found himself beset by thoughts of her, visions of her face and how she had looked last night at the ball with the golden candlelight on her creamy skin. His thoughts brought to mind how those sweet and gentle arms had felt about his neck when he had embraced her and how her subtle body had curved into his own.

Though he had once thought himself immune to the subtle ploys of women, even though he had known her for such a short time, he had begun to think he would never be free of Linnet Osborne. From the very beginning she had stirred his baser instincts. Yet much as she ensnared his thoughts, he found his dreams daunting to his manly pride, for whenever she flitted through them like some puckish sprite, he was unable to think of a means of escape from this dilemma that had suddenly presented itself and he had no will to resist.

Breakfast was over and Linnet was about to go in search of Toby. Looking into the smug, censorious expressions on the faces she passed, she could not leave Woodside Hall soon enough. After bidding farewell to Louisa she paused in the hall when she saw Lord Blakely walking towards her and it seemed to Linnet that his eyes never left her as she waited for him to come closer. He stopped in front of her, his eyes on her face.

'You are leaving?' he said.

She nodded. 'I think we must. You are leaving also?'

He nodded. He knew he must leave Woodside Hall,

for he couldn't handle the fact that he wanted Linnet Osborne—it was making him feel like an inadequate youth. He had seen her when she was vulnerable and had felt the need to protect her. He hadn't felt that way about anyone in a very long time and he knew he was caring too much. She was touching him deep down, in places he had thought long since dead.

'I apologise for my aunt's insistence that we marry,' Linnet said. 'One thing you should know about Aunt Lydia is that she is a strictly controlling character. She comes from a long line of rigidly up-right people with impossibly high standards for themselves and everyone else. She is always wary about any scandal that might damage her popularity in society. I think she is so eager to get me off her hands that she will grasp at any opportunity to do so. I am only sorry that you were on the receiving end.'

'I am sorry about the unpleasantness. I'm not so insensitive as to ignore what has happened, but I will not be dictated to or manipulated into anything by your aunt. You are to return to Birch House?'

'Yes. It will be a relief to get home.'

'Then I hope there is a change in your circumstances and your brother sees the error of his ways. I consider your life is far from easy,' he said unexpectedly. 'A young woman with so much to worry about. It is not right.'

If Linnet had not known that such a thing was impossible she would have thought there was a deep concern beneath his conventional words. 'After speaking to Aunt Lydia I feel our circumstances are about to improve. She has offered to help us out of our difficulties—although I know her well enough to know she has an ulterior motive—which is to see Toby marry Caroline Mortimer. Of course, Toby's situation is worse, much worse than she could have imagined and she feels no sympathy for his plight. He has brought it upon himself. She knows that if Toby went to prison it would reflect badly on her, so she cannot ignore the problem. We are family. She has to do something. Toby is no great catch, but from Aunt Lydia's point of view he is not a complete disaster—providing he leaves the gambling alone.'

'And will he?'

'I sincerely hope so. Only time will tell.'

'And she is to settle your brother's debts?'

'Yes—although as yet the final sum has to be worked out.

'I shudder to think how your brother would manage without you.'

'Quite well, I imagine.'

'I don't think so. He enjoys the gaieties of St James's too much. But what about you?' Noting how pale she was, he recalled the moment he had come upon her in the garden playing with the other girls. When she had removed the scarf from her eyes he remembered how they had been filled with a laughing mischief that enlivened her entire expression. Now he knew her a little better, the realisation of her desperation aroused the same deep desire that had afflicted him after her tumble into the rose bush.

'I'm glad your aunt is to help you. Perhaps now

you won't have your brother to worry about you'll start thinking about yourself.'

'Yes. It is indeed a relief, Lord Blakely.'

'It must be—and my name is Christian.'

'But you do not know me,' she uttered reasonably.

'You are mistaken, Linnet. I need only to look into your eyes and I know everything I need to know about you. I know your pain, your strength and your courage.'

She swallowed down the tears that threatened and bowed her head. Security seemed an almost tangible substance whenever he was close to her and somewhere deep within her a yearning grew, as if her soul commanded her to speak. 'You cannot possibly know what my life is like.'

'I believe I do. More than you realise. You cannot hold yourself responsible for the problems that are thrust on you.'

Linnet smiled up at him. 'I will try not to. Thank you. You are very kind.'

Her comment caught him off guard and he took a moment to reply. She really was full of surprises. He had known many women in his life and he thought he knew every nuance of sensation a man could experience from the female sex. Yet this fetching, unpredictable young woman had surprised him. Only a ragged pulse that had leapt to life in his throat attested to his own disquiet as he looked at her with mingled feelings of regret and concern, and he could not put from his mind that by his own actions, if the scandal of what had occurred between them in the garden did indeed hit society, he would inadvertently, but effectively, have destroyed her future. In society one's worth was measured in gossip. He knew how easily people could be destroyed by rumour. If not for his damnable pride, he might have broken his guise of stoic reticence and agreed to marry her.

His smile when it came was slow and sensual. 'Kind?' He laughed softly. 'I have been accused of being many things, but never kind.' His expression grew serious. 'I apologise for making things difficult for you. It was a mistake.'

'A mistake? Do you regret kissing me?'

'No. But what we did—what I did—was a mistake.' His voice was strained. 'You must have cast a spell on me, for I do not have the strength or the inclination to resist you.' He stepped away from her. 'I'm sorry. I take full blame for what happened.' His eyes went beyond her. 'Here is your brother. Have a pleasant journey back to Chelsea.'

In the tearing, agonising hurt that enfolded her, Linnet was ashamed at how easy it had been for him to expose the proof of her vulnerability. Tears blinded her vision. Brushing them away, she felt anger directed against herself for her lack of will and with a fear of her feelings for Christian Blakely she seemed unable to control.

She watched him walk away, feeling that something inside her, some bright and hopeful light that shone brighter whenever she thought of him, faded out of existence. What had she done? She must have been out of her mind to let him kiss her. What had it meant? She sighed, feeling depressed and listless. The answer to her silent question was stark. Nothing, she thought. To Lord Blakely it had meant nothing at all, just a casual thing, and now she would never see him again. Out of sheer pride she held herself tightly together not wanting to betray the desolation she felt on seeing him go.

Walking away, Christian turned and looked back at her to find her strange tawny eyes remained fixed on him, full of overwhelming emotion, and that was the moment that he knew in the deepest core of his being, that beside her all other women were irrelevant. His passion for her was torn asunder by guilt. Age and experience had taught him that some women couldn't be trusted and the first woman to show him this was Selina. Her affair with his own father had hurt him very badly and ruined whatever relationship he'd had with him, whose main interests in life had been Egypt and beautiful women.

He was careful to choose women whose company he enjoyed. They had to be intelligent and sophisticated, and would not mistake lovemaking and desire with love, and, moreover, they had to be women who made no demands and expected no promises. Until he'd met Linnet Osborne this had been his mantra.

In the past hard logic and cold reason had always conquered his lust—with Linnet Osborne it was different. Feeling threatened in some strange way, he told himself he had to end it. He had to purge her out of his mind before he was completely beaten—and if he continued to see her he would lose the battle. He was in danger of losing his heart to her and he would not permit that. The stakes were too high.

Chapter Six

They left Woodside Hall mid-morning. Aunt Lydia did not try to persuade them to prolong their stay, although Louisa was sorry she was to be denied another day of her cousins' company. Toby was quiet and morose during the journey. Aunt Lydia had given them both much to think about. While Toby would for evermore be at Aunt Lydia's mercy, there was a lightness to Linnet's heart she hadn't felt in a long time. For the interim Aunt Lydia had arranged for Toby to live at Woodside Hall during the week to become better acquainted with the work under the watchful eyes of the bailiff and Cousin William.

'Tell me what you are thinking, Toby. Aunt Lydia is determined to make things right.'

'Yes, I know and I am grateful.'

'It is indeed generous of Aunt Lydia to offer to pay off your debts. You must realise that things will have to change.'

'Yes, I do. This is my one chance and from now on

everything is going to be different. My only desire is to wed Caroline, so I must make good on my shortcomings.' He looked at Linnet, a softness entering his eyes. 'I've always left everything for you to shoulder, but no more. I have to confess that I have been afraid of what the consequences might be after that night at Stourbridge House,' he confided to her seriously.

'Yes, well, there is nothing like a shock of those proportions to make one sit up and take stock of one's life.'

'My course of action is clear. It's up to me. I realise that to hold on to what I have, I am going to have to work at it. From now on I'm going to make a virtuous attempt to reform my way of life.'

Linnet listened to him in astonished silence, unable to believe this was her brother speaking. She realised from the intensity of his voice that he was not speaking idly and she could only thank Aunt Lydia for giving him an ultimatum. She was happy to hear him sounding so positive and hoped he was in earnest about what he intended doing and would not hotfoot it back to London's gaming rooms. Seeing the enthusiasm lighting up his face, she saw something of their father in him, who, until their mother's death, had worked hard to keep everything intact. Sadly it all began to fall apart when she wasn't there any more. She prayed that Toby had truly seen the error of his ways and would grow to be like their father had been before their family had become broken.

Birch House had been their home for four generations of Osbornes. It was not a large house, but, set in its own grounds, it had a genteel, gracious quality about it.

Samuel Doyle opened the door to them.

'I wasn't expecting you today. I thought you were staying with Lady Milton for a few days.'

'We were, Samuel, but we decided to come back early.'

He nodded and took his leave. Linnet noted that he was moving a lot slower these days, but his total loyalty to the family remained as strong as ever. Samuel and his wife, Eva, had begun their service at Birch House forty years ago, proving themselves faithful servants to her parents and later to Toby and herself. It was Samuel and Eva who had comforted and supported them when their mother had died and later their father. They were always there when needed, Eva helping Linnet with her hair and her clothes. She smiled and her heart warmed at the memory. Whatever would she have done without them?

Linnet went to her room to change. As she climbed the stairs, seeing the bare places on the walls where once paintings had hung and knowing that behind the closed doors objects and precious heirlooms were missing, which they had been forced to sell when times became more desperate, wrenched her heart.

Now Toby seemed to be turning his life around with a healthy energy Linnet had not seen in a long time, she took time to consider her own future. The first decision she made was that it was time to leave Birch House. When Toby married Caroline Mortimer they would not want her here, which she could understand. Since their parents' deaths, she had spent her life trying to fill the void in her brother's heart, trying to be his advisor, trying to guide him on the right path. In that she had failed and now it was time for him to find his own way.

It was time for Linnet to stop believing she had no choices. It was time to begin deciding her own destiny. She was twenty-two years old and answerable to no one. She would not wait for Aunt Lydia to foist on her a husband of her choosing. It was an intolerable prospect. She wanted to be needed, valued, appreciated and loved. When, and if, she married, it would be to a man of her choosing, someone who truly loved her and wanted her.

Her parting from Lord Blakely had been a painful wrench, but she told herself that the human heart was strong and resilient. She wasn't broken hearted and if she had been she didn't know of anyone who had died of a broken heart. She remembered the times he had kissed her. Tongues of heat curled inside her body at the memory. She remembered every moment, what it had felt like to have his hands on her, his mouth on hers, that indescribable pleasure of anticipating more. That he had desired her, she knew, but she realised that just because a man desired a woman, it could mean nothing more than that.

One week after their parting, although she missed Christian and thought about him all the time, her heartache had lessened. She grieved for the painful destruction of the hope in her heart—for him to have wanted to see her again and to hope for his affections. However, considering her conduct since their first encounter, when he had initially believed she was a thief and she had compounded her fault by doing what no proper young lady would dream of doing and seriously considered spending the night with him in return for that wretched necklace—she could not in all fairness blame him for walking away. Although a vestige of pain still lingered and she called herself all kinds of fool for her unrealistic illusions. But where could she go? What could she do? She had already thought about looking for a post as governess to a wealthy family, so that was what she would do.

She had given little thought to her meeting with Mrs Marsden since that day in the Strand, so she was surprised when a carriage drew up in front of the house and Mrs Marsden climbed out. Linnet went out to meet her, her black taffeta skirts rustling crisply as she guided her into the house.

'Mrs Marsden, it is so nice to see you again. What can I do for you?'

'Well, Miss Osborne, I am hoping we might be able to help each other.'

When they were sitting in the drawing room, over tea and some of Eva's delicious cakes, they chatted about trivial matters. Linnet was conscious of Mrs Marsden's eyes studying her, not critically, but rather an assessing frankness and even an admiration one woman directs at another when she sincerely believes that woman is worthy of it. Eager to learn the reason for her visit, Linnet asked her again what she could do for her.

Mrs Marsden placed her cup and saucer down. Her face, which had been firm with some inner resolve, softened imperceptibly. 'It concerns the child, Alice. I recall you told me you were thinking of seeking a position as a governess. I have come here today to ask for your help. I wondered if you would consider the post as Alice's governess. His Lordship—the Earl of Ridgemont—has been intending to get her a governess but, being such a busy man with many issues to worry him, he hasn't had the time to get round to it. He's away at present, at his estate in Sussex, but I have his permission to employ anyone I consider suitable—on a trial basis, I must point out.'

'Alice is his daughter?'

Mrs Marsden seemed to hesitate, and then she said, 'Yes.'

'And Alice's mother?'

'She—she died in childbirth.'

'That is very sad, Mrs Marsden. Tell me, how is the Earl with Alice?'

'He—he doesn't see her very often—his work kept him away from her when she was younger. I am telling you this in compete confidence for he hates tittle-tattle—he doesn't take much interest in her, which is a crime really. She's such a lovely child. I know I shouldn't criticise him, but his visits are more of a duty than a pleasure. I can only hope that there will be a change for the better in the future. What do you say, Miss Osborne? Does my offer appeal to you?'

'Mrs Marsden—I don't know what to say. I freely admit you've taken me by surprise. Tell me about Alice.'

'She is a well-behaved child, quiet and shy of others, which I put down to her not often being in company—of adults or children. I have looked after Alice since she was born five years ago, but I think I told you when we last met that I am not in the best of health and I find caring for a child of Alice's age difficult at times. Milly, one of the maids, helps me out and she is very good with her. But it's time she began learning her letters and the things that will prepare her for the future.'

Linnet smiled, a compassionate warmth lighting her eyes. She could almost feel the tension inside her visitor. Linnet didn't take any persuading to accept her offer of employment. Getting away from Toby for a while as he began his work in Richmond appealed to her.

'Then what can I say? For a long time now I've been undecided as to what to do with my future, which path to take, and it is true that I am considering seeking employment as a governess. I will accept your offer and help in any way I can with Alice. I will do my best to make her happy. When would you like me to begin my work?'

Mrs Marsden's eyes were bright with tears of gratitude. Linnet's acceptance had evidently lightened her spirit, and it was as though a great weight had been lifted off her shoulders. 'Thank you, Miss Osborne.

I can't tell you what a relief that is to me. You can begin as soon as it is convenient to you.'

'I will have to speak to my brother and settle a few things here, so perhaps in a few days.'

When Linnet told Toby that she was to take up a position as a governess, he was so taken with his improved situation that he didn't voice his objections. Aunt Lydia was not so understanding, saying that her outrageous decision to earn her own living would besmirch the family name. Far better that she found a rich husband. Linnet paid her no heed. She was twenty-two years of age, her own mistress. She would do as she saw fit and taking care of a five-year-old child would suit her very well.

Linnet felt when she entered the Earl of Ridgemont's town house in Kensington that she was entering a house different to anything she had seen before, different to anything she could have imagined. The house had been built both to provide gracious living and to impress upon visitors the wealth of its owner. A wide gravel drive led to the front door and a circular lawn surrounded by tall trees and shrubs beyond. There was luxury in every room, the windows exquisitely curtained with the finest fabrics and carpets in lovely shades covering the floors.

It was still a bemused little girl who gave Linnet a direct look, regarding her seriously. Linnet prayed silently for acceptance, hoping Alice would not reject her. On impulse she reached out and took Alice's small hand in hers and smiled warmly into her eyes.

'I know this must be as strange for you as it is for me, Alice, and as much of a surprise, but I've looked forward to meeting you. Mrs Marsden has told me all about you. I've never looked after a little girl before so I'm hoping we can help each other and you can help me find my way around this lovely house of yours. It looks so big I shall be sure to lose my way without guidance.'

Alice made no attempt to pull away and a little smile began to tug at the corners of her mouth. She seemed to be assessing Linnet, and when her eyes ceased to regard her so seriously and her smile gradually broadened, which was a delight to see, Alice and Mrs Marsden began to relax. They looked at one another, certain that Linnet's approach had worked and that a good start had been made. It brought a relieved smile to Mrs Marsden's features, which told Linnet how apprehensive she had been about this meeting between herself and Alice.

'I'll show you,' Alice said, with a bright, eager light shining in her wide eyes, her face taking on a look of enthusiasm, no longer seeing the beautiful lady as a stranger. 'The house is very big. Sometimes I get lost, too,' she confided to Linnet with a considerable amount of childish gravity.

'Then we will get lost together and have fun finding our way out, Alice.'

'This house is not as big as the other house. I

haven't been there yet, but Mrs Marsden says that we will—one day.'

Linnet looked to Mrs Marsden for the location of the house Alice referred to. 'In Sussex,' she informed her.

'Then I am sure you will.'

'And do you dance? I like to dance, too,' Alice said, doing a wobbly twirl on her tiptoes.

'I do dance, but I have to confess I'm not very good at it.' Linnet smiled, cradling Alice's chin in her hand. 'I'm so glad you and I are going to be friends.'

'So am I. What shall I call you?'

Linnet looked at Mrs Marsden.

'Miss Osborne is how you will address her, Alice.' She smiled gently.

Linnet was kept so busy that she gave little thought to Alice's father, the Earl of Ridgemont, whom everyone referred to as 'His Lordship'. Alice was a delightful child, warm and eager to please. Her eyes were dark brown framed with long black lashes. Her hair was dark, with curls framing her exquisite face. Yet there was a distress in her, an anxiety that was unusual for one so young.

Linnet realised that, despite her lack of experience with children, she had a talent for entertaining Alice and in no time at all managed to win her trust. They went walking in Kensington Gardens and she enjoyed showing her some of the major places of interest in London. Alice loved to draw and colour the pictures she created, which they hung on the walls of the nursery. She became extremely fond of the child and found pleasure in her company.

Linnet had been her governess for three weeks and had no reason to regret her decision. But that was before the Earl of Ridgemont returned.

After an absence of four weeks, Christian entered his London house, surprised to hear girlish laughter coming from an upper storey. Handing his hat and gloves to his butler, he looked questioningly at Mrs Marsden coming down the stairs. He regarded her a moment, thinking how tired she looked. He really must do something about employing someone else to look after Alice. Caring for the child was taking its toll on the elderly nursemaid.

On seeing her employer, Mrs Marsden smiled a welcome. She had a warm personality and a willing nature, and never let him forget how grateful she was to him for letting her stay with Alice when they had come to England.

'Lord Blakely! You're back. I trust you had a good journey up from Sussex.'

'Thank you, yes, Mrs Marsden. Alice appears to be in good spirits.'

'Since the new governess arrived she's come out of her shell. I hope you don't mind, but when you went away and left no instructions as to the hiring of a governess for Alice, I took it upon myself to employ someone with the right credentials. Well, Miss Osborne's were more than suitable. She is proving to be an absolute treasure and she has become fond of Alice. She is an extremely capable and competent young woman, intelligent and well read. I've never seen Alice reach out to anyone as she has to Miss Osborne and Miss Osborne's interest and feeling towards Alice is obviously sincere. The child adores her.'

A world of feelings flashed for an instant across Christian's face. He stared at Mrs Marsden in disbelief, wondering if he had heard her correctly. 'Miss Osborne?'

'She is the young lady who came to our rescue that day in the Strand. Her prompt action saved us from being flung into the street, if you remember.'

'I do remember, Mrs Marsden, but I had no idea it was Miss Osborne who had come to the rescue.'

'Oh, yes—how remiss of me not to have said. She began work three weeks ago and has settled down remarkably well.'

Christian's expression hardened. The knowledge of her presence in his house stunned him. 'Has she, indeed?' He cursed his own inadequacy in not having been more attentive when he had returned to the carriage that day. Relieved that no one had been hurt, he'd been so preoccupied with his chance meeting with Linnet Osborne that he'd failed to question Mrs Marsden further. He had no idea Linnet was the young lady he had seen from a distance dash out into the road and settle the frightened horse.

And now she was employed in his house to look after Alice. Had Linnet Osborne not created enough havoc in his well-ordered life by creeping into his heart and mind so that he had been unable to think of anything else for a time? Now he was back in London and she had begun to recede into the dark recess of his mind where such things were kept, never to be resurrected. Yet here she was, having infiltrated his home and about to disturb his life once more.

'Miss Osborne, you say—Miss Linnet Osborne?' he queried—there must be more than one Miss Osborne.

'Why, yes.' She frowned. 'You are acquainted with her?'

He nodded. 'We have met.'

'I hope you are not displeased, Lord Blakely. I did do the right thing in setting her on?'

'Yes—yes, of course. I'll go and have a word with her. Is she in the nursery?'

'She is.'

Without more ado Christian strode swiftly up the stairs, pausing for an indecisive moment outside, before hesitatingly pushing open the door, unprepared for the scene his eyes beheld. He stood for a moment, taking in a scene of domesticity and harmony. The nursery was filled with bright sunlight and colourful childish paintings on the wall. There were books and baskets of toys, a child-sized table and four chairs, occupied by dolls and a stuffed rabbit and a teddy bear.

He would have known Miss Osborne was there, even before his eyes lighted on her. It was the perfume she wore—that was the thing he remembered about her—a subtle smell of roses, hardly noticeable at all, but nevertheless a part of her. He could not believe she was here. His eyes were drawn to her automatically, his muscles taut from some unconscious force. For the first time in his life he was totally surprised. She was heartbreakingly lovely. He should have been prepared for this, but he was neither prepared for the sight of her nor what it did to him. He stood quite still and looked at her, his face drawn, his eyes wide, fixed and unbelieving. A hundred questions and emotions swept through his head. Then he was moving forward, very coolly, to stand before her.

For a moment a deathly hush fell on the nursery. The man who had just entered caught Linnet's attention, for the grim expression on his face as she looked at him made her wary. She was seated on a sofa with Alice beside her, looking at a story book. The smile on her lips faded when she saw him. Immediately she got to her feet and stared at him as if she could not believe her eyes.

'Christian—Lord Blakely… You—you are…'

'The Earl of Ridgemont.'

'Oh—I—I had no idea.'

'Clearly. I prefer to use one of my lesser titles. Mrs Marsden informs me that you are Alice's new governess?'

'Yes. Alice is my charge,' Linnet said, totally bemused and beside herself with embarrassment. Her heart contracted. Slowly she turned to look at the child and then back to him, so distracted by her own rampaging emotions that she never noticed the sudden hardening of his face. 'Is—is anything wrong?'

'You might say that.'

'You are surprised to find me here—and are not best pleased, I take it.'

'This is no place to discuss the matter. We should go into the drawing room. Mrs Marsden can take care of Alice.'

Christian went ahead of her down the stairs. Holding the door to the drawing room open as Linnet passed through and ignoring a hovering servant as if she were not there, he closed the door when they were inside. Standing in the middle of the room, Linnet turned and stared at him, her hands folded in front of her, her mind already realising what her heart couldn't bear to believe. How could she have been so stupid? Not for one moment had she connected the Earl of Ridgemont with Lord Blakely. And why, having been absent for a month, had he not acknowledged Alice? And Alice? Why had she not run to her father as any doting child would have done?

She could feel the very air move forcefully and snap with a restless intensity that Christian Blakely seemed to discharge. Clad in an immaculately fitting brown coat that deepened his complexion, he looked lethally handsome and incredibly alluring. But he didn't want her here. He never had.

'I'm sorry,' she said. 'I had no idea who you were. Had I known I would never have taken the position. Do you want me to go?'

He looked at her, his face hard and cold. 'Yes, I do,' he said, without preamble.

No slap on the face could have hurt so much. A sudden weight fell on her heart at what was happening. She was stunned, bewildered, and a thousand thoughts raced across her brain and crashed together in confusion. There was no room in her heart or her mind for anything but this vast disappointment, which had already become an aching pain.

'I'm sorry you feel like that. I will be sorry to leave Alice.' Moving closer to him, she met and held his eyes. 'Tell me why you want me to leave—your reason for terminating my employment?'

'Does there have to be one?'

'Yes, there does.'

He moved closer to her, his hands on his hips as he bent his face to her. 'You, Miss Osborne, are too much of a disruption.'

Linnet stared at him, utterly confused by his reply and momentarily stunned to silence. After a moment, she said, 'A disruption? How? To your household? Because if that is the case then I will tell you that I have been treated with unaffected warmth by everyone. Courtesy and mutual affection rule in perfect harmony.'

'I'm glad to hear it, but I wasn't talking about the household.'

The truth dawned on Linnet as she looked at the granite face of the man who had kissed her into mindless oblivion on two occasions. 'You!' At any other time and on another occasion she would have laughed, but the matter was too serious to be amused by. 'You are the one disrupted by my presence here!

I am flattered. I had no idea when you tried to seduce me that I'd affected you so profoundly. Weren't you satisfied with the humiliation you inflicted on me in Richmond that you must add further humiliation on me by dismissing me from your employ for no other reason than if I continue living in your house you might not be able to keep your hands off me? Well, I will tell you this, you conceited, supremely amoral beast. If you ever touch me again…' she told him with quiet firmness, 'I will fight you with my dying breath.'

Her words scorched Christian's soul with its fierce, despairing passion. They hit the target with such force he tensed, his jaw tightening. Linnet could have pressed her advantage further, but she knew that his mind was made up and nothing would change it.

'You won't fight me, Miss Osborne. I know how you feel.'

'No, you don't,' she contradicted angrily. 'You couldn't possibly.' Her cheeks and eyes were blazing hot, her fists tightly clenched as she struggled to contain her rising emotions.

'Enough! Alice is not your concern. It is up to me who I employ to look after her.'

'Why are you being like this? What have I done?'

Everything, Christian thought wretchedly. Ever since he had first set eyes on her she had stirred his baser instincts. She was too much of a threat to his sanity. He couldn't possibly live in the same house with her if he was to have any peace. Everywhere he went she would be there, ready to ensnare him, and when she was absent his need to see her would make him seek her out. He was furious with himself for feeling like this—for wanting her. He realised that sexual desire for her had become a complication. Better if she was away from him altogether, out of his sight, before she disrupted his whole life.

Not to be so callously dismissed and stiffening her spine, Linnet raised her head defiantly. 'I came here with nothing but good intentions. They were honourable and completely honest. I did not expect to have them flung back in my face.'

'Then it's unfortunate you've wasted your time, but it's hardly a tragedy.' Christian would not allow himself a moment of weakness. His pride was his strength.

His words sliced through her, laid her open and left pain in their wake. They seared through her and brought a rush of colour to her face. He was being cruel and her stung pride would not allow that. It brought her chin up defiantly. She glared at him. 'Contrary to what you might or might not think of me, I will not tolerate it.'

Christian's jaw tightened and his eyes were glacial. 'Then deal with it, but be careful what you say,' he said harshly. 'And don't be misled by the fact that I once showed myself indulgent in my dealings with you—'

'One might say rather more than indulgent,' Linnet retorted. 'It infuriates me that I allowed such liberties to be taken by a man who thinks of me as no more than a moment's pleasure when you get me alone.'

'I don't recall you complaining at the time.'

Something welled up in Linnet, a powerful surge of emotion to which she had no alternative but to give full rein. It was as if she had suddenly become someone else, someone bigger and much stronger than her own self. Her eyes flashed as cold fury drained her face of colour and added a steely edge to her voice.

'Which is to my regret. As a matter of fact, it did mean something to me. To you, what happened may have seemed commonplace,' she upbraided him, her words reverberating through the room. 'Just another one of the many titillating flirtations and infidelities that give society something to gossip about. But I am not in the habit of kissing gentlemen who are relative strangers to me, or any other kind for that matter.'

'I was not accusing you of such.'

'You may be an earl, of noble birth, but your lofty rank does not intimidate me. You are not the sun around which the world revolves. I know who I am and I do not need you to remind me, and I am aware that you not wanting me here has nothing to do with me not being suitable to teach Alice, but that it is personal—to do with you and me. You are heartless, inconsiderate and arrogant and I cannot believe I let you touch me. When I leave here it will be your loss, Lord Blakely, but it will be my loss, too—and Alice's.'

'Nevertheless I want you to leave. Don't test me further.'

'I wouldn't dream of it.'

'You will be reimbursed for your time, of course. I don't think Alice will suffer any adverse effects from your leaving.'

'And you're sure of that, are you, Lord Blakely?'

'Alice is my responsibility and I will guide her as I see fit.'

'Then I would say that, with the attitude you've got, you will not make a very good job of it and you will end up with a very unhappy child.'

'Don't you dare lecture me on how to bring up Alice, Miss Osborne.'

'I wouldn't dream of it, but it's high time someone did. Oh—perhaps I should be more explicit. You already have an unhappy child, Lord Blakely. I didn't have to be told because I could see for myself. She does not mean to criticise you—indeed, she does not know the true meaning of the word—but she has mentioned that she rarely sees you—she believes that you do not want her here. Maybe you have issues concerning your daughter—it is not for me to speculate on that—but I can see in her manner and her drawings that your daughter is crying out for your attention and you choose not to see it. It is breaking her heart. She has been deprived of her mother. It isn't right that she is deprived of her father, too, of his own volition—which is unforgivable.'

Christian's face had gone white with anger. 'You are right. It is not for you to speculate on things that do not concern you,' he said, speaking to her as he would anyone else in his employ for their impudence. 'I think you have said quite enough.'

'I agree. Would you not allow me to stay until you have found someone else? You may not have noticed, but Mrs Marsden does not enjoy the best of health. Will you not consider it?'

He spoke through gritted teeth, his eyes hard. 'I have. It took precisely one second. The answer is no.' His tone was implacable and left no room for argument.

'I see. When we were in the garden at Woodside Hall you asked me if I would allow you to help me. Do you remember?'

He nodded. 'Of course I do. You didn't accept my offer.'

'I wanted to, but I did not know you well enough.'

'And now?'

'I still don't—not really. But if you still want to help me, then you will let me stay to look after Alice.' When he didn't reply she stepped back. 'I can see there is nothing more to be said. I thank you for your hospitality,' she said with the polite cordiality of one who might have been his guest. 'I trust you will find another governess who will suit your needs—if not your daughter's. I am sorry to have inflicted myself on you. Will you allow me to say goodbye to Alice? She will be upset if I just disappear. She is a beautiful child and we get on well.' Her words were of resignation, not defiance.

Suddenly Christian looked at her with unexpected softness. Surprised by the change in his expression, she opened her mouth to speak, but he stopped her and, taking a deep breath, continued, 'Of course. But then you have to go, Linnet,' he said, using her Christian name for the first time since they had parted at Woodside Hall. 'You must. There are some things you cannot understand.' He was thinking of Alice and the complications that would arise in time when he would have to explain that Alice was not his daughter, but his half-sister. Having to explain the unfortunate circumstances of Alice's birth and his own father's unacceptable behaviour was anathema to him.

Linnet's face was a pale, emotionless mask. Displaying a calm she did not feel, as she swept from the room she managed with a painful effort to dominate her disappointment. She had to ask herself why it should hurt so much, and to question what was in her heart.

Christian watched her as she walked out of the room without another word, undecided whether to go after her or remain where he was until she had left the house. When she had closed the door, he raked his fingers through his hair in consternation, thinking over what she had said. When he had told her he wanted her to leave she had not tried to play on his sympathy or his chivalry with a sad tale of how she was desperate and needed the post. Instead she had turned the tables and taken him to task for his treatment of Alice. No one had done that before.

Her concern for Alice had been evident. Protective and loyal towards her young charge, with a will of burnished steel, defiant and brave and with blaz-

ing eyes, she had stood up to him, had berated him
for his conduct of the child. Challengingly ready to
defend Alice, she had subjected him to the most mas-
sive dose of guilt, coercion and emotional blackmail
that he had ever seen anyone hand out.

Alice was inconsolable—she began to sob, clinging to Linnet in desperation. Mrs Marsden was beside
herself. Clearly she had displeased Lord Blakely, but
she'd had no idea he felt so strongly against employing Miss Osborne.

Linnet would have been surprised if she had
looked up and seen Lord Blakely's face as he stood
in the doorway, watching her comforting Alice, her
cheek resting on the child's dark curls held up by
a shiny red ribbon. Mesmerised by the lovely picture the woman and child created, his expression
had softened. He listened intently to her trying to
soothe Alice, which was something that came quite
naturally to her. Gradually Alice became quiet and
ceased to cry, looking at the face of the woman with
something akin to adoration and responding to the
warmth in her voice.

For the first time Christian absorbed the sweet
innocence of the child and suddenly felt a profound
need to protect her. Alice looked across at him shyly,
much in awe of this dark, forbidding man. As Miss
Osborne placed a soft kiss on her cheek, his throat
tightened with emotion. He could see Alice's need of
her. He had to admit that there were times when he
didn't even know the child existed, but now, struck

by the various emotions playing over her features as she looked up at Miss Osborne, the fondness in Miss Osborne's eyes could not be concealed.

Mrs Marsden stood looking on, wringing her hands, giving her employer a pleading look. Surely he only had to see how fond Miss Osborne was of Alice and how much Alice had come to love Miss Osborne.

The scene and the words Miss Osborne uttered, words of comfort and love, bewitched Christian and reached out to some unknown part of him that he had not been aware he possessed. It was fleeting, but it touched and lightened some dark corner of his heart, then it was gone.

Becoming aware of his presence, Linnet raised her head. With his shoulder propped against the door, he was a towering, masculine presence in the nursery. He was dressed in the same clothes he had worn for his journey from Sussex. He was watching her intently. Removing Alice's arms, which were wrapped around her waist, she got to her feet. Mrs Marsden took her place, gathering Alice to her.

'I'm sorry. I'll go to my room and pack my things. It shouldn't take long and then I'll leave.' She looked down at Alice, who was shy of Lord Blakely, hiding her face in Mrs Marsden's neck.

With her heart breaking for the child in her distress, Linnet walked along the landing to her room. She was surprised when she reached for the handle only to find Lord Blakely reached out and place his hand over hers.

'Wait. We have to talk,' he said without preamble.

'I don't think there is anything further to be said. And if you are about to take me to task again I should not like you to do so where the servants might overhear.'

Christian abruptly opened the door to her room. They went inside and he closed it behind him.

'Perhaps I was too hasty to dismiss you. Whatever I thought of your audacity to come here to look after Alice, I should have had the courtesy to listen to you.'

'Yes, you should.'

'I appreciate the advice you gave me concerning Alice, but you do not know the facts and I am not prepared to speak of it. Be assured that I make sure all of Alice's needs are taken care of and I want what is best for her. If she wants you to be her governess, then so be it.'

Linnet bowed her head in defence of his superior knowledge of Alice. 'It was most ungentlemanly of you to order me to leave the way you did.'

A wry smile added to his hard features. 'According to your blistering tirade, I haven't done anything to give you the impression that I am a gentleman.'

Linnet stared at him, her anger forgotten. 'No, you have not. Are you apologising?'

He looked puzzled for a moment, then he nodded. 'Yes, I am.'

'Then I apologise for my harsh words. I had no right to accuse you as I did. How you deal with your daughter is your affair. It was most undignified of me and I should have known better.'

'Do you regret it?'

Linnet lifted her brows, eyeing him with an impenitent smile. 'No. You deserved it.'

'You're right,' he admitted, taking a step closer and holding her eyes with his steady gaze. 'But don't let it go to your head.'

A sudden smile dawned across his face and Linnet's heart skipped a beat. Christian Blakely had a smile that could melt the hardest heart—when he chose to use it. She drew a deep, steadying breath, trying to ignore how near to her he was. 'I won't,' she said, turning away from him, but before she could step away from him, his fingers curled over her wrist, stopping her.

'When I saw you just now with Alice, I could see how close she has grown to you. It was unforgivable of me to ask you to leave so abruptly.'

For a moment Linnet was too surprise to speak. His thumb caressed her wrist and she felt her pulse quicken in response. Angry with herself, she pulled her wrist free of his grasp. 'And now? Are you saying you would like me to stay?'

'I am.

'So I don't have to pack my bag and return home with my tail between my legs?'

'I'm not completely heartless. There is another matter I wish to raise. Mrs Marsden told me about the incident in the Strand. I want to thank you in person for your prompt actions when you stopped one of my carriage horses from bolting—the day I saw you and you disappeared before I had a chance to find out more about you.'

Linnet stared at him in disbelief. 'That was your carriage? Your horses?'

'Indeed. The horse you brought under control is a peppery beast at the best of times. It was immensely brave of you to do what you did and for which I am truly grateful. You handled him admirably. Mrs Marsden is frail—I am sure you have seen that for yourself. I doubt she would have survived being flung out of the carriage into the road.'

'I'm happy to have been of help.'

'You brought the horse under control with superb skill, calming it down until it was almost docile. You weren't afraid of the danger?'

'Not in the least. I saw no danger.'

'Naturally I was concerned when I discovered that Mrs Marsden had decided to employ you without discussing the matter with me first, but now, having seen you with Alice, I am happy to let you stay.'

'What you must understand is that I did not seek the position she offered me. Indeed, when we did speak in the Strand that day I mentioned in passing that I was considering seeking a post as a governess. I was surprised when she called on me and offered me the post.'

'I see. Mrs Marsden is not well and taking care of a small child is not easy for her. It would seem you came along at the right moment.'

'For Alice, too. I have many household accomplishments I can teach her.' She smiled, a smile that lit up her whole face. 'Alice has also expressed a desire to learn to dance. I am not the best dancer in the world—and having partnered me in the waltz I am sure you will be in agreement—but I can teach her the rudiments of the dance until she is old enough for you to employ someone with the expertise to teach her better. I also like children—especially Alice. I look forward to getting to know her better. Where she is concerned I take my responsibilities seriously.'

He leaned against the door, folding his arms casually across his chest. She was standing facing him, surveying him with a steady gaze. He was taken aback by the sheer magnetism of her presence. She was dressed in a plain yellow high-waisted dress, her hair arranged in glossy twists about her well-shaped head like a beacon of light. Hers was a dangerous kind of beauty, for she had the power to touch upon a man's vulnerability with a flash of her wonderful tawny-coloured eyes.

'Well, now that's sorted out, I think I should go and give Alice and Mrs Marsden the news.'

'Perhaps you should. You surprise me, Miss Osborne. You are not intimidated by me, are you?'

Their eyes met, measuring each other up, thoughtfully, calculating, aware of the differences in their backgrounds, but aware, too, of a personal interaction.

'Not in the slightest. Should I be?'

'No.' He smiled. 'I must congratulate you. Alice has taken to you. Mrs Marsden has told me how much she likes you.'

'And I like her. It would be difficult not to. She's a delightful child.'

'Did your brother raise any objections to your taking up this position?'

'Not at all, although Aunt Lydia was livid. She was determined to marry me off to the first man to ask for me, but when she saw how determined I was to take care of my own future, I fear she has washed her hands of me. If everything goes to plan Toby will marry Caroline Mortimer—Sir George Mortimer's daughter.'

'I saw them together at Woodside Hall. They did seem to be enamoured of each other. Does Lady Milton have the power to force you to marry?'

'No. I've reached my majority.'

'You will miss your home when your brother marries and Caroline moves in.'

'Birch House has always been my home—it will always be an integral part of my life—as it will come to be Caroline's.'

'And you wouldn't want to get in the way of that.'

'No. I want Toby to marry and settle down so much. They will find their own way. I should hate to be looked on as some interfering spinster sister-in-law who has no other life than to live my life through them.'

'And you have no other family—apart from Lady Milton?'

'No, and heaven forbid she would want me to go and live with her—which is why—despite disgracing myself—I have taken paid employment.'

'Then if you are to avoid the clutches of your Aunt Lydia,' he said, opening the door, 'it's as well I have agreed to keep you on.' He moved on to the landing. 'I think you should go and give Alice the good news.'

Chapter Seven

Now Christian had seen Linnet again all the feelings he had tried so hard to suppress in the past month came back to torment him. He wanted her more than he had ever wanted anything in his life.

He immersed himself in his work. The usual duties and matters of business, and meetings with other business associates, all took place in town and kept him from the house. This he welcomed, for it kept him fully occupied, away from thoughts of Miss Osborne and her tawny eyes and his increasing desire for her. What was it about her that made him unable to dismiss her from his mind? She liked him well enough. She had liked him when she had melted in his arms. Christian knew he was liking her more and more as the days passed into weeks and he saw her day in and day out, heard her laughter coming from the nursery, saw her walking out with a happy Alice skipping along beside her. He desired Linnet far too much and she invaded his mind every time he lowered his guard. She had become an obsession and continually took his mind from his work.

Christian had been away from the house all day. It was dark by the time he returned home. When he had changed and eaten, he went in search of Miss Osborne—because of her position he had reverted to the formal way of addressing her, Linnet being too familiar. Such familiarity would cause unwanted gossip and speculation among the servants which would not be appropriate.

She was alone in the nursery, curled up in one of the two big leather chairs by the fire, reading a book, her feet tucked beneath her. The firelight washed a soft glow over her. She looked up when he knocked and entered, placing her book on the small table beside her chair.

'Lord Blakely,' she said, getting to her feet and smoothing down her skirts. 'I did not expect you. If you are here to see Alice, she went to bed over an hour ago. I took her to the park earlier and she was quite worn out by the excitement of seeing a hot air balloon soar up into the sky. She went to bed telling me she was going to draw a picture of it tomorrow and paint it all the colours of the rainbow.'

He smiled, nodding his head slightly. 'I shall make a point of looking at it when it's completed.'

'If she knows you will do that, then I can guarantee it will be the best picture she has created so far.'

'I knew she would be asleep now. It is you I have come to see.'

'Oh?'

He had never seen Linnet at this time of the day. She had loosened her hair and it was gathered in a loose ribbon in the nape of her neck. At that moment there was a defencelessness about her, and the small smile on her lips brought a softening to his heart. Her face mirrored her confusion at being caught unawares. She looked vulnerable and much younger and she had the innocent appearance of a bewildered child. Her long lashes quivered and her eyes were clear as they looked up at him.

He walked into the centre of the room, distracted by the pictures Alice had painted hanging on the walls. His eyes did a quick sweep of them, then he looked away, focusing his attention on Linnet.

Linnet watched him, her throat tight with emotion. Every day she could see that Alice's need of her father, to have him in her life, to protect her against all things, was a role he did not play. There were times when she thought he didn't even know his daughter existed.

'I've come to tell you that I intend leaving for Sussex the day after tomorrow. It should give you enough time to prepare.'

'You—want me to go with you—and Alice?'

'Of course. I have some business to take care of at Park House and I thought you might like to accompany me. I'm not sure how long we will be there, but a jaunt in the country and the country air will do Alice good.'

'Yes, I am sure it will. Alice will be thrilled—even more when she realises she is to travel with you.'

'We shall see.'

His reply was abrupt, giving Linnet reason to believe there was some underlying trauma that made it difficult for him to be close to his daughter. She sensed it went back to the time of her birth, but what it could be was a mystery. She was certain Mrs Marsden was fully aware of the facts, but she was not forthcoming and Linnet didn't want to appear too inquisitive.

'I'm looking forward to seeing Park House. I've heard so much about it from the servants. Everyone who has been there has told me how splendid it is.'

'My ancestors would be pleased to hear it,' he remarked. 'I know I've only recently returned to London—I have business meetings to attend and I have to take my seat in the House of Lords occasionally—but I must get back to Sussex. It's a busy time for the tenant farmers, harvest being in full swing. I have an excellent bailiff, but there are matters only I can take care of.'

'Park House must be such a welcome change after the hustle and bustle of the city.'

'I cannot deny that. I would like to spend more of my time there, which I intend to do eventually. When I went to Egypt to sort out my father's affairs, which were quite extensive, I had to put everything here on hold. It's amazing how things build up.'

'Lord Blakely, when you returned from Sussex and found Mrs Marsden had offered me the post to be Alice's governess, it was wrong of me to say what I did.'

'What? When you accused me of neglecting her?'

'Yes. I behaved in an impertinent and presumptuous manner. I didn't even allow you the chance to defend yourself. When you refused to be drawn on the matter I couldn't help myself.'

Christian looked at her, thoughtful for a moment, and when he continued his voice was serious. 'You also told me Alice is an unhappy child. Is that still the case?'

'I think so, but she tries not to show it. I have seen the hope, the fleeting joy on her face at any mention of her father, only to be replaced with a quiet hurt and disappointment when you fail to come to her.'

Linnet's face was composed and her eyes clear and untroubled. In fact, she looked as she always looked since he had taken her in his employ. She went about her work with a cool reserve and looked unapproachable and detached when they met in the house. It was hard to believe she was the same young woman he had held in his arms, the woman who had returned his kisses with such abandon. The memories of those kisses reminded him that he had detected untapped depths of passion within her and he knew her well enough to know she was not as prim as she appeared. The impact of those memories brought a smouldering glow to his eyes. She excited him, made him imagine those pleasures and sensations she could never have experienced without being aroused by him.

It would not be too difficult a task to demolish her pride and have her melting with desire in his arms.

Briefly the idea of conquering her appealed to Christian's sardonic sense of humour—if that was what he had a mind to do, which he didn't. It would put him on a par with his father, who had been the most debauched man he had known. Christian was his son, but there the association ended. He was not like his father and never would be.

Where Miss Osborne was concerned he must remember that—because of the post she held, to him she was untouchable. But she tempted him daily. When he retired to his bed at night, he was fully conscious that within a few strides of his room, she was there.

A hectic two days had followed as preparations to leave London began in earnest. Alice was excited to be going to the country and Linnet was looking forward to seeing Park House. She wrote to inform Toby of her plans and where she could be contacted if need be. With everything packed up, after an early breakfast, they climbed aboard Lord Blakely's impressive shiny black travelling chaise, which boasted a crest on the door panel and was drawn by four sleek bay horses.

Linnet was glad when they left London behind and the lovely English countryside slid by. Christian travelled on horseback for much of the journey. Alice was so excited she never stopped chattering, but eventually, with the warmth and the rocking of the coach as it trundled along country lanes, she fell asleep with her head resting on Mrs Marsden's knee.

* * *

It was early evening when they approached their destination, after stopping twice to take refreshment and stretch their legs. Park House was set in glorious countryside in the high heathland of the Western Weald in Sussex. They passed through huge wrought-iron gates bearing a family insignia, travelling on up a long, curving drive lined with tall elms. Linnet was not disappointed when she saw Park House, the grand country residence of the Blakely family. The house was situated on a low hill and consisted of two wings embracing a central court. Its many chimneys and courtyards looked out over the still waters of a lake, presenting a stirring sight which could be seen all over the surrounding countryside.

The closer the carriage carried Linnet to Park House the more vulnerable and weakened she became, feeling that this was very much Lord Blakely's territory, where he was master and reigned supreme.

He was the first to alight the carriage. Holding out his hand, he assisted Linnet and then Mrs Marsden, before lifting Alice out and placing her carefully on the ground.

'Welcome to Park House,' he said.

Stepping inside the great timbered hall, Linnet was overwhelmed by the magnificence and antiquity of the house. The staff had gathered to welcome Lord Blakely home and Linnet had a strange feeling of passing into another world. She could feel the past closing in on her, wrapping itself around her, but it was in no way unpleasant or threatening—in fact, it was quite the opposite, for it gave her a warm welcoming glow deep inside. The magnificence of the house was well matched by the view of well-planned gardens and acres of parkland, which could be seen from the terrace.

Lord Blakely instructed the housekeeper to be so good as to show Miss Osborne the rooms that had been allocated to her and Mrs Marsden. They both connected to a sizeable nursery that had housed generations of Blakelys. It was a lovely room—large, light and warm since it faced south. Alice immediately began to explore. She was soon dragging toys out of boxes and was thrilled to find a rocking horse.

Everything became chaotic as their trunks were unpacked. They ate their evening meal in the nursery and then it was time for Alice to go to bed. When Linnet had read her a story—the exhausted child falling asleep before she was halfway through—Linnet left the nursery, wanting to spend a little time by herself.

Standing close to the French windows and drawn by the coolness the terrace offered, she slipped outside. Dusk was falling and the sky was a blaze of colour on the horizon. Linnet began to stroll along the length of the terrace, tilting her face to allow the light breeze to cool her cheeks. Reaching the end, she paused on top of a short flight of steps that led down to the gardens. The air was filled with the scents of late summer flowers. She looked towards the lake in the distance, its waters still and dark. Linnet was irrevocably touched by the timeless splendour of the house. She felt helpless in the grip of something she could not name, or escape. Sighing deeply, she experienced a feeling of contentment she had not felt in a long time.

Stepping down into the garden, she was unaware that Lord Blakely had come to stand beside her until he spoke, his voice soft and warm to her ears.

'I'm glad you came with me to Park House. Have you settled in?'

Smiling softly and falling into step beside him, she glanced up at him. 'Yes, thank you. Everything is perfect. This is a lovely house—a beautiful place to live and bring up children.'

'The house never changes,' he murmured. 'My mother loved it and I have loved it since I was a child. It means a great deal to me and when I've been away it always feels good to be back. It invites and welcomes all who come here.'

'I know. I can feel it,' Linnet answered, looking towards the lake. At that moment she felt that Park House was part of her destiny, that she belonged here. Coming back to awareness, she told herself not to be silly, that such fanciful thoughts were not possible, that things did not happen like that, especially not to a woman who was as poor as a church mouse.

'Speaking of children, Alice is in bed?' Christian said.

Linnet nodded. 'The poor lamb is exhausted with all the excitement. With almost every one of your servants fussing over her, I do not think she would notice my absence. Mrs Marsden is keeping an ear open for her. I understand this is the first time she has been to Park House—Mrs Marsden also.'

'And no doubt you are wondering why.'

'I can't pretend that I am not curious, but it is not my concern.' She didn't want to pry into information that Lord Blakely and Mrs Marsden didn't want to offer, but she would like to get him to open up and tell her something about himself and why he was finding it difficult to bond with Alice. This was something she had quietly observed over the time she had been in his employ. Over time she hoped everything would become clear to her.

'Alice spent the first five years of her life in Egypt. When I had settled my father's affairs and I was able to return to England, she came with me.'

'And her mother died in childbirth, I believe.'

Christian looked at her, then looked away. For the briefest instant she saw a flash of—what? Remorse in his dark eyes—or was it anger? When he looked at her again his expression was unreadable.

'Who told you?'

'Mrs Marsden.'

He nodded and stopped to look at her. 'And what else has Mrs Marsden told you, Linnet?'

'About Alice? Nothing.'

They walked on in silence, each occupied with their own thoughts—Linnet even more curious about Alice's mother. Lord Blakely had sidestepped her query and she wondered why. The mystery about her deepened.

Christian turned his head and looked at his companion. He beheld a vision of her washed in light. A prickling sensation raced down his spine. His stare followed the graceful curve of her throat downwards to her slender body. Graceful and serene, her pale cream gown had sheer long sleeves and a scooped neckline. She wore her honey-gold hair piled and coiled in glorious chaos atop her head. Tendrils wafted against the flushed curve of her cheeks. He quivered and forced his gaze away, his pulse hammering.

Dear Lord, she was lovely, he thought with a catch of longing in his throat. Her eyes were dark and glittering with sensuality as she swept him with an assessing gaze, smiling her welcome. How could mere reason stand against the sensory power of her presence? Just having her here at Park House, his home, sent ripples of unrest into his soul. He would like to say that what was between them was nothing more than a practical arrangement, that it suited them both that she was Alice's governess. But he couldn't.

More than anything in the world he wanted at that moment to take Linnet Osborne to bed. Had she then made the smallest seductive gesture—had she indicated that she was willing—he might have taken her to his bedchamber and made love to her. But she was not merely a body, a thing of the flesh. He desired her, oh, yes, but as his gaze caressed every inch of her lovely face, her eyes whispered to him of the gentling influence—the elevating companionship—he had long been starved of.

Unable to resist her any longer, taking her hand he drew her into the shelter of the trees, away from prying eyes. She made no attempt to draw back. Towering over her he looked at her for a long moment, tracing the tips of his fingers along the curve of her jaw. He could feel the warm, beguiling sweetness of her soft breath on his skin.

Once again Linnet felt that melting sensation between her legs as his finger made sensuous movements on her flesh. She did not speak or move, but her eyes darkened as her pupils dilated. For weeks she had been telling herself that she was drawn to Christian Blakely because of his compelling good looks and his powerful animal magnetism. She had almost convinced herself that it was so, that this strange hold he had over her was merely his ability to awaken an intense sexual hunger within her. But that was just the tip of the iceberg, for what she felt for this man went way beyond anything physical. It was something deeper, something dangerously enduring, which had been weaving its spell to bind them inexorably together.

Without warning or hesitation, he bent his head and brushed her parted lips with his own. At first Linnet hesitated, with the uncertainty of innocence, then with an eagerness that would surely astound Christian, as it did her. Parting her lips, she welcomed the invasion of his tongue, sliding silken arms tightly about his neck and pressing herself to the hard contours of his virile form, little realising the devastating effect she had on him as her lips blended with his with an impatient urgency. Impatiently his fingers caressed her breasts straining beneath the fabric of her gown. Linnet closed her eyes and let the hot, flickering flames of desire sweep through her when his lips left her mouth and travelled down the silky softness of her throat, his hand searing through her gown over the hard peaks of her breasts.

Finding her lips once more, he lightly traced his tongue over her lower lip, his kiss deepening with all the persuasive force at his disposal as he held her tight against him. So lost was she in the desire he was skilfully building in her that she almost drowned as wave after wave of pleasure washed over her. Her body came keenly alive, all her senses heightened and focused on him and herself and the touch of his mouth until nothing else mattered. His kiss was deep, his lips teasing hers. In his arms, with his hand gently cupping her breast, she felt wanton and joyously alive. Caught up in sensation, she was floating on a cloud of euphoria.

This, heaven help her, was exactly what she had wanted, needed him to do, ever since she had come to live in his house. Linnet slid her hands over his chest, marvelling over the breadth of his shoulders. Then they were about his neck like tendrils of ivy, clinging to him as an ache spread through every part of her, a sensation she had felt before when he had kissed her. She ran her hands through his hair and pressed against him, wanting to bring him even closer. It was as if her entire body knew what to do, even if her mind did not. Hesitantly she half-opened her eyes and met his intense gaze, hearing the drumming of her heart until her ears were full of the sound. Faintness drifted on the edge of her vision. She wanted more of him. She ached for him with the awkward desperation of inexperience.

Fighting a rampaging desire, Christian took her face tenderly between his hands, caressing her cheeks with his thumbs and gazing down into her passion-bright eyes, knowing she would be a willing partner as his wife. The moment his lips had touched hers and he'd felt her body mould itself to his, he knew she wanted him. She was too young and inexperienced to conceal her feelings, too genuine to want to try.

'My God, Linnet,' he said, his breathing ragged. 'You are so lovely. You are a temptress, angel and courtesan all in one. You see how much power you have when you choose to use it. Ever since I saw you that day as Alice's governess I have wanted to do that.'

Linnet did see that she, who had convinced herself she had no influence over anything in her life, felt as captivating and alluring as the most beautiful woman on earth, and a joy she had never felt before blossomed inside her.

'Thank you—but why are you smiling?'

'I was just trying to make up my mind if the kiss was as good as the last time.'

'And what is your conclusion?'

'I confess to being delighted at your eagerness. If the kiss, like the last time I kissed you, is an indication of your feelings then I am encouraged. You certainly kiss me with more enthusiasm than your Aunt Lydia would consider proper. You melted in my arms as you did the last time. In fact, your passions were in grave danger of running out of control. Still, I am not complaining,' he uttered softly. 'I confess to enjoying the moment. Your eagerness astounded me. Nothing you can say or do will change what happened between us. You do want me, Linnet,' he told her with a knowing smile. 'You cannot deny it.'

Linnet swallowed nervously and stared at him before turning and taking a step away from him. From the very first, Christian had awoken feelings inside her that she had not known existed. She was no longer a naïve young innocent, but a woman, with a woman's wants and needs that could match those of any other—and she knew only this man could fill those needs. But what she felt for him she could not begin to analyse or understand. It was dark and mysterious and all consuming, a highly volatile combination of pleasure, danger and excitement, and the force of it terrified her.

All the pleasurably wanton feelings he had awoken in her tore through her. More than anything in the world she wanted him to make love to her—and he knew it. Never again would she misjudge his strength or his ardour. She had felt the strength of his hands exploring the secrets of her body with the sureness of an experienced and knowledgeable lover. The smell of his elusive scent lingered in the air and she could still taste his kisses and remember how urgent and hungry his mouth had been on hers.

Instead of trying to stifle her feelings, she allowed them to flow through her. Not even in her wildest dreams had she imagined that a man could make her body come to life like that and she doubted that anyone else ever would but Christian Blakely.

But she should not have let him kiss her. The stability of her position as Alice's governess had shifted dramatically.

'We—we should not have done that.'

Christian's lips quirked with wry amusement at her gravity, then, raking his fingers through his hair, he sighed, clearly no longer in any mood for the light banter that had laced their conversation so far. 'I'm sorry, Linnet. I never meant for it to happen. It was wrong of me to take advantage of you.' He gazed down at her, his expression tender. 'I would like to say that I would like you to forget it happened, but I can't.'

'I was supposed to forget the times you have kissed me before—one of them in a garden similar to this— but no matter how hard I have tried, it's impossible.' That's the trouble, she thought. The memory of those kisses lingered far too strongly for her to discount their effect on her. 'So are you telling me your intentions weren't honourable when you took advantage of me in my weakened state?'

She tried to sound light and flippant when she spoke, but somehow it didn't sound like that to Christian. When he heard the tell-tale hurt in her voice, it was so touching that he was moved in spite of himself.

'The times we kissed we had mutual understanding, Linnet. You understood what was happening. When your aunt ordered us to marry, I recall you saying you didn't want to marry me any more than I wanted to marry you. Have you changed your mind?'

'Why—I—no, of course not.'

'And you're sure about that, are you?'

'Of course I am. I've never harboured any aspirations like that.'

He arched a questioning brow. 'No?'

'No.'

He shrugged. 'I'm offended.'

'Offended? Is that all you feel? Christian—Lord Blakely—you are a peer of the realm. I am so far down the scale of things. I am your daughter's governess. Peers of the realm do not marry governesses.'

'And you harbour no ambition to snare a wealthy husband?'

'Material wealth does not interest me. But if I did marry, I would marry the meanest pauper if I loved him and he returned that love.'

'I suppose you think when you marry it should be a love match.'

'It is important in a marriage. If two people have to spend the whole of their lives together, then they would be considerably more miserable without it. Don't you agree?'

'I have to confess that I haven't thought about it to any degree. Was your parents' marriage a love match?'

'Yes, very much so. They had a depth of devotion and companionship few can boast.'

'Which, I imagine, is what you want for yourself.'

'Yes. When I marry I want the kind of love my parents had. There is nothing wrong with that.'

'Don't you think that looking through the eyes of a child you might have idealised their relationship?' Christian remarked, watching her closely.

'No. I know that they had and I won't settle for less. Of course, I do realise that there are some people who are of the opinion that love and marriage need not have anything to do with each other. My own opinion is that there is no other reason to marry.'

'That is a cynical opinion, Linnet.' He watched her with a good deal of interest. 'But I consider children an excellent reason for two people to marry.'

Linnet's lips twitched into a smile and a mischievous light danced in her eyes. 'I did not realise it was necessary for people to marry for children to arrive.'

Christian laughed low and playfully tapped Linnet's cheek. 'What a deliciously wicked thing for you to say, Linnet. Were you to utter such a comment in society, it would make people think you are too forward by far and quite outrageous.'

'I suppose they would and I would condemn them for being shocked only because I dared to say such a thing, not for the content. It is my opinion that children need the stability of a loving family environment, but I am not so naïve or ignorant as to know that sadly this is not always the case.'

Christian's expression became almost melancholy as he studied the young woman. 'What a wise head you carry on your shoulders, Linnet Osborne, but, you know, love can also bring its own measure of pain.'

'If it is one-sided, then I'm sure it can. But what of you? I'm sure half the female population in London has been in love with you at one time or another.'

He smiled wryly. 'I've had my moments.'

'I don't doubt. But what do they love about you, Christian? Your wealth? Your title? Don't any of them love you for yourself?'

He smiled a bitter smile. 'I don't need love. If my father taught me anything at all, it is that love is more destructive than hate.'

Linnet looked at him hard. 'That's not true. Love is what is essential to make a marriage work. Money has no place when it comes to happiness.'

'That is just sentimental nonsense spoken only by romantic young girls,' Christian remarked with biting scorn.

'I am not a girl, Christian. I am twenty-two years old.'

'And still naïve.'

'By your standards perhaps I am. Where does all this bitterness come from? Your notion of love is nothing more substantial than mere indulgence. Why are you so disenchanted with life? What has happened to you to make you so cynical? And please don't tell me that men in your position only marry to beget an heir because I do not believe it. I can only think what a miserable state of affairs that must be. Don't any of the ladies of your acquaintance fall in love with you? One must have for you to have married her—but it must have been a difficult time for you, to suddenly find yourself a widower.'

Christian fixed her with a steady gaze.

'You must have had someone you were close to,' she went on. 'Your mother, perhaps.'

Before her disappointed gaze, his expression became aloof and she deeply regretted asking him the question.

'Oh, yes, I was close to my mother. She was beauty and grace personified and I adored her. Unfortunately, my father didn't give a damn. He broke her heart. She died three years ago.'

'I'm truly sorry, Christian.'

'I know you are. Come, let us walk back to the house.'

They walked back in silence. Linnet went inside and turned to Christian.

He seemed about to walk away, but then hesitated. 'There is something I should tell you, Linnet. I was not married to Alice's mother. Her name was Selina.'

'Oh—I see. I didn't know.'

'How could you? I have never spoken of it.'

It had crossed her mind that Alice might have been born out of wedlock, but she had heard nothing to clarify this. 'Please do not think you have to explain anything to me. But remember that Alice did not ask to be born,' she said quietly. 'She is a lovely, charming little girl and deserves to be loved.'

Christian gave her a tortured look. There was a deep sadness about him. He left her without another word.

* * *

The following morning Linnet had cause for some serious thought. The kiss they had shared had changed everything. *She* had changed. How could she have been so foolish, so incredibly naïve? Oh, yes, she had feelings for Christian Blakely. She felt sure she always would, but she knew that as far as he was concerned she was just another woman who had fallen into his arms—so very gullible—and she would pay dearly for it if she let it.

She was employed by Lord Blakely to be Alice's governess, yet she felt he had other ideas and that he was setting her up to be his mistress. That could not happen. She must not let it happen. She was beginning to realise that taking on this post had been a mistake. Much as she would hate leaving Alice after such a short time, she must, but she would wait until they returned to London before she told Lord Blakely.

Over the days that followed their arrival at Park House, Christian saw little of Linnet. He was busy riding about the estate, often with his bailiff, consulting with his tenant farmers, seeing what needed to be done. It would have surprised Linnet to know how often his thoughts turned to her.

He found as he went about his business that he anticipated seeing her when he returned to the house. Then it crossed his mind that he was looking for her, looking forward to seeing her. Whenever she was in a room with him he had difficulty keeping his eyes off her, and, when they were alone, he found it almost impossible to keep his hands off her. She had teased and intrigued his male sensibilities from the start, stirred his senses, her sharp mind stimulating his own. She was possessed of a strong determination, was waywardly confident and showed a capacity to think for herself. He admired her spirit, her sweetness and her honesty. The longer they were at Park House the more he began to marshal his thoughts with the precision taught him by years of doing business.

Eventually clarity made a breakthrough and a smiled quivered, lurking at the edges of his mouth, quivered as though longing to burst into laughter.

He had a choice to make. It was time. Either he could go on fighting what he felt for Linnet, or face head on the ever-strengthening bond that was between them. Every time he thought of her, of kissing her, he felt a sharp needle of exasperation drive through him, directed at her, as though, like a witch, she had cast a spell on him, which was totally absurd. It wasn't her fault that he was unable to put her from his mind. No woman had clouded his judgement and stolen his peace so completely. Never in his life had he felt a bond so great and a feeling so all consuming. Suddenly he found himself wondering what it would be like, having a wife to light up his life with warmth and laughter—a woman to banish the dark emptiness within him.

Linnet's belief that it was possible for love to exist in a marriage, that people did marry without regard to wealth or power, appealed to him. But could he risk his heart—could he risk bearing his soul? He caught himself up short, dispelling such youthful dreams and unfulfilled yearnings. He had witnessed all that with his father when he had been with Selina and others before her. His father had been so smitten with Selina that he'd failed to see the avarice and ambition behind her smiles. Christian had had many affairs, but not one woman he'd considered marriage to. As a consequence, he had not come near to forming an association with any woman that had anything approaching permanency—until Linnet.

His mood veered from grim to thoughtful to philosophical, and finally gladness when he decided it was time for him to act out his desire.

Park House employed a large staff, including footmen and grooms. The housekeeper and the butler ran things so smoothly that one wasn't aware of their presence except when they were serving.

Alice raised her head from playing with her toys when a maid entered the nursery and placed a wicker hamper on the table. The inquisitive child went to look.

'Is it for me?' she asked, her eyes wide with excitement.

'In a way it is,' Linnet told her. 'It's a hamper—a picnic hamper.'

'What's a picnic?'

'Well, Alice, I thought we might take a little walk around the lake, in which case we might get really hungry. So I asked cook to prepare us a hamper of food so we might stop and eat it somewhere. What do you say? Would you like that?'

Alice clapped her hands excitedly. 'Ooh, yes please. Can I take Pol with me? She would like a picnic, too.'

Linnet laughed. Pol was Alice's stuffed doll. She had hair the colour of straw, a squashed nose and a floppy ear. But Pol was Alice's pretend friend. She adored her and took her everywhere. 'Of course you can bring Pol. The more the merrier.'

'And Mrs Marsden? Can she come as well?'

Mrs Marsden gave her a hug. 'I don't think so, Alice. I'm not really one for eating outside. But you go. It will be like one big adventure and then you can tell me all about it when you get back.'

When Alice was ready and Linnet had fastened on her bonnet, they took hold of the hamper and went downstairs. Suddenly the door opened and Lord Blakely walked in. His eyes went from Linnet to Alice holding her hand and back to Linnet.

'What have we here? Are you going somewhere?'

'A picnic,' Alice said, moving closer to Linnet, but unable to take her eyes off the man she called Chris. 'We're going to eat some cake on the lake.'

'Well, not on the lake, Alice,' Linnet explained, smiling at her young charge. 'We're going to sit on the grass at the side of the lake and eat our picnic.'

'I think a picnic is a splendid idea,' Christian remarked. 'It's a beautiful day and it will be lovely by the lake.'

'Would you like to come with us?' Linnet ventured to ask, her look direct and challenging.

Christian frowned, seeming to consider this.

'Please come with us,' Alice uttered shyly, much

in awe of the dark, forbidding man. 'You can share our picnic if you like.'

Much to Linnet's delight and more than a little relief—any opportunity to get him involved with his daughter had to be a good thing—he nodded.

'Very well. I would love to share your picnic.'

'Then if you are coming with us, you can make yourself useful,' Linnet said, handing him the hamper.

The afternoon was glorious, the surface of the lake shimmering beneath the sun. Fascinated by the swans and ducks that glided along, Alice insisted on running on ahead. After walking around the lake to the other side, they chose a spot to have their picnic in the shade of a huge willow tree. Christian stretched out on the grass, watching in fascination as Linnet supervised an excited Alice. They placed the food on a cloth spread out on the grass. Linnet sat back on her heels and looked around as Alice ran to pick some daisies that sprinkled the grass.

'What a lovely place this is,' Linnet remarked, twisting her body and sitting with her legs stretched out in front of her. Discarding her bonnet, she turned her face up to the sun and closed her eyes.

Christian watched the sunlight playing on her hair, caressing her upturned face. Aware that he was watching her, she opened her eyes and looked at him.

'What are you thinking?' she enquired softly.

He grinned at her and a devilish light gleamed in his eyes. 'I wouldn't corrupt your sensitive young mind with the content of my thoughts, Linnet. But I was also thinking that this is much nicer than attacking all that paperwork waiting to be done in my study. But have a care. With the sun beating down on me and finding myself close to a lovely woman, my imagination is in danger of turning to rustic pleasures.'

Linnet looked at him in mock amazement. 'Why, Lord Blakely, what on earth can you mean?'

Chuckling softly, he shifted his position. 'Don't pretend to play the innocent,' he said, pulling off his jacket and tossing it aside, loosening his neckcloth and stretching out his long booted legs. 'Perhaps we should call them country pleasures instead.'

'Careful,' Linnet said, laughing lightly, indicating Alice, who had ceased picking daisies and was watching them with interest. 'Little ears and all that. I do not think this is the place to indulge in such things.'

'What do you think I am, Linnet? Have you no idea how I am tormented, being close to you and forbidden to touch you?'

Slanting him a speculative look, Linnet wondered if that was really true, or if he was being deliberately provoking. She stared into his fathomless brown eyes while his fingertip traced a line up her arm. His voice caressed her, pulling her under his spell. Averting her eyes, she sighed and gave him a reproachful look. 'Perhaps you should have retired to your study after all.'

'What—and miss taking tea with my two favourite ladies?'

Linnet stopped smiling and looked at him. 'I wish I could believe that.'

Reaching out his fingers, he gently brushed a tendril of hair back from her cheek. 'Believe it, Linnet. It is true.'

'Then it will be nice for you to spend some time with Alice.'

Christian glanced at Alice, who was sitting on the grass, still watching them, as if too shy to approach them. He looked at her hard, as if seeing her for the first time. Linnet was right. She was a lovely child, her dark hair and eyes resembling his own. There was a look in her eyes that pained him. Alice was his half-sister. In a way they had both been abandoned by the same father. That was something they had in common. His father's neglect while he had been growing up had hurt him profoundly. He would not wish that on Alice. She was as much a victim as he was. When he'd brought her from Cairo, he'd found it difficult coming to terms with having her around. She was a constant reminder of that terrible time in his life. But he could not blame her for that.

Oddly touched by something he saw in her eyes, suddenly, impulsively for him, holding out his hand, he said, 'Come here, Alice. Come and sit with us.' Gathering up her bunch of daisies, she came hesitantly towards them, sitting between them. Tucking the child in close to him, he raised his eyes to Linnet.

She smiled, looking from one to the other. 'There is a striking resemblance between the two of you.'

'Alice and I have much in common. And now,' he said, getting to his feet and lifting the child into his arms, 'while you finish preparing the picnic, I'm going to take Alice to the lake and show her how I used to make boats out of leaves and twigs when I was a boy. Would you like that, Alice?'

'Yes, please,' she whispered, her eyes shining with adoration.

Chapter Eight

Entranced, Linnet watched him put Alice down by
the edge of the lake, collect broad leaves from the
bulrushes and sticks, and painstakingly make a boat
out of the bulrushes, sticks and leaves with a stick
as its mast and a leaf for its sail. She continued to
watch as they pushed the little boat on the water,
Alice releasing peals of happy laughter and clapping
her hands with delight. Linnet was utterly captivated
by the scene. Their heads were so close together that
it was impossible to distinguish where Alice's gleaming dark curls stopped and Christian's began.

Linnet continued to watch them, her throat tight
with emotion. She could see that Alice's need of him
as the father she had never had; the man in her life to
protect her against bad things. It was a role she prayed
Christian would learn to relish. Mrs Marsden had told
her that, up until now, he'd played no part in Alice's
life, and there were times when Linnet thought he
didn't even know the child existed, but now, struck

by the various emotions playing over his features, the tenderness in his eyes could not be concealed.

When they wandered back to partake of the delicious food, Alice sat close to Christian, watching two swans glide majestically by. Linnet's heart warmed as she listened to Christian inventing stories about pirate ships and buried treasure. Wide-eyed, Alice listened, enraptured, clutching the little boat in one hand and Pol in the other.

As they talked and ate, Linnet was vaguely aware of Christian's appreciative gaze on her face as she handed Alice a cup of lemonade. When the child had eaten and drunk her fill, Linnet picked some thin reeds growing by the side of the lake. Sitting beside Alice on the grass, she proceeded to show her how to plait them together. When Alice had become completely absorbed in her task, Linnet left her to it and returned to Christian, who was sitting with his back resting against a tree, one knee drawn up against his chest and his arm draped across it, completely relaxed.

'I must spend more time with her,' he said. 'She's a delightful child.'

'Yes, she is—and a delight to teach. She's intelligent and creative and never bored.'

When it was time to return to the house, after packing the picnic away, Linnet noticed that Alice's eyelids were beginning to droop.

'I think we have a tired little girl on our hands,'

she whispered to Christian. 'She's exhausted—although I usually put her down for a nap at this time.'

'I'll take her.' Immediately Christian swung the child into his arms, settling her head in the crook of his neck.

'You have a way with her,' Linnet said as they headed for the house. She was carrying Pol and the little boat Christian had made for her. It would take pride of place in the nursery. 'It's good to see her so happy.'

Reaching the house, Christian carried the still-sleeping child up to the nursery.

'Shall I take her?' Linnet asked, holding out her arms.

'Allow me to put her to bed.'

'Of course. She is your little girl, after all.'

Momentarily their eyes met and then he looked away and carried Alice to her bed. He tenderly laid her on her bed and pulled the covers over her. Gazing down at her fragile features, for the first time he placed a kiss on her soft cheek, inhaling the sweet innocence of her.

Linnet accompanied him out on to the landing. 'Thank you for coming with us on our picnic. I don't think you realise how much it has meant to Alice having you with her.'

His expression was grave. 'I do. It's been a pleasure for me, too. Thank you for inviting me.'

Linnet watching him go with a warm feeling glowing inside her, feeling that something worthwhile had been achieved.

* * *

The hour was late and, feeling restless and unable to sleep, and pulling her robe over her nightgown, Linnet left her room to go down to the kitchen to warm some milk. The house was quiet, and only the chimes of a distant clock tolling one o'clock broke the silence. She glanced about her, peering into shadows and dark recesses as she went down the stairs.

Christian was in the drawing room. After a hard day out of doors, he was enjoying some time alone before going to bed. The room was in semi-darkness. Having removed his jacket, he was seated before the dying fire with his legs stretched out in front of him. Glancing through the open door and into the hall, he was amazed to see Linnet move smoothly down the stairs, looking like a waif—flowing white in ribbons and lace.

Immediately he was on his feet and moving quietly to the door. Linnet turned and gasped when he suddenly appeared in front of her. His bold brown eyes raked her quite openly.

'Ah! Another night owl.'

His voice, as soft and smooth as the finest silk, stroked Linnet like a caress. She felt its impact even as she realised how intently he was studying her face. Her heart turned over, for despite his dishevelled appearance, with a heavy lock of hair dipping over his brow he looked remarkably impressive with his crumpled white shirt half-open to reveal the strong muscles of his neck. The memories of the times they had been alone together, the intimacies they had shared, and with them the emotions she had felt, the feelings she wanted so desperately to deny, swept over her and she knew that what she felt for him had not changed. It was still very much alive inside her. She was scandalised by the stirrings inside her that the mere sight of him commanded and she resented this hunger, this need, that held her captive to her emotions.

She could not allow herself to continue in this way. The sooner she left Park House and put Christian Blakely behind her, the better it would be for her peace of mind.

'Looking for me?' Christian enquired.

'Actually, I wasn't,' she replied. 'I'm sorry. I didn't mean to disturb you.' She flushed, tightening her robe about her. 'I couldn't sleep so I thought I'd come and get myself some hot milk.'

'How about a nice Madeira instead?'

'Oh—I—I don't usually...'

'Drink? Now's the time to start.'

Christian stepped back and swept his arm inwards in a silent invitation for her to proceed. Linnet complied and Christian watched as she boldly crossed the room. He was fascinated by the play of firelight on her hair falling in loose waves down her spine. His breath caught in his throat as the outline of her lithe body was subtly betrayed through her flimsy night attire. He was quickly brought back to the present when she sat in front of the fire and looked at him.

'Well?' she asked. 'You offered me a glass of Madeira. How long do I have to wait?'

Grinning wickedly, he crossed to a sideboard and poured two glasses of Madeira. Handing one to her, he sat opposite, watching her closely, unable to believe his luck that he should find his heart's desire wandering about the house in her night attire at the dead of night.

Linnet sipped the amber liquid slowly, savouring the flavour, feeling its warmth flow through her.

'Are you usually up this late?' she asked.

'Occasionally. I like some time to myself and my thoughts after a busy day.'

'And I have to intrude. I apologise.' She raised her glass and gulped down the Madeira, then put it on a small table beside her before getting to her feet. 'I'll leave you to your thoughts.'

Christian's long, lean body unfurled and he stood up. 'What if I tell you that I don't want you to leave?'

There was a moment of silence. Both of them were rather ill at ease now, the implication of his last words all too clear.

'Would you like another glass of wine?'

She shook her head.

Reaching out, he took her hand. 'Don't be in such a hurry to go. I can't think of anything more pleasurable than whiling away the night hours with such charming company.'

Reading the sudden glow in his eyes, Linnet felt a frisson of alarm. 'I really think I must go.'

'Must you?' He didn't want her to leave and was

reluctant to let go of her hand. He was content to let his eyes dwell on the softness of her lovely face, to gaze into the depths of her eyes, to glory in the gentle sweep of her long dark lashes which dusted her cheeks.

Almost without conscious thought of what he was doing, he moved his head closer to hers, overcome by a strong desire to draw her mouth to his and taste the sweetness of her quivering lips, which he did, succumbing to the impulse that had been tormenting him ever since she had entered the room. The moment he placed his mouth on hers Linnet parted her lips to receive the longed-for kiss, her heart soaring with happiness. He kissed her slowly and deliberately, and Linnet felt a melting sweetness flow through her bones and her heart pour into his, depriving her of strength.

With a deep sigh Christian drew back and gave her a searching look, his gaze and his crooked smile drenching her in its sexuality.

'There are times, Linnet Osborne, when you confound me,' he murmured.

Her cheeks aflame, Linnet drew a long, shuddering breath, her whole being bent on recovery. 'We really shouldn't be doing this. Someone might come in.'

'No, they won't. Everyone is in bed. We are entirely alone.'

Christian wasn't concerned that they might be interrupted—the servants were usually in bed and left him alone at this hour and he was determined to use the time alone with Linnet to complete advantage.

Linnet couldn't have said when the exact moment occurred when she sensed a change in him, but she became aware that when he looked at her his eyes narrowed and the atmosphere seemed suddenly charged with subtle tension. It seemed a lifetime passed as they gazed at each other. In that lifetime each lived through a range of deep, tender emotions new to them both, exquisite emotions that neither of them could put into words.

Linnet recognised her emotions were in danger of getting the better of her and she stepped away from him, away from the gentle touch of his finger on her cheek. Though sorely lacking experience in the realms of desire, instinct assured her the wanton yearnings gnawing away inside her were nothing less than cravings that Christian Blakely had elicited from her before. At that moment she wanted him to kiss her so badly, to taste all she had experienced before in his arms. She wanted to taste all he was offering now and was growing heady with anticipation, but, she asked herself, could she live with the pain afterwards?

She suffered only a moment's uncertainty. She would feel the pain when it was over and they parted anyway. But she didn't want to go without feeling the passion first.

His face lowered slowly to hers and his lips captured hers, taking possession, searching, demanding, consuming the delicate sweetness in a delicious assault. His kiss was slow and evocative, his tongue invading her mouth in a rhythm suggestive of something more erotic. When he finally raised his head he held her at arm's length, doing a slow sweep of her body.

Linnet laughed softly. 'Hasn't anyone told you that it's rude to stare.'

'Frequently, but tonight I have something worthwhile to look at. You, my love, have far too many clothes on.'

'As you do, my lord.'

'Then I suggest we do something about it.'

Pressing her back to lie full length on the *chaise longue*, her head supported by soft cushions, he left off kissing her.

'Dear Lord, Linnet, see what you do to me. You want this,' he said, 'say it.'

His voice was low with a husky rasp and his eyes held hers captive, gleaming in the dim light. The effect of his warmly intimate expression made Linnet's heart turn over. She knew she should say no, that she mustn't stay, but his potent virility was acting like a drug on her senses, the tug of his voice, his eyes too strong for her to resist. Sensations of unexpected pleasure washed over her, making her want to stay, making it impossible for her to leave. She realised it was no longer possible to put a stop to what she had so dangerously begun when she had entered the room—and did she want to? she asked herself. The answer was clear—no, she didn't and what she felt had nothing to do with what was right or wrong. At that moment she wanted so badly for her life to be different, to be daring—perhaps even a bit shocking—to taste all that she had missed. This was what she had been wanting from that first time he had kissed her, she was not going to risk losing this opportunity to finally feel like a woman. Just once, she promised, sliding her hands over his chest, revelling in the exhilarating experience.

What was happening to her? Linnet had never felt like this, but she recognised the feeling. It was happiness, a feeling she had not felt in a long time, and never with such warmth, such intensity. Christian touched her lips with his own.

'I think the answer is yes,' he murmured.

'Yes. I want the same thing you do.'

'Then I think we should continue this conversation in more comfortable surroundings, don't you, Linnet? Come. Let us retire to the bedroom, where neither conscience nor servants will intrude.'

Linnet took little notice of the magnificence of the bedroom with its many exquisite objects and works of art, of tasteful furniture, and thick carpets into which her feet sank. The only thing she was conscious of was the huge bed, waiting—and the man she was to share it with in such a short time.

Slowly Christian moved towards her, towering over her, his physical presence rendering her weak.

'This,' he said, glorying in the tender passion in her eyes, feeling the heat flame in his belly as he drew aside the curtain of her hair and placed a kiss in the warm, sweet-scented hollow of her throat, 'is the moment I've been thinking of ever since I first saw you.'

As his lips trailed over her flesh, with a gasp of

exquisite pleasure she threw her head back and closed her eyes. 'I cannot believe I am letting you do this,' she breathed softly. 'I am heading for something I cannot possibly know how to handle.'

'Then I will teach you,' he replied softly, seductively.

Linnet shivered as the delightful sensations were renewed when he began kissing her once more. Lost in the stormy kiss, she was not at first aware when his fingers began to pull at the belt securing her robe, but when she realised what he was doing a wave of panic swept over her. Pulling away slightly, she opened her eyes, warmth flaring in the pit of her stomach at his scorching look.

'What are you doing?'

Seeing the apprehension in her eyes, her uncertainty, Christian smiled slowly. 'What do you think I'm doing? I don't want to make love to you with your clothes on.'

Linnet's lips trembled into a smile. 'I usually disrobe myself, but if you insist…'

'I do,' he murmured. 'Someone has to remove your clothes and, when the need arises, I make a perfect lady's maid.'

He began to disrobe her, eager to view her perfect body unfettered by clothes. His fingers fumbled with the fastenings on her robe, slipping it from her shoulders when he succeeded in releasing them. Her thin white nightdress, trimmed with fine lace which clung to the perfect orbs of her breasts, received the same attention and when it lay in a pool at her feet she heard his quick intake of breath as her body was revealed to him, his eyes fastening hungrily on her naked beauty. Her skin was white and cream and gloriously lovely, and he was bewitched, helpless to temptation.

'Truly, my love, I have never seen such perfection.'

'I am flattered that you think so. You are handsome, too, my lord, with few imperfections if any.'

Then it was his turn. Linnet was more than happy to assist. When his shirt was removed she drew back, somewhat in awe of her handsome lover with almost adoring reverence. She stroked the muscles of his chest, following her hands with her lips, tentative at first, as if she'd had time to reconsider what she was doing, but as she felt the heat of him, she seemed to relax a little and began placing tantalising, featherlight kisses on his warm flesh. Christian watched her, amazed by her gentle passion.

Stripping off the rest of his clothes, Linnet caught her breath at the marvellous perfection of the powerful body displayed before her eyes—so earthy, so vital and strong. His arms came around her and he lifted her up, and with exquisite tenderness he kissed the soft flesh of her breasts, her shoulders, her neck. She tasted faintly of her own perfume and he was suddenly hungry for an even more intimate taste of her.

As passion flared between them, suddenly they were on the bed, although she could not remember how they came to be there, with his mouth moving lingeringly over hers, unable to stifle a gasp when his lips left hers and took possession of her breast.

She would never have suspected that the feel of a man's lips on such a secret part of her body could create such incredible pleasure. As he stretched out beside her he knew he would need patience to wait for her to reach fulfilment. A woman was supposed to be terrified of the experience which lay ahead of her, terrified because she was ignorant of what it entailed, but told to endure it because gentlemen liked it. Even though he burned to possess her, he would be gentle with her. He didn't want to risk alienating her from his bed. Placing his arm about her waist, he drew her against his taut, tightly muscled length, touching her hair with his lips.

'I want you to relax. There will be a drifting of the senses, soft kisses, an initiation in the art of love, moving towards a climax that will please us both,' he murmured.

Linnet pressed closer, warming her shivering body against the satin of his bare skin. Fingers caressed her spine, moving lower to the roundness of her buttocks, her thighs. Linnet sighed, her trembling hands reaching to hold him. The scent of his flesh filled her with a heated glory of wanting, with desire.

She stirred restlessly beneath his tender assault. The way his hands moulded to the roundness of her body was making her feverish. Then his lips joined his hands, capturing the aroused peaks of her breasts, his tongue flicking and pulling at her, nipping softly, tasting her. He was determined that she would feel pleasure, not to satisfy himself until he knew she was satisfied, as well.

He moved his hand slowly up her inner thigh.
To his delight and amazement, Linnet's hips slowly
began to writhe sensually, pressing, arching herself
closer, as if an unknown force was compelling her as
he continued touching her here, caressing and kissing
her there, so that no part of her escaped. Her trembling innocence was incredibly erotic—he longed to
bring her to ecstasy.

She gasped with shock, shocked to her ladylike
core. She had no idea how to respond to his scandalous attentions. She lay there, open to him. He was
stirring such sensations in her. She tried to draw away
from him, but Christian moved his hands beneath her
in a relentless grasp and he began to raise her hips to
make her more accommodating. They came together
almost instantly. Now there was no gentleness in him,
nor in her, and when she wrapped her legs about him,
she moved her hips beneath him.

'Try to be still,' he murmured, his voice deep and
soft and utterly determined.

'I'm all right. Truly—please—don't stop now.'

She gasped as he renewed his wicked assault, but
she was powerless beneath his experienced hands
and could only let her head fall back in helpless abandon. Just as it had been at Woodside Hall in the gardens that night, and again on her first night at Park
House, she felt herself being drawn into the same
hypnotic spell that had trapped her then. As Christian
moved inside her, she felt something wild and primitive growing, something so wonderful that her consciousness receded as she unwittingly drove him to

unparalleled agonies of desire, and just as she thought she must cry out, ask him to stop, the sheer pleasure at being with him took her over. Their need for each other overwhelmed them and Linnet's body, released at last from its long-held virginity, became insatiable for him. Her mind and all her anxieties seemed to dissolve so that she was aware of him and only him as he controlled all her senses. She seemed to be hurtling through space where there was no past, no future, no responsibilities, only this moment.

Linnet's passion devastated Christian and when they lay spent, their bodies entwined in moisture, the hot climatic world that had held them in its grip began to subside. Linnet's hair spilled over them both like a silken sheet and he lifted if off her face, seeing that her face was one of peace and perfect tranquillity. She was magnificent, exquisitely soft in his arms. From the moment his mouth had touched hers, he'd known they were an oddly combustible combination. What had just passed between them had been the most wildly erotic, satisfying sexual experience of his life. Lying there while she slept in his arms, he marvelled at the intoxicating primitive sensuality of her. Whatever he'd felt for her during their coupling had been real and uncontrived. He had no doubt about that. No woman could have feigned those responses, not without a great deal of practice.

When she opened her eyes she appeared to be awaking from a deep sleep. Her eyes were huge and warm with passion. Christian was lying on his side, looking at her in wonder, his face strangely calm and his dark head supported on one fist, the waving locks of his hair drooping over his moist brow. He was well aware that her feelings for him were deeper than even she knew. She would not have responded to his kiss so ardently if that weren't so. She was too sweet and innocent to feign those emotions.

Linnet lay quite still. She was transfixed by a profound pleasure that felt almost holy. It shook her to the very core of her being. Nothing would ever be the same again. She savoured the memory of what had happened, recalling the details and storing them away. She felt that, deep down, Christian had been shocked at her abandonment, at her eagerness, at her wanton display. If he had expected a hesitant lover, he had found instead a full-blooded woman ready and eager to enjoy their loving. They had taken pleasure in one another's bodies. She had been shy at first, but not embarrassed, uncertain without clumsiness. Christian had made her feel like a real woman. She wanted to experience more and she hugged the pleasure she had felt to herself, feeling wanton.

Taking a lock of her hair and twisting it around his finger, Christian said, 'I have something I want to ask you, Linnet.'

Her eyebrows arched in faint surprise. 'Oh?' Her lips curved in a smile. 'I am intrigued. What is it?'

'Would you do me the honour of becoming my wife?'

Linnet had not seen this coming and she gasped with the shock of it. 'Your wife?'

He nodded. 'My proposal seems to have taken you by surprise.'

That was true. 'Forgive me if I seem surprised, but—is this a jest?' She was unable to imagine what madness could have caused him to ask her.

'Not at all. I would not jest about something so serious.'

'But—marriage! You must be mad.'

He chuckled softly. 'I imagine there are others who would venture to agree with you, but I assure you I am quite sane. Although I suppose when emotions are running high people do mad things.'

'And your emotions are running high now?'

'When I'm with you my emotions are always running high—in fact, they're often pretty chaotic, even though I firmly try to suppress them. I realise this must come as a surprise.'

'Indeed it does. But—isn't it a bit extreme?' Tilting her head to one side, she gave him a questioning look. 'Please don't feel you have to ask me because of what we've just done. We do have some control over this. It was a mutual decision, Christian, for my feelings are comparable with yours.'

'You must know that I have come to have a high regard for you and a strong and very passionate desire and affection for you.'

Desire and affection were all very well, Linnet thought, but she wanted a deeper, more loving understanding with the man she married. 'Naturally I am honoured,' she said, knowing he was offering her a way of life unknown to her—a way of life akin to royalty. 'May I ask what has prompted you to ask me?'

'You may. I know I must marry some time and there is no other woman I would want to be my wife, Linnet.'

She stared at him. Her mind was in a turmoil. Christian Blakely was the last man she'd ever thought would offer for her. 'Christian, I thank you for your generous offer. I am flattered that you have come to think so highly of me, but I cannot accept your offer.'

He looked surprised. 'Might I ask why not?'

'I'm not a suitable wife for you.'

His eyebrows rose. 'Surely I must be the judge of that.'

His smile was disconcerting, but she went on. 'My behaviour since meeting you has been somewhat circumspect. I do not think we are compatible.'

'You don't?'

'No,' she said firmly. 'For a number of reasons.'

'Shall we discuss the reasons you believe make us incompatible? Although I don't think we should take too long in discussion,' he murmured, nuzzling her ear. 'And don't imagine you're going to sleep. I have not done with you yet.'

She giggled softly. 'You're incorrigible,' she remarked, snuggling closer to his naked body. 'I shouldn't have to remind you that you are a titled gentleman—an earl—with friends in high places and far above my status in life, while I am the sister of an impoverished gambler without a dowry—and initially you thought I was a thief, even though you were mistaken. You must realise that that alone sets us apart.'

'No, I don't. Besides, that has all been explained. I understand what you were doing and I hold no blame.'

'But—how can you trust me after that?' She glanced at him obliquely, laughter bubbling on her lips, mischief lighting her eyes. 'Aren't you afraid I might run off with the family silver?'

Quite unexpectedly he smiled broadly, a white, buccaneer smile, and his eyes danced with devilish humour. For a moment he couldn't breathe. She was indeed beautiful, perfect, and there was no sound more delightful than the sound of laughter from Linnet Osborne's lips and the mischief brimming in her lovely eyes. Desire clenched his chest. He wanted her more than he had wanted any woman in his life. Equally intense, and far more disturbing, was a need to protect and a tenderness that made his throat ache.

'My darling Linnet. I am offering you my name and all I possess. If that includes the family silver then you can have the lot if you agree to be my wife. My Countess.'

A pleasurable shiver ran down Linnet's spine. A countess—the Countess of Ridgemont… Lady Blakely. It would take some adjusting to. 'And you won't mind taking on a pitiable, penniless waif?'

'You're a far cry from that.'

'You could marry someone from the aristocracy with a generous dowry.'

'That doesn't concern me. I have enough wealth for the both of us. So, what do you say? Would the position as my wife be to your liking?' He cocked a quizzical eyebrow. Amusement glinted briefly in his eyes which crinkled briefly at the corners, then vanished. 'Is there anything else that makes us incompatible?'

'We—we hardly know each other, for one thing, so how can you wish to marry me? We have known each other for such a short time and that time has been fraught with trouble. We know nothing about each other.'

'What would you like to know?'

'Everything, I suppose—but even then I don't think I can accept and can only hope that you will withdraw your offer.'

'I will keep asking you. I will wear you down until you accept. We are compatible in bed—you cannot deny that.'

'No,' she said, a little shyly. 'I cannot deny that.'

'Good, because I believe that you and I would be well suited and have a very pleasant life together.'

Linnet had listened to him in wide-eyed wonder. He fell silent and awaited her response. A lump of nameless emotion constricted her throat.

'I want you, Linnet. You *will* marry me. Here you are with your hair spread about us both—naked and beautiful. We are lovers—we must look upon this night as a gift from fate. Ever since we first met my mind has been full of you. When we parted at Woodside Hall I realised that knowing you had brought disruption to my life, a disrupting I did not want, and I honestly did not believe we would meet again. When I returned to London and found you ensconced in my home, I suppose I panicked and wanted you gone because of the effect you had on me. But I soon realised that I wanted you to stay and now I want you to become an integral part of my life. I'd like this to be a new beginning for us both. Say you will be my wife.'

He spoke in a low, husky voice that was half-whisper, half-seductive caress. Linnet remained silent, too afraid to speak at first. She could scarcely believe this was happening. Tilting her head, she looked deep into those sober brown eyes, so gentle, so tender. His expression was serious.

For the first time in his life Christian was finding it difficult to tell a woman—this woman—that she was the most alluring and as desirable as any he had ever known. She had become a passion to him, a beautiful, vibrant woman.

Linnet was looking at him closely. Was it possible that she would marry him after all? Her heart was whispering, *Yes, perhaps...*

'Well?' he asked, his voice deep and husky with desire. 'Do not refuse me, Linnet. I beg of you.'

She opened her mouth to utter a denial, but her conscience chose that moment to assert itself and strangled the words in her throat. She'd already decided to leave his employ when they returned to London. Perhaps she had been too hasty. Could she be falling in love with him? she wondered and then firmly dismissed the notion. For her there would always be the ideal. Not only must she love, but she

must be loved equally in return. Anything less was
unacceptable. Yet she had gloried in his kiss, in his
body and his loving, and she could not bring herself
to tell him otherwise. And what if there was to be a
child after this night? She would not want any child
of hers born out of wedlock. The thought was beginning to form in her mind that marriage to Christian
might not be so terrible after all.

'Damn you, Christian Blakely, you know I can't
do that,' she whispered. 'In this instance I concede
victory to you. There is a part of me that doesn't want
to want you. I don't think I want to feel like this. It's
unendurable.'

She didn't see the tenderness in Christian's slow
smile as he bent his head and planted a kiss on her
neck, caressing her cheek, relieved when she didn't
draw back. 'My poor little Linnet. It needn't be. It
could be something wonderful if you would let it.'

It was his tone, not his words, that conquered her.
'I know,' she whispered shakily.

'Then don't fight me. You will tire yourself out
with the effort. In the end you will succumb to what
is in your heart and you will not want to fight it. Have
I given you sufficient time—and persuasion—to consider my proposal? Do you have an answer for me?'

'Yes,' she murmured, finding it difficult to hide
her treacherous heart's reaction to the deep timbre of
his voice. Remembering all the times she had been
alone with him and the consequences of letting him
come close, those brief, private flirtations had been
thrillingly dangerous and had added a zest of ex-

citement to her life that had decidedly been missing before. 'Very well. I will marry you.' She sighed. 'How strange life is. Aunt Lydia has agreed to pay off Toby's debts—he has to work for it, I know, but it is indeed generous of her. And here you are—asking me to be your wife. It would seem luck is on my side at last.'

'Say it again. Let me hear you say you will.'

'Yes,' she whispered. 'Yes, Christian. I will marry you. I shall be proud to marry you.'

'Thank God for that.'

His lips were warm when they covered hers, touching her mouth with an exquisite gentleness that stunned her into stillness. They caressed, lazily coaxing, hungry and searching, fitting her lips to his own, and then his kiss deepened and he kissed her endlessly, as if he had all the time in the world.

The following morning Christian marched into the nursery and told Linnet he was taking her riding. Stopping what she was doing, she stared at him askance.

'But—I couldn't possibly—and I have Alice to take care of.'

'Mrs Marsden will take care of her, won't you, Mrs Marsden?' he said, playfully ruffling Alice's hair and giving the old nurse one of his melting smiles.

Mrs Marsden was only too happy to oblige.

'There you are, you see. How easy was that.' The smile curled and his lips lifted slightly at one corner, his lids drooping seductively over his dark eyes.

'Come, Linnet,' he said teasingly. 'Be adventuresome. I can assure you that you will enjoy it. Put on something suitable and I'll meet you in the stables. I have a beautiful little mare, extremely docile—'

'Not too docile, I hope.'

He laughed. 'She's a frisky mare. You'll love her, I know. I also have a ladies' riding saddle so you need not be afraid of losing your dignity.' His attention was drawn to Alice, who had climbed on to the rocking horse. 'And when I've found a quiet little pony for you to ride, Alice, you can come with us. Would you like a pony of your very own?'

Alice nodded and giggled as Christian proceed to rock the horse faster.

'A pony of my very own? I would like a white one.'

'Then a white one you shall have. Then I will teach you how to ride. Would you like that, Alice?'

Alice nodded her enthusiasm, rocking the horse even harder.

Attired in a dark green skirt and matching jacket over a white blouse, her hair tucked beneath her bonnet, excited at the thought of riding again, Linnet hurried to the stables. Christian was leading a grey mare into the yard. She looked at Christian admiringly, thinking how attractive he was, with his darkly handsome face and the breeze lightly ruffling his dark hair. He was resplendent in an impeccably tailored, tan riding coat. His gleaming white neckcloth was perfectly tied and snug-fitting buckskin breeches disappeared into highly polished black riding boots.

Already saddled, the horse whickered and stretched out its nose to greet her, shaking her mane vigorously.

'So, I'm to ride you today. What a lovely horse, you are,' she whispered, removing her glove and rubbing her velvety nose affectionately. 'Does she have a name?'

'Delphine—her name is Delphine,' Christian provided. 'She was my mother's horse. She bought her at a horse sale in London—fell in love with her the moment she saw her.'

Linnet frowned. 'Are you sure you want me to ride her, Christian? Any other horse will do.'

'No. I want you to ride her. My mother would be more than happy for you to do so.'

'That is indeed generous of you. Well—if you are sure, I promise I will take good care of her.' She smiled, running her hand down the horse's glossy flank. 'I think Delphine and I are going to be good friends.'

'I know you will.' The heat of his gaze travelled the full length of her in a slow, appreciative perusal, before making a leisurely inspection of her face upturned to his. 'I'm pleased to see you appropriately dressed for the ride.'

'Why—did you think I wouldn't be?' she asked, smiling provocatively at him out of the corners of her eyes, marvelling at the thought that this man would very soon be her husband. 'Now,' she said, turning her attention to the horse. 'Does Delphine have any peculiarities I should know about before I risk life and limb?'

Christian lifted one eyebrow lazily. 'She's as gentle as a lamb. Now, give me your opinion of her.'

'I'll be able to do that better when I've ridden her.' The mare rubbed her head against her, her soft dark eyes alive with intelligence.

Placing his hands on her waist, Christian lifted her effortlessly into the saddle, watching as she hooked her knee around the pommel and placed her foot in the stirrup before settling her skirt. Taking the reins as Delphine moved restlessly, Linnet controlled the horse effortlessly and slanted Christian a glance.

'Are we ready?'

They set off at full gallop towards the lake. Linnet was happy that Delphine turned out to be a spirited little horse, certainly less docile than she had first thought. Leaving the lake behind and riding through the park to the fields beyond, after a time they slowed their horses to a leisurely walk.

'My compliments, Linnet. I know few men who ride as well as you.'

She laughed, her eyes shining and her cheeks having turned a delightful pink with excitement of the ride. 'That is a compliment indeed.' The genuine warmth and admiration in his voice and in his eyes flooded her heart with joy.

'Is Delphine to your liking?'

'She most certainly is and I know we are going to get on well.' She smiled, leaning forward and stroking Delphine's neck when she saw the mare prick her ears back, as if aware that she was being talked about. 'She's a beautiful horse.'

'I'm glad you like her. She's yours.'

Linnet stared at him, almost speechless with pleasure. 'Mine? Oh, Christian. No one has ever given me such a wonderful gift. I—I can't possibly accept it.'

'Yes, you can—unless you wish to offend me.'

She smiled a little shyly. 'I wouldn't dare.'

'Good. Let's walk a while.'

They were on the edge of a wood which gave way to fields. It was late morning. Sunlight slanted through the boughs of the tall trees, making patterns on the ground, flecks of sunshine alternating with shadows. Harvest was well underway in the fields full of men and women working together; the smell of freshly cut corn was heavy on the air. Although he had a very efficient bailiff and a number of assistants, Christian took his duties seriously. He took an interest in all the families of the tenant farmers. Linnet smiled at him and he slung his arm casually across her shoulders. They walked slowly along the edge of a field, the stubble crunching beneath their boots. Watching the workers stack the sheaves of corn, some paused and gazed at them, curious to know the identity of the unknown woman by Lord Blakely's side. He made no attempt to approach them, but waved good naturedly.

'When will you tell everyone we are to be married?' Linnet asked.

'Soon.'

'Would you mind if I told Mrs Marsden? She gave us both a peculiar look when you came to the nursery—which I suppose is to be expected. It's not the normal procedure for the master of the house to take his daughter's governess riding.'

'I suppose not. Feel free to inform her. I think she'll be relieved to know that as my wife you won't be going anywhere.' He looked at her. 'You know I would never ask you to leave or hurt you, Linnet.'

'Not intentionally,' she said.

'I want to give you the world.'

She stopped walking and looked up at him, the sun making her squint her eyes. 'I don't want the world,' she told him. 'I don't want wealth, a title or a grand estate. The things that matter to most people aren't important to me.'

'You're all that matters to me.'

Later, Linnet bathed Alice and put her to bed, where she quickly fell asleep after Linnet had read her a story.

Mrs Marsden, who was putting away some sheets brought up from the laundry, looked up and smiled.

'Is she asleep?'

'Pretty much straight away.'

'I'm not surprised. I took her outdoors when you went off on your ride so she's had plenty of fresh air. The country air agrees with her. You won't hear a peep out of her until morning. She's such an angel.'

'She's much too quiet, though. It would be good for her to mix with other children, Mrs Marsden. Were there any children for her to play with in Egypt?'

'No, bless her. Being in a hot country, her mother

was always afraid she might contract some disease of some kind and kept her indoors.'

Linnet glanced at her sharply. 'But I—I thought her mother died in childbirth.'

Realising she had unthinkingly divulged something Lord Blakely wanted kept secret, mortified, Mrs Marsden sank into a chair. 'Oh, dear. I seem to have forgot myself. Lord Blakely will never forgive me.'

'Lord Blakely won't know, Mrs Marsden—at least, not from me.'

'It's good of you to say so, but he'll find out.'

'I will not speak of this, Mrs Marsden,' Linnet assured her, having no wish to upset her. 'Your secret is safe with me.'

'Thank you, my dear. It's so difficult trying to keep something so important to myself.'

'What happened to Selina? Where is she now?'

'Please don't ask me.'

Seeing she was becoming agitated, Linnet declined to ask further questions about Christian's former love. But it left her wondering. If Selina did not die in childbirth, why had she left her daughter?

Selina had been a woman who had borne Christian a child—a woman he might have loved, a woman who had abandoned him along with her child. Where was she? Who was she? Was she likely to come back into his life? The thought was so immediate, so dreadful, that Linnet didn't even want to think about it, for she couldn't bear it. She felt she had just awakened from a glorious dream to a nightmare.

Chapter Nine

Christian and Linnet agreed that it would be more convenient for everyone if they were married in London. Linnet wrote to Toby to give him the news that she was to marry Christian. She also wrote to Aunt Lydia.

The society columns were full of the impending marriage. Aunt Lydia was pleased at the prospect of Lord Blakely marrying into the family, but many of those in society, eager for fresh gossip, could not believe that the extremely wealthy and powerful Earl of Ridgemont should take for a wife a dowerless daughter of a deceased businessman, especially one who had been of such little account when he had been alive.

Linnet found herself in some kind of indeterminate state, suspended not only in time but in emotions as she was swept along on an unfamiliar path towards her nuptials. She could hardly believe how deep her feelings were running, and the joy coursing through her body melted the very core of her heart. She was falling in love with Christian. She knew that now and that perfect certainty filled her heart and stilled any anxiety she might otherwise have had.

When they reached London, Linnet went to Birch House, where she was to remain until her marriage to Christian. Mrs Marsden along with one of the maids had resumed full charge of Alice. The child was so excited about the wedding that she could talk of little else. Toby had been taken by surprise when he had received Linnet's letter telling him of her betrothal to Lord Blakely, as Linnet barely knew him, but nevertheless, he wrote to say he was delighted that his sister was settled.

When Lady Milton met Lord Blakely at Birch House she was determined to take the credit for the marriage.

'I'm so pleased you have seen the error of your ways at last and that you are to do the right thing by my niece after exposing her to a public scandal.'

'Not at all,' Christian said, his patience with Lady Milton wearing thin. 'Linnet and I were of the same mind when we parted after your daughter's betrothal party. We neither of us saw any reason for us to marry then and she came to no harm.'

Lady Milton opened her mouth and when she spoke her voice dripped icicles. 'That may be so, but you could have ruined her just the same.'

'Not necessarily. There was some gossip, I grant you, but it did not amount to much and was soon forgotten. If anyone can make a scandal out of a young woman being kissed, they need their minds examined.'

'Not when that young lady is my niece.'

'A niece who is twenty-two years old and answerable to no one when it comes to choosing who she will and will not marry. We have both had time to get to know each other better and decided marriage is what we want, so I hope you will come along and witness our union.'

His remark rendered Lady Milton momentarily speechless and then she appeared to relent, her attitude softening enough to accept the glass of sherry Toby handed to her.

'I was hoping we could enlist your help, Lady Milton,' Christian went on in an attempt to placate Linnet's formidable aunt, thinking it conducive for their future relationship to have her on side than against them. 'Since Linnet's mother is not here to take on the task of preparing her for her wedding, I was hoping we could rely on you and your experience on protocol and the fashions of the day and such things to assist her.'

Lady Milton straightened her back and positively purred. 'Of course. I shall be delighted. I was going to offer my expertise in any case.'

Linnet shot her future husband a look that he could not determine—was it one of relief for mollifying her aunt or was she put out because she would have preferred to arrange her own wedding? Whatever her expression was trying to tell him he merely smiled in the face of it, hoping for the best.

* * *

Over the days that followed, although she was busy with the arrangements for Louisa's marriage, Lady Milton, true to her word, took on the responsibility of making sure Linnet was well turned out.

'But what will you wear for all these events Lord Blakely insists upon attending?' she remarked, flitting about Linnet's bedchamber like a restless wind, looking thoughtful as her eyes moved over her niece, clearly absorbed in dressing her in only the finest since Lord Blakely insisted on footing the bill.

Christian, looking on, smiled his encouragement, his eyes appraising his future wife. 'Whatever you come up with, with that hair and those eyes, you cannot fail.

And so Linnet became firmly fixed under Aunt Lydia's wing as, with the help of Christian's instruction, she arranged Linnet's vast wardrobe, employing modistes who enjoyed her own patronage.

Linnet was extremely nervous about appearing in society beside Christian for the first time. Christian was the personification of the doting swain as he escorted her to all the stylish gatherings, accompanied by Lady Milton or Toby. There were strolls and carriage rides in the park, visits to the gardens at Marylebone where they drank tea, or visited the Pleasure Gardens at Ranelagh. Linnet particularly enjoyed the evenings when they went to see a play at the theatre at Covent Garden or Drury Lane. Like a bird set free, she was surprised to find herself revelling in the fun of it and most of all she was happy because she was with Christian. He was always politely attentive and considerate, and her days became a kaleidoscope of shifting emotions.

In all of this Alice was not to be forgotten. She was so excited about the prospect of Linnet marrying Christian that when he visited her in the nursery she gave him a hug, her pretty face shining with happiness as he lifted her off her feet and hugged her back.

'Linnet will look lovely in her wedding dress,' the little girl whispered, her mouth against his ear.

'And so will you, Alice,' he replied. 'You are going to look like a fairy princess in your new pink dress and carrying a posy of flowers.' After gently kissing her plump cheek, he put her down. He watched in amused silence when the little girl immediately began playing with Pol and telling her all about the forthcoming wedding.

Entering the room, Linnet watched Alice scamper off. She went to sit across from Christian, who had come to see his 'two favourite ladies'. Already so perceptive of his mood and able to read every nuance in his dark eyes, she knew he was impatient for their wedding day.

Christian continued to watch Alice as she played with her dolls and was moved to an emotion that was happening all too frequently when he was with the child. The resentment he had felt when he had learned of her birth had nothing to do with the child, but towards her mother and his father. He had tried to distance himself from her, but when her mother had abandoned her she had no one, apart from Mrs Marsden. He was glad he had done the right thing by her and was grateful that Linnet, who seemed to have a talent for motherhood and was warm and loving and never afraid to show her feelings, had helped him to embrace Alice.

When Linnet attended her first ball, it seemed as if everyone in London was there. When Christian arrived at the house, she was just coming down the stairs. She paused and looked down at him. With a stunned smile of admiration, he took in the full impact of her ravishing cream-silk gown. High waisted, it fell from beneath her breasts into panels that rested gently on her graceful hips and ended in a swirl at her feet. Her hair was drawn back in a sleek chignon, its lustrous simplicity providing an enticing contrast to the sophistication of the gown.

Smiling his approval, Christian stepped forward, taking her hand to help her down the last step. 'You look positively enchanting, Linnet. After tonight you'll take the shine out of all the London belles.'

Contrary to Linnet's expectations, the evening was a success. Every pair of eyes seemed to shift to them as their names were announced. Having read the announcement of the betrothal in the newspaper, heads turned, fans fluttered and whispers began. But on the arm of her future husband, with her head held high, Linnet was a new distraction, drawing admiring glances from males and females alike.

When the orchestra struck up a dance and began to play a waltz, Christian proudly led his betrothed into the centre of the floor and took her into his arms. Gazing down into her upturned face, he whirled her around in the dance. He was a superb dancer, and as he spun her round she seemed to soar with the melody. It was as if they were one being, their movements perfectly in tune. Linnet could feel his long fingers splayed across the small of her back. All the while he was looking at her, and she at him, as if there was no one else present.

An unbearable sense of joy leaped in Christian's heart. The yielding softness in her eyes, the gentle flush that bespoke her untainted innocence and youth, brought faint stirrings of an emotion he thought long since dead.

'Thank you,' he murmured.

'For what?'

'Agreeing to be my wife. If at times I have seemed indifferent in my behaviour, it is because I found it difficult coming to terms with how I feel about you. Are you nervous?'

'Terrified,' she amended, pinning a smile to her face. 'Everyone is looking at us. Don't they know it's impolite to stare?'

'You look radiant and very beautiful,' he said, studying her upturned face closely. 'You appear to be very happy with the situation.'

'I am—very happy—but I am also apprehensive,' she confessed.

'You are? Why?'

'Because I'm afraid it might all go terribly wrong.'

'And why should it do that?'

Her gaze fell from his and she looked at his frilled white shirt front. 'I'm being silly, I know, but it's a feeling I have.'

'Put it from your mind. Nothing will go wrong. In just four days you will be my wife. You dance divinely, by the way. You are as light as thistledown in my arms.'

Linnet laughed. 'I feel as if I'm floating on a cloud.'

A wicked, devilish grin stretched across Christian's lips. 'I hope that's the way you will feel when I make love to you on our wedding night,' he said, having made up his mind after their shared night of love at Park House that he would not make love to her again until their wedding night.

Before she could reply to the *risqué* remark, he had spun her round so that her feet almost left the floor. There was a warm, underlying excitement within Linnet that Christian had kindled, a promise and a tingle of anticipation of that moment when she would be alone with him as his bride.

Just four weeks to the day that the arrangement had been struck, Linnet and Christian were married.

There was a small assortment of guests made up of a handful of Christian's close friends and Lady

Milton, William and Louisa, having travelled from Richmond for the occasion. Aunt Lydia seemed well pleased at the way everything had turned out and that a connection had been formed between her own illustrious family and that of Lord Blakely's. She was also no doubt thankful that the marriage was a low-key affair and not the grand wedding she was planning for Louisa. At least she had been spared the expense.

Louisa had taken Linnet aside to speak to her privately at the first opportunity.

'I can't tell you how surprised I was when I learned you were to marry Lord Blakely, Linnet. I did not expect it. What you did—at my betrothal party—the gossip—was it so very bad that you were left with no choice but to wed?'

'Be assured, Louisa, that my decision to accept Christian's proposal had nothing to do with that.'

'Are you telling me that you are in love with him—after such a short time?'

Linnet laughed. 'As to that I cannot say—not yet.' Her tone was light, her manner unconcerned, but Louisa was not convinced and inclined to argue.

'You have been persuaded, I can see that.'

'Christian can be very persuasive, Louisa. My circumstances do not permit me the luxury of choice. I am a woman in need of a husband and yet I have no dowry. Christian is a wealthy man. He does not care about that. What I care about now is having a home of my own. This is a very good match for me. He is to take me to Park House in Sussex to live. I welcome that.' She looked at her cousin and when she next spoke her tone was quiet and pleading. 'Be happy for me, Louisa. Please.'

Louisa smiled and reaching out clasped her hand. 'I am happy for you, Linnet. If this is indeed what you want then I pray you find happiness—and love—together. And when I am married I shall look forward to visiting you with Harry in Sussex.'

The short ceremony took place late morning at St George's Church in Hanover Square. It was a swift, solemn affair, seeming totally unreal to Linnet, whose feelings see-sawed between excitement and apprehension. Holding a small spray of white flowers at her waist, she wore a high-waisted gown in lemon satin with a tulle overskirt sewn with tiny seed pearls. Her hair was swept up and artfully arranged in curls, and threaded through with narrow ribbon the colour of her gown. With all the radiance in the world shining from her large tawny eyes, they were drawn to the groom.

Overwhelming in stature, he wore a superbly tailored claret coat that accentuated his lean frame and enhanced his ebony hair smoothly brushed and gleaming, his dove-grey trousers hugging his long legs. His crisp white cravat was simple but impeccably cut. Her mind wiped clear of everything but the moment, Linnet's heart gave a joyful leap at the sight of him. Unable to contain his desire to look upon his bride, his clean-cut profile was faced towards her, waiting for her in watchful silence. To her at that moment he was pure perfection.

Now the moment had arrived for her to plight her troth, Linnet could not believe it was actually happening. This was the wedding she had always dreamed of.

Toby, who was filled with cheerful optimism that one day soon he would be marrying his darling Caroline, was proud to escort his dear sister to the church and deeply moved to see her married to Lord Blakely. Having got to know him during the time they had spent together since the announcement of the marriage, he confided in Linnet that he could not have entrusted her to a finer man.

Though Linnet had agreed to marry Christian, she had originally thought little of what marriage to such a powerful man would entail. But during the days since he had proposed marriage, she had considered it a great deal and she had decided that taking everything into account, it was the sensible course of action to follow. And now, as she became snared by his unnervingly intent gaze, his dark eyes drawing her in, all other thoughts fled her mind. She wanted to be with this man so badly that she was shaken by it. She loved him with all her heart and soul. At this realisation it was as though chains fell away from her, lightening her heart.

Unable to contain his desire to look upon Linnet, Christian turned. The vision of almost ethereal loveliness he beheld, her face as serene as the Madonna's, her body slender, breakable, snatched his breath away. Sensing her trepidation, Christian reached out a hand to her and smiled in an attempt to dispel her serious expression. He was completely taken aback by the depth of her composure. Something like terror moved through his heart, and he prayed that he would cherish and protect her all the days of her life, to give her the joy and happiness she deserved.

'You make a beautiful bride, Linnet. You look perfect. Are you ready?'

Feeling pleasure in the compliment, her mood lightening, she nodded and returned his smile. With the eyes of everyone upon her, she took his hand and let him draw her towards the cleric, waiting to hear them make their solemn promises. Unaware that she was holding her breath, she watched as he placed the gold wedding band on her finger. His warm grasp sent a shiver up her arm. Perhaps it was all that the ring implied or the combination of gentleness and solemnity in Christian's eyes as they gazed into hers, but whatever the cause, Linnet's heart rate doubled and her eyes misted with tears.

When the vows had been exchanged, binding them together in a promise that must be kept, the vicar pronounced them husband and wife. Unable to believe this wonderful young woman belonged to him at last, the sweet, elusive fragrance of her setting his senses alive, Christian drew her towards him. 'A kiss,' he said, 'a kiss to seal our union, Linnet.'

Favouring her with that slow, careful scrutiny that made her feel devoured, he drew her into his arms and kissed her slowly, deliberately. Heat shot through her and then he released her.

It was a proud moment for Christian and a happy one for Louisa, dabbing away her tears, as she came forward to embrace Linnet.

It was a happy group that arrived back at the house to partake of the wedding breakfast. Standing in the centre of the salon, with glasses of champagne in their hands, Christian and Linnet received the well wishes of all those present. Linnet knew a rush of happiness She had committed her life to this man and from that moment she knew how it must be between them. Also, in that moment, she'd recognised the emotion that had struck her when he had kissed her in the church. She no longer had any doubts that she was deeply and irresistibly in love, and this revelation sealed the bond between them. She would nurse and cherish her secret, and hope that in time he would come to feel the same about her.

The wedding breakfast held in the green and gold salon of the Blakely town house was a quiet affair, without the pomp and splendour that would mark Louisa's wedding to Harry. A long table had been prepared for the wedding feast. It gleamed with silver cutlery and crystal glasses and was festooned with flowers. Christian presided over the meal with his usual calm composure. He was politely courteous and attentive to his bride and guests.

Christian leaned close to his wife, the sweet, elusive fragrance of her setting his senses alive. 'What are you thinking?' he asked quietly.

She turned and looked at him, her face flushed and

her eyes bright. 'Oh—about all this? I never believed it possible that this could happen.' A cloud darkened her eyes and a note of regret entered her voice. 'My only regret is that my parents are not here to see me married.'

Christian squeezed her hand comfortingly under the table. 'They are not far away. I am certain that they are watching you from that mysterious place we all go to one day. Perhaps our children will produce their likeness,' he said softly, his eyes gleaming into hers, lazy and seductive, feeling a driving urge of desire at the sultriness of her soft mouth and the liquid depths of her eyes.

'Children?' A lump of nameless emotion constricted her throat. Christian's casual reference to any future offspring they might produce warmed her heart.

'At least half a dozen,' Christian replied, laughter rumbling in his chest. 'But you have to promise me one thing.'

'And that is?'

He stretched his arm possessively across the back of her chair without taking his eyes off her face. 'That at least one of them looks like you.'

She smiled. 'I'll do my best—and speaking of children,' she said, glancing along the table where Mrs Marsden was seated next to a wilting Alice, worn out with all the excitement and attention she had received from admiring guests, 'I think it is time for Alice to take her nap.'

When everyone had eaten and drunk their fill and left, at long last the bridal pair were given their pri-

vacy. Linnet loved her bedchamber, with its exquisite objects, tasteful furniture and thick carpets into
which her feet sank. She was conscious of the huge
bed holding centre stage and how she would share it
with her husband this very night.

Entering through the connecting doors adjoining
their bedchambers, his robe falling open to the waist,
revealing his firm, well-muscled chest, Christian dismissed the maid, grinning leisurely as he told his
wife he would be only too happy to stand in for her.

Attired in her dark blue silk robe that clung to her
body like a second skin, Linnet sat at the satinwood
dressing table, taking the pins from her hair and shaking it free. Through the mirror she watched Christian
move towards her, towering over her, his physical
presence rendering her weak. He stopped behind her
and his hands settled on her shoulders. She was very
still, unable to move. She shivered with apprehension.
Without straightening, he met her eyes in the mirror.
He was looking at her in a way he had never looked
at her before. He was implacably calm.

'This,' he said, glorying in the tender passion in
her eyes, feeling the heat flame in his belly as he drew
aside the curtain of her hair and placed a kiss in the
warm, sweet-scented hollow of her throat, 'is the moment I've been thinking of ever since I first saw you.'

As his lips trailed over her flesh, with a gasp of
exquisite pleasure she threw her head back and closed
her eyes. 'I cannot believe this is happening—that we
are husband and wife,' she said softly. 'I feel as if I'm
in some kind of dream and I'll soon wake up. I am

certain I am heading for something I cannot possibly know how to handle.'

'You handled it admirably when we made love before. However, I am going to enjoy teaching you more of what to expect,' he replied softly, seductively. Despite having shared his bed before, she was nervous, she had to be, and yet, he thought he could sense an excitement about her. 'I'm a good teacher, Linnet. I don't think you'll have any complaints.'

Linnet's tawny eyes were shining with surrender and there was a tremor to her voice. 'I am yours, Christian, willingly. I want to hold this day in my memory, to share this time we both hold dear.'

'You're very lovely, Linnet—and quite irresistible.'

She wanted to contradict him, but her tongue remained silent. The rest of her body began to sing and her pulse raced at the warmth of his breath on her neck.

Taking her face in his hands, he looked down at her with an intensity that warmed her. 'We have a lifetime together. But were I to spend every moment with you it would never be long enough. No man has the right to feel such joy. You've done this before so you do not have to fear what is to happen. This time will be better than the last, I promise. The marital act is something to be enjoyed.'

The husky timbre of his voice, combined with the tantalising exploration of his skilful fingers caressing her neck, was already working its magic on Linnet. She had little knowledge and was eager to learn more of the intimacies that took place between men and women. She was a complete novice, on the brink of the unknown.

Drawing her to her feet, he took her in his arms. 'Do you know—have you the slightest idea how much I want you?'

She shivered slightly, for she felt the full force of his masculinity, the strong pull of his magnetism. She felt a hollow ache inside as he gazed at her. Taking her face in his hands, he splayed his fingers over her cheeks, looking into the liquid depths of her eyes.

'I wonder if you have any idea how lovely you are, how adorable.'

Linnet stood very still, barely able to breathe. He placed his lips on hers, gentle, barely discernible.

The feel of his lips and the hot, melting familiarity of them made her gasp, causing a natural hunger to stir deep within her young and healthy body. Reality faded and exciting, dangerous intimacy followed. She was a woman who had senses and emotions, whose body wanted fulfilment, to meet a need so strongly rooted within her and so fiercely suppressed that now it turned against her and overwhelmed her with its intensity.

Nothing existed but this man, her husband, and the husky timbre of his voice and his dark eyes upon her. The next moment she was in his arms, the pressure increasing as they tightened around her, his sensual need claiming her in a kiss of violent tenderness. His mouth was caressing, savouring, his tongue invading the dewy softness with his need. Linnet moaned with pleasure. Heat catapulted through her, setting her whole body on fire, and cindered every nerve beneath the crushing weight of his passion. His mouth, his hands, his powerful body were demanding things from her that she could now, as his wife, give him, things she wanted as badly as he did.

When he released her, with slow deliberation he loosened her robe, pushing it off her shoulders. It slid down her naked body, settling in a pool of shimmering blue at her feet. His burning eyes devoured every inch of her exposed flesh. Gathering her up into his arms in an act of possession, he carried her to the bed. Linnet found herself snuggling with gratitude and what seemed to be absolute contentment against his chest. She wanted him and it was enough.

His dark eyes looked into hers, into her very soul, and she was hardly aware of the moment he placed her on the bed. Christian quickly divested himself of his robe. Linnet drew in her breath, enthralled by what was happening to her—by her own nakedness—and his—to reveal the muscled, well-honed body of an athlete. Lowering himself on to the bed, he stretched alongside her. The firm, hard muscles of his body pressed against hers and the exploration of his hands on her flesh, gentle and caressing, his lips devouring and tender, had her glowing and purring like a kitten.

Her hair lay in luxuriant, tangled disarray around her head like a vibrant halo. Christian's eyes were hungry and dark with passion and, unable to resist her a moment longer, he covered her mouth with his own, snatching her breath away, teasing her lips when they opened to his. Her lips were warm, eager and sweet.

A need began to grow inside Linnet as his caresses grew bolder. It was a hollow feeling that ached to be filled. Passions were inflamed. She felt on the threshold of some great and already overwhelming discovery. She quivered as his fingers stroked the swell of her breasts and continued over her flat belly and on to the curve of her hips and inner thighs and her feminine instinct whispered to her that her body held some incredible surprises in store for her. His lips followed where his fingers led, touching her here, kissing her there, so that no part of her escaped, her sighs and moans feeding his ardour, fuelling his passion. She would never have had suspected that the feel of a man's lips on such secret parts of her body could create such incredible pleasure. What he was doing to her was like being imprisoned in a cocoon of dangerous sensuality.

Christian was slow, in no rush to possess her, but one thing he was sure of—he would not stop until he had achieved what he intended and sealed their vows securely in a physical show of passion. He would make her body sing with rapture before he was done. He thrilled to her, his hands sliding lower to search and caress her womanhood.

Linnet's instinct at such an intimate invasion was to object, to thrust him away, but he filled her with such exquisite promise as he continued to stroke, to arouse her, that she moved her hips instinctively against him, pressing herself closer, as if an unknown force was compelling her. She could not believe the pain of ecstasy increasing within her.

Trapped beneath the exquisite promise of his aroused body and the persistence of his mouth, she began to tremble with uncontrollable need. When he finally entered her, his carefully withheld hunger released itself in a frenzy that demanded that he possess her fully.

His breath quickened against her throat as he began to surrender to a primitive and powerful, desperate need that became a torment inside, the restraint he had shown so far vanishing in his desire to possess the woman writhing beneath him, her hands soft as they moved feverishly over the muscles of his shoulders, down his long, hard back, lingering on his narrow waist and taut hips. Her response was unrestrained, everything but the present obliterated from her mind as her body became a stranger to her and developed a life of its own.

Her passion devastated Christian and when they lay spent, their bodies entwined, the hot climactic world that had held them in its grip began to subside. Sated, he pulled her into his arms as he came down from the unparalleled heights of passion she had just sent him to. In all his years of amorous liaisons, not once had he ever come close to the shattering ecstasy he'd just experienced. His wife was innocence and wantonness, passionate and sweet. From the moment his mouth had touched hers, he'd known they were an oddly combustible combination. If he had expected a hesitant bride, he had found instead a full-blooded woman ready and eager to enjoy their marital bed together. Whatever the circumstances that had brought about their marriage, they were forgotten as he wrapped his arms around her.

Linnet sighed and melted into her husband's embrace, unable to believe that she could feel such joyous elation quivering inside. Nothing could be so sweet, so perfect, as she lay with this man, her husband, a man she loved so desperately. Nothing would ever be the same again.

'I imagine this means that we are truly husband and wife in every sense,' she murmured, savouring the memory of what had happened while placing tiny kisses on his chest. 'I shall never be ordinary Miss Linnet Osborne again.'

'Ordinary is not how I would describe you, Lady Blakely,' Christian said, chuckling softly as he addressed her by her title for the first time.

It was mid-morning the day after the wedding when Stainton, the butler, apprehended them in the hall, rather agitated. 'There is a gentleman to see you, Lord Blakely. I've shown him into the library.'

'Oh—who is it? Someone here to wish us well?'

'It's an army officer, my lord, from India. He arrived while you were having breakfast.'

Christian's face hardened, his gaze shifting from the butler to the closed library door. 'An army officer, you say, Stainton. Then I'd better see what he wants.' He turned to Linnet, kissing her hand. 'I'll try not to be too long.'

As he turned away Linnet saw his jaw clench and his hands ball into fists as, in frigid silence, he strode towards the library and went inside. Her instinct told her that the army officer's arrival boded ill.

Linnet immediately went to the nursery to speak to Mrs Marsden. Her intuition told her that she would know what was going on, what Christian wasn't telling her. Mrs Marsden was in a chair by the fire, Alice playing with her dolls. She looked at Linnet.

'What is it, dear? You have a worried look.'

'I have, Mrs Marsden. My husband has a visitor— all the way from India, would you believe.'

Mrs Marsden was clearly taken aback. 'India—? Oh, dear.'

'Yes. Christian didn't look at all pleased to see the gentleman—an officer in the army, apparently.'

'Really?'

'Mrs Marsden,' Linnet said, going to sit opposite. Leaning forward, she took her hand. 'I am sure that whatever his reason for coming here has something to do with Alice's mother. Please tell me what you know about her. I know that she is alive—you said as much when we were at Park House. Whatever it is that is being kept from me, as Alice's stepmother I have to know what it is if it affects Alice. I have a right to know.'

'Then you must ask Lord Blakely. I am sure that now you are his wife, he will explain what you want to know.'

'Where is she, Mrs Marsden? Please tell me.'

Mrs Marsden sighed. 'As far as I know Selina is in India. She fell in love with a soldier in the English army and went with him to India. As far as I am aware nothing has been heard of her since. And that poor motherless mite,' she said, glancing at Alice playing happily with her dolls. 'What is to become of her?'

'She has us, Mrs Marsden. She knows she is loved.'

'Yes, yes, she does. I'm so sorry, my dear,' Mrs Marsden said, sympathetically. 'I cannot tell you any more than I have. You must ask Lord Blakely. You have a right to be told.'

Linnet was confused by what Mrs Marsden had told her about Selina. When she had given birth to Christian's daughter, being an honourable man, why had he not married her? Unless, of course, she was married to someone else. And what was she doing in Egypt? Unless, unable to bear being apart from her, she had accompanied him when he had travelled there to sort out his father's affairs.

That he had made love to her, Linnet, and told her he wanted to marry her had made her happy. She believed he did care for her and that his fondness was growing into something deeper and stronger. Their loving had delighted her and it had seemed satisfying to Christian. She had been encouraged by it and believed they would have a good marriage and that in time he would grow to love her—when all the time he was grieving for the mother of his child so much that he could never love another. She had married him knowing he didn't love her—and now she knew why.

And what of this woman, Selina? Had he given to her what she wanted—his whole inner self a man gives to the one woman he loves? She, Linnet, had given him her heart, although she supposed he was not aware of it. In fact, she had given him the sum and substance of herself.

In wretched disbelief she got up and went to the window, so Mrs Marsden couldn't see how her disclosure had upset her. She stared out of the window, feeling a great sense of loss.

The window was at the front of the house, overlooking the drive that led down to the road so she saw the moment when the army officer left. She waited a while, hoping Christian would come looking for her or send word that he wanted to see her. After waiting a little longer, unable to quell her curiosity any longer, she went in search of him. He was in the library, looking into the fire in the hearth, deep in thought.

Entering and closing the door behind her, she leaned against the cold wood, looking at him.

'Your visitor has left, Christian. What did he want?'

Half-turning, he glanced at her. 'Nothing—nothing to concern you.'

Linnet was hurt by the direct snub. She let her eyes dwell on his face. How well he shielded his thoughts. 'Does it concern Alice's mother, Selina?'

Christian's face twisted and darkened. 'Leave it, Linnet. I have no wish to discuss it. I have just learned that Alice's mother—Selina—is dead,' he bit out. Pushing a hand, which had a curious tremble in it, through his thick hair, he turned to look at her, his face blank. 'And now if you have nothing further to say I would be obliged if you would grant me a few moments to myself.'

His face was set hard. It was as if he had thrown a bucket of cold water over her. She stared at him with huge, bewildered eyes. 'And I will not be so easily put off,' Linnet was quick to retort, trying not to think of the woman—dear God—the woman he had clearly loved so much, a woman who had borne him a child, a woman he still mourned. The thought was so terrible, so profoundly hurtful, she didn't want to think about it. 'I am sorry she is dead, truly, but you should not have kept the fact that she was still alive from me. It was cruel and despicable. How did you think I would react when I found out?'

'Selina's death will make no difference to how things are between us.'

Could this be Christian speaking to her? Linnet asked herself. She had never heard him use that tone of voice before. Lowering her eyes, she smoothed the skirts of her gown with a hand that shook. Her dejection was caught by Christian. The muscles worked in his cheek as his jaw tightened and he turned and strode to the window. With his rigid back to her, his shoulders taut, he thrust his hands into his pockets. Angry with him for shutting her out, she straightened.

'I beg to differ, Christian. I feel it does—very much so, as it happens. Excuse me. I, too, wish to be by myself for a while.'

It was with a heavy, aching heart that she returned to her room. Changing into travelling clothes and ordering the carriage, she went down the hall. Christian came out of the library. Seeing she had changed her clothes, he frowned.

'Are you going somewhere?'

'Yes.'

'Do you mind telling me where?'

'To see my brother.'

'Today?'

'Yes, Christian, today.' Pulling on her gloves, she looked at him. 'Do you have anything to tell me?'

'No. Should I?'

'Not if you choose not to. You have met that particular gentleman before—the army officer?'

'We have never met.'

'Did he know Alice's mother personally—the woman who ran off to India with a soldier, abandoning her daughter?'

Christian went white. 'How do you know this?'

'I asked Mrs Marsden. Poor woman didn't want to tell me, but I persuaded her. Anyway, I can imagine that what the tragic news the army officer came here to impart has upset you grievously and given you food for thought, so I'll leave you to think it over.'

'Have a care what you say, Linnet. What time will you be home?'

'I don't know. I haven't had the chance to talk to Toby for a while—there wasn't time at the wedding. I may decide to stay at Birch House tonight. If I do, I'll send a message.'

'Stay over? Linnet, we have not been married twenty-four hours and already you are planning to separate yourself from me. You are my wife.'

The authority and the arrogance with which he spoke infuriated Linnet. 'Then you should have shown

me that courtesy,' she threw back at him fiercely.
'Prior to our marriage you should have told me about
Selina—the mother of your child. You led me to believe she was dead, that she died in childbirth. That
you didn't was deceitful and despicable.'

'Have you come to hate me in such a short time,
Linnet?'

'I don't hate you, Christian. I happen to love you—
very much, as it happens—but I must be given time
to think through how best to deal with this. In the
meantime, with time to myself, I will then be able
to determine my desires and hopes for the future.'

Christian's eyebrows rose in amazement, then
dropped swiftly and ferociously into a frown. He
crossed the hall towards her. 'Stop this foolishness.
There's no need for all this melodrama.'

'Melodrama? I am many things, but never dra-
matic. What were you thinking? You must have
known I would find out about Selina some time. Now,
excuse me. The carriage is ready.' She turned from
him and walked to the door.

'Linnet—wait…'

She turned. 'Don't, Christian. Not now.'

She went out and closed the door. Climbing into
the waiting carriage, she tucked the woollen travelling rug over her knees. She had learned many things
since her father had died. Now she'd learned another,
too. Anger was a great hardener and it was this that
stopped her asking the driver to turn back.

Chapter Ten

Toby was surprised when she turned up at Birch House without her husband. Unfortunately he was about to leave for Richmond so they had no time to talk. On a sigh Linnet waved him off. Feeling the need to get out of the house, she walked through the gardens to the field beyond, with nowhere particular in mind. She was beginning to feel that something momentous had happened and that her life had changed beyond recall. She felt the cold of the late autumn weather, the sudden breeze that rose and stirred the grass, swayed the trees and went searching and whispering through the branches and dry leaves.

Four hours after Linnet had stormed out of the house, Christian had gone through a fog of desolation. He knew that the combination of not being honest with her and his attitude had hurt her. He supposed it had been arrogant of him to assume he could keep what had happened to him in life from her. He shouldn't have. He should have been straight with her from the start.

He recalled their wedding night, thinking of her incredible passion when she had lain in his arms, her sweetness, how she had driven him mad with desire. She was like a drug to his senses that he could not name, but could not get enough of. She had fed his hunger and ever since she had left, a dull listlessness had followed him. There was something in Linnet that calmed him, that moved him imperceptibly away from the misery which had caused him so much pain and desolation in the past.

For most of his life anger and resentment had kept him going. He had fed on them for so long that they were the only emotions he recognised, the only ones he still knew how to feel. But Linnet Osborne had done the impossible. She had given joy to his life and brought him peace.

His life before she had entered it had been empty. And then she had come and suddenly he felt feelings he had never believed existed and saw things he had never seen before. She had resurrected a part of him that had been dead for many years and given him strength and a reason to look forward to the future rather than flounder in his past. He realised how much she had come to mean to him and so, driven by need and desperation and the desire to look upon her face once more, he left for Chelsea.

Having followed his wife to Birch House to try to make amends, Christian found her sitting on a fallen log in the field beyond the garden. She didn't turn when he approached but, seeing her back stiffen, he knew she was aware of his presence. Shoving his hands into his trouser pockets, he propped his back against a tree, his narrow gaze trained on her. Having half-expected to find her in a distressed state, he was surprised to find her looking unruffled.

When she turned and looked at him, Linnet saw Christian was wearing the same grim expression she had seen when she had last seen him. He looked strained with the intensity of his emotions, but slowly, little by little, he was getting a grip on himself. His shoulders were squared, his jaw set and rigid with implacable determination, and even in this pensive pose he seemed to emanate restrained power and unyielding authority. There was no sign of the relaxed, laughing, loving man who had married her the day before, who had kissed her and made love to her so ardently last night.

'I'm glad to have found you alone.'

'Toby's gone to Richmond. He won't be back tonight. What do you want, Christian?'

'I want to apologise for my boorish behaviour. I spoke to you in a way that I am ashamed of.'

'Ashamed, Christian?' she uttered coolly, giving him no help. 'I am certain there is nothing for you to be ashamed of. As for apologies—don't you agree it is a little late to withdraw anything you may have said—or not said—to me?'

'Please, Linnet,' Christian said in a low, rapid tone.

'I know I spoke hastily and you have every right to be angry. I was stunned when I found out about Selina's death.'

'I imagine you were. She was Alice's mother, after all.'

Christian wanted to shake her. He knew she was playing a part. He believed that behind the bright expression and glib speech the real, warm, passionate Linnet was still to be found. That army officer coming to the house had angered him to such a degree that he had vented his anger on her and driven the woman he loved underground. Shrugging himself away from the tree, he went and sat beside her on the log, taking hold of her hand, encouraged when she didn't snatch it away.

'I shall not be happy until you tell me you forgive me.' He smiled crookedly at her, willing her to respond in the old way.

'I will tell you whether or not I will forgive you when you have taken me into your confidence and told me the truth about Selina.'

'I want to tell you everything. I owe you that at least. I should have told you everything at the beginning. I promise it will be the truth.'

Linnet gazed at him. 'I sincerely hope so, Christian.'

'It's difficult to know where to begin.'

Linnet settled herself next to him, crossing her legs, watching him calmly, her heart going out to him. 'At the beginning would be a good place to start. But tell me first what has happened to Selina.'

He nodded. 'She died in India—a riding accident, apparently. She was killed outright.'

'I'm sorry. How awful—particularly for Alice.'

'She will be told what happened to her mother, but not just now. Keeping everything to myself has only made matters worse between us. I can see that now. I want to tell you everything that has affected my life—Selina, Alice, my parents.'

'You must miss them—your parents.'

'My mother, yes. As far as my father was concerned, no. We were not close.'

Thinking of his father darkened his mood. He turned his head away, but the tension pulsating from him began to play on Linnet's nerves. She wished that he would open up to her about his family and why he felt such antipathy for his father. She felt sure it had something to do with his time in Egypt.

Her anger diminishing, Linnet looked tenderly into his eyes. 'Tell me about him, Christian. I realise that you are entitled to your privacy and, if you choose not to talk about it, it is your decision. But until you face what happened and allow me, as your wife, to understand, you will never be at peace. Tell me why he made you unhappy. Did your father hurt you?' His expression turned glacial. She knew she should heed the warning in her head, but ploughed on regardless. 'Why do you hate him?'

'Hate? I didn't hate him, but I hated his inconsistency and his heartlessness. There were issues between us that were unresolved when he died.' This

was his only response, but his eyes were full of secrets, as unyielding as cold, hard steel.

'Was he hard on you?'

'There was not the affection that should exist between father and son. He always demanded a great
deal from me. He hated Park House. He always said
it was too confining, too demanding. He scorned the
long traditions that automatically make a man lord
and master in his own house, regardless of his competence—or incompetence.'

'But is that not how it is in every house?'

'Sadly, yes. The law decrees that any greedy, self-
seeking fool is entitled to chance the well-being of his
family on the outcome of a horse race, or wager their
safety on the turn of a card. With my father, the well-
being of his family was decided by his obsession to
follow his own interests and to hell with everyone and
everything that had to do with Park House. Because
he was the head of the house my mother and I were
subject to his every whim. At every opportunity he
was off on one of his archaeological digs, be it Egypt
or some other place where there was something of
interest to be dug up. From an early age he insisted I
learn all there was to running the estate. Fortunately
we had a loyal staff—some had worked on the estate
in my grandfather's time. I learned more from them
about the running of things than I did from my father.'

'What about your mother? Did she mind him being
away for such long periods?'

He nodded. 'She adored him. He didn't deserve
her love. He was free to take advantage of the many

privileges of position and his sex, the woman he so casually abused no more free to question his authority than the menials who worked in his house. He had a weakness for beautiful women—his affairs were notorious.'

'Did your mother know?'

'Oh, yes, she knew. There was nothing she could do about it. Her submissiveness to his amoral behaviour was something I was never able to understand. It infuriated me when she tried to make excuses for him. I wanted her to stand up to him, to berate him. He humiliated her, spurned and shamed her. All my life I tried to ignore what he was doing, getting on with the running of Park House and looking after my mother, while all the time resentment was burning inside me because of his indifference and his neglect.'

'And Selina? You must have loved her for her to have borne you a child. Did you know her family?'

'She came from a military family in Berkshire. The first time I saw her was in London.' He paused, thinking over his next words, aware that he was about to shock her. 'Selina was my father's mistress, Linnet. Not mine. My father was a fool. He believed she loved him—for how persuasive and soothing her voice could be. I saw through her as soon as I set eyes on her. I found it hard to grasp the guile behind her soft smiles and fond words. My father did not realise for a moment what weight of treachery they concealed. She was ambitious and always looking for the main chance—a woman not to be trusted. Finding herself with child, she followed my father to Egypt.'

Aghast at what he was telling her, Linnet stared at him in horror. 'She was your *father's* mistress?'

'Exactly.'

She looked at his proud, lean face, moved by the pain that edged his voice. 'And you are still tortured by what they did to you, I can see that.'

'Selina inspired me with nothing but disgust and loathing. As long as I live I shall never forget the day when I saw her with my father—how much my mother was hurting. It sickened me.'

'And Alice?'

Still holding her hand, he raised it to his lips, taking a moment to consider his next words. 'You will have gathered by now that Alice is my half-sister, not my daughter as I would have had you and everyone else believe—although I never lied to you about that. I can't ever remember saying she was my daughter. When my father died and I went to Egypt to sort out his affairs, Selina was living in Cairo—or so I thought. Before I left Egypt I went to the house where she was living with Alice—paid for by my father— although he rarely visited. His work came before anything else. Alice was five years old. I sent a letter informing Selina of my intended visit. As much as I hated what she and my father had done, I could not forget that Alice was of my flesh and blood—an innocent. I had a responsibility towards her. Mrs Marsden, who had been taking care of Alice from birth, put me in the picture. Apparently there was a new man in Selina's life—a captain in the British Army. He'd been posted to India. Selina had gone with him, leaving Alice with Mrs Marsden—the Captain didn't want any encumbrances and insisted she left Alice behind. Before she left she told Mrs Marsden she didn't know when she would be back—if ever.'

'So you brought Alice back to England. You said you felt responsible for her. Did Selina not have family?'

'Her father was dead and she had no siblings. I wrote to her mother, explaining the situation, but she had washed her hands of her years ago and wanted nothing to do with Alice.'

'That poor child. I'm glad she is in your care.'

'Our care, Linnet. We will take care of her together.'

'Alice is like a daughter to me, Christian. You know that. And your mother? Tell me about her.'

'She died three years ago. I think her heart was broken.'

'I'm so very sorry, Christian. What an awful time that must have been for you. Are you still tortured by what your father did to you?'

'There have been times when the pain was deep. On his death I felt a kind of relief—a thankfulness. I suppose there are those who would think that is a terrible thing for a man to say about his father, but one had to know the nature of the man to understand why I felt like that.'

'Why did you let everyone believe Alice is your daughter?'

'Because the truth is too sordid—and to protect my mother's memory. She died in ignorance that he had fathered a child. It would have destroyed her. At least my father kept his debauchery with Selina confined to Egypt.'

'Mrs Marsden knows the truth, doesn't she?'

'Yes. Thankfully she is devoted to Alice, as you will have seen for yourself, but she is in failing health. She made it plain from the beginning that she only has Alice's best interests at heart. Whatever I decided where she is concerned I could count on her support.'

'And now? Will you go on letting everyone believe she is your daughter? And Alice? Where does she feature in all this? She must be told the truth, Christian. It wouldn't be right to keep it from her.'

He nodded, thoughtful. 'I know and I do intend doing the right thing—more so now I've met you. When Selina climbed into bed with my father I persuaded myself that I would never let a woman have control over my emotions like that—that I would have the strength to withstand such debilitating emotions.'

'And has that now changed?'

'Everything changed when I met you. You are not Selina. You are nothing like her—thank God. When I took you to Park House it was there I decided I wanted to marry you—before that night we spent together. I have fallen in love with you, Linnet. In fact, I believe I have loved you from the moment I set eyes on you at the Stourbridge ball—replacing that precious necklace your brother had taken. I wanted you then and I continued to want you despite refusing to marry you at Woodside Hall when Lady Milton tried to force my hand.'

Linnet's lips curved in a smile, her mind and body

rejoicing at his declaration of love. 'If you only knew how much I have wanted to hear you say that—that you love me as I love you.'

'I am not going to let the bitterness and resentment that has almost eaten me up destroy everything I have now. That is not going to happen. What I have now is too precious. But, in addition, what I have with you is something deep, open and honest. It transcends all else. You are a rare being, Linnet Osborne and I love you.'

'Blakely,' she corrected with a teasing smile. 'My name is Blakely now.'

Having no reason to remain at Birch House, they returned to Kensington, where they took Alice aside. After tactful and sensitive explanations from both Christian and Linnet, she accepted that he was her big brother and Linnet her new sister and then went back to playing with her dolls.

After a scented bath and perfumed oil rubbed into her skin, Linnet sat in her petticoats while her maid brushed her hair until it shone. Deciding on a pink-satin dress for her relaxed, intimate dinner with her husband, satisfied with her appearance, she went down to the dining room.

Christian was waiting for her. She felt his gaze glide leisurely over her, taking in every detail of her appearance. Her heart refused to stop its wild thudding. She halted in front of him. Her eyes had to raise slightly to meet the shining glimmer in his.

'I compliment you, my love. You look perfect.'

Placing a light kiss on her lips, he handed her a glass of ruby-red wine, raising it in a toast.

'To you, Linnet.'

She smiled, raising her own. 'To us, Christian. To many, many years of happiness.'

Hyde Park was where the world of fashion congregated and paraded every afternoon. The gentlemen were mounted on superb horseflesh and the ladies in their carriages, attended by their chaperons and liveried footmen. It was a colourful, frivolous place to be, where people went to see and to be seen.

It was a lovely afternoon, the air sharp and the breeze that rustled the trees made the blue ribbons on Alice's bonnet bounce as she trotted along. Attired in her blue velvet riding habit, she was riding her white pony, the promised gift from Christian, its long silky mane and tail dancing as she trotted along. Christian had gone to a great deal of trouble to make sure it would be suitable for Alice. When he had decided that it could be trusted, only then was Alice allowed to ride it.

Alice adored Daisy, almost as much as she adored Christian. The feeling was mutual. Christian's pride in Alice's beauty, her tangled curls and her effortless ability to communicate with others was boundless. She had become a great source of comfort to him. The shy little girl he had brought from Egypt had been replaced by a confident and spirited lovable child. She had a certain way with her and had everyone eating out of the palm of her hand. All those who came into contact with her immediately came under her spell. She learned to ride quickly and when they were in London, the three of them could often be seen riding in Hyde Park.

'Watch me—watch me, Chris,' she called as she gleefully urged Daisy to jump a very small shrub.

'No more jumping today, Alice,' Christian called after her, unable to hide his concern that she might fall off Daisy and injure herself. 'Are you listening to me?'

'I do—I do, but did you see? I did it.' Laughter followed her as she rode on.

Riding at a steady pace behind her, Christian and Linnet took equal pride in Alice.

'See how she sits her horse,' Christian said, admiring the child's straight back and the proud set of her head.

'She's a natural,' Linnet said, looking sideways at him. 'I'm so glad you have got to know each other. You make a wonderful big brother.'

'I have some time to make up. It was wrong of me to ignore her as I did.'

'It's understandable why you acted as you did. The fates played against you. She wasn't your child. Your father and Selina had put you in a difficult situation.'

'If only I had done things differently back then, but I was so intent on settling my father's affairs that I paid no attention to Alice.'

'There's no turning back the clock to right the wrong. It's the future that counts—a future that includes Alice.'

Christian's gaze warmed to her. 'I don't deserve you, Linnet. When I consider the way I treated you when the army officer came to tell me Selina was dead, you were already convinced I behaved the way I did because I still loved her and was mourning her passing. How wrong you were. I'm sorry for hurting you. I never imagined you would actually retaliate by leaving me and returning to Birch House. Did you intend coming back?'

'Of course I did—I was a bride of less than twenty-four hours, but when I thought you were still in love with Selina—that I could not compete with a dead woman—it came as a great shock to me and I needed time alone to think.'

Riding close to her he reached out and took her hand. 'Your imaginings were unfounded.'

'I know that now,' she murmured, suddenly wishing they were alone in the close intimacy of their bedchamber, where his ardour had already taken away all her inhibitions and she always gave herself to him with unrestrained delight.

'How I have agonised over my treatment of you,' Christian said, releasing her hand. 'It was both cruel and indefensible. I should have been more understanding.'

'All that is in the past—let us forget it.'

'I agree. There are other, more important matters to interest us now. I want you to tell me how much you love me.'

Linnet smiled happily, seeing the need in his eyes that matched her own—a need that would not be satisfied until the sweet agonising moment of fulfilment. She tilted her head and looked at him, happiness giving her an inner glow that shone through. Joy and happiness welled inside her, filled her because this wonderful, vital man belonged to her. She sighed, a happy sight of contentment.

'Have I not convinced you of it yet? I will—later. I promise.'

'How lucky I am to have such a lovely wife—and how amiable,' he teased gently. 'There is scarcely a trace of the reckless young woman I met at the Stourbridge ball.'

'Do not be deceived, for she is still there, lurking somewhere in the background.' Linnet laughed softly, letting her eyes feast on his handsome features. She adored this man, her husband, and everything about him, and she had come to know him like she did no other—the smell of him and every muscle and contour of his fine body. He was her destiny, her future. His ardour had taken away her inhibitions and she always gave herself to him with unrestrained delight, but how she wished he would not remind her of their first meeting, when he had thought she was a thief. 'We will leave the past in the past. The only thing that's important is what's between us, you and me.'

His eyes blazed suddenly with their own vivid light. 'That is true. There are other, more important matters to interest us now. Ever since Toby developed a liking for the gaming tables your world has been spent in torment and strife. This is a time to forget the past and seek out the better moments of whatever the future has to offer as my wife. We have Alice to take care of and before long there will be a child of our own and, God willing, more and laughter will ring within the walls of Park House.'

'I truly hope so. It's a beautiful house, Christian. How could anyone not be happy there? I am impatient to return. Your ancestors must have been very rich to build such a grand house.'

'They were. The first Lord Blakely was a powerful politician and a trusted adviser of Queen Elizabeth. He later became the first Earl of Ridgemont. Park House means a great deal to me. It is mine to safeguard and one day bequeath to my offspring and their offspring that follow. I also realise that it is a heavy responsibility, but with you by my side I will carry it with honour and pride.'

'Thank you. It makes me happy to hear you say that. It will be the perfect place to bring up our child.'

'When we have a child.' A wicked light entered his eyes. 'I will give the matter more serious consideration.'

Staring at his handsome face, she felt a surge of love. 'My darling Christian,' she said softly, 'perhaps you should consider it seriously now.'

He stiffened. 'What do you mean? Linnet, are you—?' He broke off to stare at her incredulously. 'Linnet, are you with child?'

'I am, Christian. Your child.'

'So I should hope.' He ran his fingers through his dark hair, at a loss for further words.

She looked at his unsmiling face with dismay. 'Are you not pleased?'

'What are you talking about? Of course I'm

pleased—but it's a hazardous thing to bear a child. I could not bear it if you should come to harm—and you should not be riding. What are you thinking? We will return home at once.'

Linnet broke into laughter. 'Nothing is going to happen to me, Christian. Having children has been a natural function for women from the beginning of time—and I certainly won't be giving up riding just yet. It is perfectly safe.'

No matter what she said, he insisted they return to the house.

When they were alone in their bedchamber he drew her close to him. 'How long?' he asked. 'How long have you known?'

'A little while. It's still early days. Will you not speak a few words of welcome to our child? He or she is barely alive as yet, but I am certain that he or she will be happy to hear your voice.'

Her words seemed to galvanise him into action. With a swift movement he swept her up into his arms and carried her to the bed. 'You must not stand around too long. I will make sure you get plenty of rest.'

Trying to control her laughter, she wriggled to sit up. He was bending over her and, touching his face with a caressing hand, she said, 'Come now, Christian. I will come to no harm, I promise you.'

'Am I being foolish?'

Linnet smiled at him, loving him. 'No, my love. They are the natural fears of a man who has just been told he is to be a father.'

* * *

Viscount Charles Richard Blakely was born at Park House. Linnet was holding her son in her arms when Christian and an excited Alice, eager to make the acquaintance of her new nephew and feeling very important and grown up on becoming an aunt, entered the room.

Stopping near the bed to kiss his wife, Christian looked down at his sleeping son, having much to be thankful for. There was an unnaturally bright glitter in his eyes as he took the child into his arms and he had difficulty swallowing past the constriction in his throat.

'Is he not perfect?' Linnet said, stroking Alice's hair. Alice was perched on the edge of the bed, eager for her turn to hold him.

'In every way,' Christian agreed. 'But then, how could he not be with a mother like you?' Walking around the bed, he laid him in his crib, covering him.

Alice immediately homed in on Charles. Sitting on the bed, Christian put his arm about his wife, drawing her close. Together they watched Alice peering adoringly down at the child, each content with the way things had turned out for them.

'How fortunate we are,' Linnet murmured, a tender smile curving her lips as she listened to Alice whispering words of endearment to Charles. The words echoed in the fullness of her heart, filling her with a tune too sweet to be sung.

Christian looked down at her smiling face. 'What are you thinking?'

'That I never believed I could feel so happy.'

'You deserve to be happy. You're the best thing that has happened in my life.'

Linnet sighed happily, snuggling closer to him. 'And I love you so much, Christian Blakely. Believe it, for it is true. You have given meaning to my life— to everything I do. Not only are you my husband, but my friend—a very special friend.'

Moved by her words, Christian looked at her with admiration and respect and love, and when he spoke his voice was husky. 'Then I am indeed blessed. I ask for nothing more.'

'Thank you, Christian. That is the nicest, most wonderful thing you have ever said to me. I hope you mean it, because now that you've said it, I couldn't bear it if you didn't.'

'I'll never lie to you,' he promised quietly and she believed him.

* * * * *

*If you enjoyed this book,
check out these other great reads
by Helen Dickson*

Royalist on the Run
The Foundling Bride
Carrying the Gentleman's Secret
A Vow for an Heiress

LTB J.7 X00

FEB 2 5 2020